Kinship of the Twilight Moon

Legacy of the Twilight Dragon

Book One

Kiersten Renée Nichols

ISBN-13: 978-1483983943
ISBN-10: 1483983943

This book is dedicated to all of the trees that had to die in order to make Kinship of the Twilight Moon a reality. May their deaths never be in vain.

Special Thanks goes to Allison Spetrini for sticking with this story from its very first incarnation as a writing assignment gone out of hand back in the 8th grade; and Carissa McIvor, Richard Mowry, and Herbie Hicks for reading through the final version's manuscript and giving me much needed feedback. This story has come a long way since its initial creation, and I could not have done it without all of your wonderful and sometimes rather critical input.

Table of Contents

Chapter One
Vanish and Follow

~~~

Deep in the White Forest of Eldra, in a world of mystery and magic known only as Eidolon, there was a great emptiness that was setting in. Or rather, had already set in. With this emptiness came sadness, loneliness, and a deep and unsettling silence. Wind scarcely sang its airy melodies anymore, as even it seemed to be wary of the emptiness. Animals of the earth and sky alike fled far away, and even the vegetation ceased its growth. All that remained were the tall, bleached, pillar-like trees that made up the entirety of the Wood that gave it its name, though those, too, had become petrified and lost the life that had once filled the trunks and branches. Colorless bark gave way to bright, white leaves, and those in turn fell to the ground and carpeted the hard earth in a soft substance somewhat akin to the appearance of snow.

In the entire Wood, there was but one living being who still remained there, and she only stayed because of stubbornness. Her family had long since died out, driven away by the malevolent *Sídhe* given physical form by the pure energy of their intense hatred of death. Those who remained behind eventually died of old age or were wiped out by the Plague of Twilight. The people who had lived in the forest had become faders left and right, and the magical potency in their blood acted as a catalyst to their own demise.

That Girl was Áine Nic Maoilriain.

She herself had remained unaffected by the Twilight Dragon, something she believed had occurred due to her diluted blood. She

1

was the only one of all her people who hadn't been killed outright by the Plague of Twilight. The only one who hadn't been directly affected.

Oh, but it had certainly cursed her, for now she was bitter...bitter and alone.

She was the only survivor in her entire home, and all she had to remember her people by was an enchanted violin carved from the White Wood before its trees had turned to stone, whose strings would never snap nor lose their tune, and whose wood would never wear nor rot. She carried it with her, always.

Her full name was Áine, Nic Crae by her mother and Nic Maoilriain by her father, and she was the last of the Tuatha Dé Danann, the People of the Hills, the Faeries of the Seelie Court. Or at least, she would have liked to call herself the last. In truth, however, the last had died off many years ago, before a drop of blood had ever stained her hands, back when she was but a child who still clung to innocence. That was her father Lord Egobail Maoilriain, High King of Eldra, and father of many daughters and sons, all full-blooded Faeries, all dead. All except for Áine. All except for her.

She was nothing more than a mere Halfie, one born of Human and Faerie blood, born of the union between her father and some nameless human trespasser of the White Wood. Regardless of her diluted blood, however, she was still once a favored daughter of the Fey King.

She once lived deep in this White Forest of Eldra, alone in the Crystal Palace at its maze-like center that her great, great grandfather had built in ages past. She once guarded it tooth and nail from any intruders; as she was loathe to giving up this nexus to any but those of her family's bloodline. It was her right to be here, and no one else's. If need be, in order to protect her home, she had once been willing to kill.

And kill she had, though every drop of blood she spilled to the floor of the forest tainted her heart and made her weep tears filled with sorrow and regret. But it was all she could do to keep them out.

2

Áine no longer made her home in those woods, but she remembered well the day she had left. As she stared up at the night sky in a world so unlike her own, she counted the stars as she recounted her final mistake.

She remembered years ago when she had gone into the darkness, not even caring that the silver mist that had been creeping into her home as of late had all but dissipated. Áine had only been fifteen at the time. Her cover was gone, but the humans couldn't have seen her all that well in the darkness either, could they? No. They weren't nocturnal like the creatures of her Wood. They weren't unsleeping like the Fey of her world. She knew both sides of her advantage. Being a Halfie had certainly been of use to her that night.

Áine crept along the walls of the canyon surrounding the eastern boarder of the White Wood, taking care not to make any noise. She came upon the first traveler she had encountered in a weeks, but was wary of getting much closer to him. There were no crevices to hide in or things to crouch behind to avoid detection if perhaps by some slim chance he could detect her in the darkness. She suddenly became more aware of her own quiet footsteps. They sounded louder to her somehow, echoing ever so slightly by the aid of the canyon walls. Could he hear her? Would he turn around? She had certainly hoped not.

Áine crept onward, disregarding her fears. After all, what could one mere human do? They had no powers, no magical prowess. That right was given to Faeries and Faerie kin alone. Even the Fianna, powerful human warriors who borrowed magic from the Gods of Old would be hard pressed to defend themselves against a Feral Fey. Humans were just lowly fools, taking a similar guise to the Fey. They were powerless husks who wore the faces of the Tuatha de Danann. It's why they could breed together. It's why they could dilute the blood pool. It's what had happened to Áine.

It was why she thought they had to be driven out of the Wood.

Her next step warranted a crackling sound. She had stepped on a soft clump of sand and soil, and it crunched loudly beneath her

3

bare foot. She had miscalculated. "*Is cuma liom!*" she muttered to herself. "*Go hifreann leat!*" The language of the Tuatha Dé Danann... Though she knew the basics of the common-tongue, it was all she had to hold onto as memory of her family. Even in curses, that was once the only tongue that she would allow to flow from her lips.

"Who's there?" called out the boy's voice. Áine's heart stopped. Though she was loathe to admit it, she could understand the words he spoke, and when she knew that he had heard her. Áine had been discovered, or at the very least, her presence had been announced. "Hello?"

The Halfie pulled back, squeezing herself against the side of the canyon. She knew that it would be a fool's errand to follow him any closer. Blend, blend, blend, she had to meld in with the scenery. She could hear his steps echo through the area as he backtracked and headed straight towards her. Then she closed her eyes, took a deep breath, and vanished completely. Her body was still there, nearly unseen to untrained mortal eyes, but all that remained to be seen where she once stood was a single firefly with shimmering wings. The boy approached, and Áine perched gently on his shoulder while in her insect glamour. As the sun sank low beyond the pale horizon, he began to leave the forest and head due east. She only hoped that he would lead her to his base before her energy was spent.

Chapter Two
Memoirs and Regrets

~~~

Grian Nic Crae found herself taking a brisk stroll through her manor garden, as she did every evening just after she finished with her duties for the day. The way the sun hung low over the horizon, just before it had finished setting, released the most beautiful golden twilight over the emerald hedges and marble grave markers. It helped her to relieve the stress of ruling and guarding the entirety of the Fianna household and branch members. It was where she came to think to herself for a change.

Though she did her best to lead by just laws and hold a harmonious connection to her clansmen, she still couldn't help but feel that, just perhaps, she had made a mistake or two along the way. Some that she could never undo. Her rash decision to send countless of her kin to their deaths in search of a single blood-thirsty Halfie, putting too much responsibility on her brothers, and even before that... No, she mustn't think of that. It was so long ago. She had duties to uphold now, and they were more important even than her love for Áine, her love for him...

Her body shuddered as she realized that her thoughts and feelings had only begun to go astray once she had arrived at the foot of his monolith. The one she had painstakingly etched his last words onto. Paragraphs and paragraphs of long-winded truths and explanations that had once been contained in a stack of crinkled paper were now carved in clear print on this enormous slab of rock and enameled in silver. It had taken her years to complete, but here now it stood, tall and beautiful and terrible. It was the very least she could do to honor him and what he died for after she had taken away his life and abandoned their son with her own two hands.

She gazed sorrowfully upon the monolith, where his words still remained, etched in stone, echoing out the truth.

I write these words for they must be known. Too long have I waited already. The Peach and The Cat have been taken from me, and I can no longer tell these words to those who were meant to hear them.

The world has drastically changed from the way it once was, from the way none who live now remember it as.

It all started many, many years ago, long before I was even born. People had become completely dependent on technology and automation. In an effort to reduce deforestation, all production of paper books were stopped, though those that already existed were not banned. They became collectible items, their prices skyrocketing, though not many people bothered at all with books. As it stood, all information existed on The Net or on other digitally managed databases. People stopped going to work, as the machines could handle literally anything that required manual labor. Society became a paradise of pleasure, with life consisting of naught but play and pampering. Life was wonderful for a time, even for the less wealthy members of society.

But then the End of the World came, and everything changed. The end came not from mass destruction, rebellion, unrest, or even war. It came not even from the people who inhabited the earth, but by the earth itself.

A geomagnetic reversal suddenly encompassed the whole planet and anything in its orbit, including all satellites both man-made and The Moon, effectively destroying all electronic, magnetic, and even many biological wavelengths in one fell swoop. Many records of what once was were lost. There was widespread chaos, spawning horrific wars and mass destruction across every nation. Libraries burned, schools and businesses were torn to the ground, and with the information wipe of nearly the entire internet, we were lost. The violence allegedly ran rampant for nearly one hundred years, though there is still scholarly debate for precisely how long it lasted.

Without the protection of Earth's magnetic field, radiation poured down to the surface of Earth, brutalizing all that lived down below. Many people escaped to the enormous underground country-wide bunkers that had been implemented during the Nuclear War of 3030 A.D., though still many perished beneath its harsh and twisted touch. The chaos began mere moments after what is now dubbed The Collapse, but that was only the tip of the iceberg.

Not long after the shift, strange white-winged people began to fall from the clouds, at first one by one, but then in whole droves. When they touched the ground, they were unharmed, though extremely disoriented. They had no memories of who they were or where they were from, but they could fluently speak every last language on earth, in every known and forgotten dialect, from the most widely-spoken Mandarin and English to the most obscure tribal languages of the more primal regions of the world. When more began to descend all over the world, people began to fear that perhaps it was Armageddon at last, and these winged ones with no memory but knowledge of languages were nothing less than angels who had come to take us to heaven.

First taken in by a pair of scientists who had found them just outside the bunker they were residing in off the coast of Japan, they were dubbed "Shironohane" after their white feathers, and the winged ones' adamant denial that they were tenshi, or angels. Having no name for themselves, they adopted the name as their own.

They were, at first, welcomed with open arms as the saviors of humanity who would restore knowledge and order to the people, but as more and more descended from the heavens, this notion was quickly abandoned. To prevent overcrowding, they were turned away from the bunkers and forced to live on the surface tainted with radiation, which the Shirohane were miraculously resistant to.

7

Angry with the disdain they were being treated with, the Shironohane declared war on the subterranean bunker-dwellers.

So soon after the end of their own war, the humans feared going to battle with these strange people. And so, a compromise was made. The Shironohane would go back to living above the clouds, and the humans would cease the hostilities. In return for forcing the white winged ones back into the sky, they would send them peace tributes of food, water, and anything else they would have need of.

Though the Shironohane accepted the terms, The Collapse had left little to nothing for the humans to even give as tribute. The Winged Ones began kidnapping the humans themselves as tribute, taking them to their floating cities, never to return. All lived in fear of these anti-angels.

None were safe from The Collapse.

But then came a man by the name of Dr. Ryu, a brilliant scientist who had with him the last remaining, and most significant, of all technological achievements - the A.I., or Artificial Intelligence. When the Collapse first struck humanity, he was very young, not yet out of diapers, and very bright. He had spent his life thus far dedicated to his studies and to gathering information, as his parents had alongside him. When the Collapse began, he and his family went into hiding, far away from any public bunker, to work on a plan to restore humanity to its former glory.

Though his parents died during the Collapse, his will did not. Decades passed, but still he gathered and stored what knowledge he could find so that he might continue to construct his great creation. He persevered through the darkness and the loneliness, and at long last, his life's work was done.

His Artificially Intelligent construct was a great scientific breakthrough, even by pre-Collapse standards, that ended the unnumbered days of The Collapse. Because of her biomechanical make-up, she was made to be immune to the same sort of data wipe that began The Collapse in the first place. She could not be harmed by radiation, could not be destroyed by physical force, and could not be controlled by anyone except for the doctor himself. And he called her Momoko, the Peach.

Dr. Ryu immediately began uploading all of the stored data he could into the AI's memory banks. Hundreds of thousands of books, both fictional and informative, that he and his parents had spent their life scavenging, were now recorded in its mind. Mathematical equations, fables, histories, artistic critiques, philosophies, proper ways to farm and build, medicinal knowledge, and much, much more was all given to this manufactured being.

The fact that it was now the only remaining storage library of the Old Knowledge due to Dr. Ryu's and his family's foresight made it an invaluable asset to humanity. He shared his creation, though not his schematics, with the world, ending the modern Dark Ages and bringing about the rebirth of humanity. Ryu's A.I. began to reconstruct and improve the lives of billions as soon as it was released to the world. People had the technology to create weapons to fight off the wicked Shironohane as well, and were able to drive them all back and keep them from kidnapping humans. Because of Dr. Ryu and his Bio-machine, the world was saved. The calendar was changed once more, to A.R., or "After Rebuild."

Now, there is little poverty, no hunger, and no pollution. Poverty was practically eradicated because of the systems of society that the new governments had implemented based upon data supplied by the A.I., as well as the way that the cities and towns had been reconstructed. Hunger was ended by a new way of farming through multi-storied green houses the length of football fields that towered as high as skyscrapers. These greenhouses were spread throughout the many countries of the world. The remaining effects of the geomagnetic reversal, including the influx of radiation, were successfully stopped, and even reversed by the invention of vehicles that ran on the fumes, toxins, and gases that had already been released into the atmosphere. Once that source was depleted, they ran on natural energy such as sunlight, and later merely a refined version of water power. On top of that, they were no longer built with machinery that relied on electronic or magnetic foundations, and were now being constructed using clockwork engineering.

Even overpopulation of humans had its own solution...though that will not be discussed at this particular moment.

Each individual country had been rebuilt, remodeled, modernized, and renamed. Sections of the countries had been divided into individual provinces known as kingdoms for more intimate government structures. Though leaders reigned as "Kings" and "Queens" whose children were schooled in the ways of politics so that they, too, might one day rise to govern the nations, no family held absolute political reign. Elections were regularly held once every decade, and it was fair game for everyone with a background in political education, not simply family members of current leaders, to run.

However, in a world with so many enchanting enhancements, undesirable things were sure to come along as well. There soon came the day that Dr. Ryu was assassinated by a group of terrorists who dubbed themselves as "Eidoliths." It was rumored that they were anti-A.I. rebels who feared that if my father's creation was not destroyed, she would one day learn enough to take over the world and make slaves of humans. After they murdered him, they took The Peach and tried to destroy her, though thank whatever Powers That Be that the Eidoliths did not succeed in their endeavor. Though she could not be altogether eradicated, the Eidoliths were able to split her into two separate entities and wipe her functionality somehow by infecting her core programming.

When I found The Peach, broken and disabled, I fashioned a new body for the part of her that had been broken off, since my lack of knowledge left me incapable of truly putting her back together. And since my knowledge was limited to that of animals, I fashioned it the body of a tiny cat. I was surprised to find that when it awoke, it had taken on the persona of a male. I called him Nekotarou, and he became The Cat.

I tried to hide The Peach and The Cat away, but in their new blank states, they wandered away from me and became lost. Rather

10

than pursue them, I foolishly hunted down the Eidoliths that did this to them and ended up in the predicament I find myself in now.

Rumor has it that The Peach and The Cat began wandering the globe from that day forth, though no one, not even I, now knows where they are. Even now, while I sit here waiting to receive my sentence, I should be out there in search of what remains of my father's AI. Instead I am stuck here in this prison with no method of escape.

But I digress.

The truth was far different than what the rest of the world would come to know, however. I had to know why they had murdered my father and tried to destroy his creation, and I had to avenge his death. There simply had to be a reason. I didn't believe the terrorist bullshit for a second. I tracked down the Eidoliths myself, going so far as to leave Earth for its Phantom Sister. When I found him, I questioned him, but he refused to speak. I unfortunately let my anger get the best of me, and I killed him.

I knew of no way back to my home on Earth, and I had just killed my only ticket back. It was then that I began to wander through the expanse of this new world, and I happened to stumble into the grounds of the great warrior clan known as the Fianna. There I met and fell in love with the Daughter of the Fianna and learned of what had really happened.

The Eidoliths were from this other world, the spirit realm of Eidolon, the phantom sister to Earth, and they had tracked Dr. Ryu down at last after many, many years of searching. They believed that he had been harboring the seed of the Twilight Dragon within him, so they slaughtered him in his sleep before dispersing and hiding out all around the world. Only one of them ever returned to Eidolon, the one I had followed and killed, where before I had done such a thing he no doubt told his cousin, the Fey King, all that had come to pass.

Though Dr. Ryu's death was tragic, something happened that day that no one could either explain or understand. All at once, previously known diseases just seemed to miraculously disappear

11

without reason...including HIV, AIDS and all forms of Cancer. No Polio, no Chicken Pox, no anything. Even such things as the common cold or the flu were nonexistent. Only bacterial based illnesses remained, as the shift had no power to completely eradicate living organisms. Those who were already afflicted with the illnesses that had vanished were cured without exception or explanation.

It was then that the general public began to fear Dr. Ryu's legacy, just as the Eidoliths had. It couldn't have been mere coincidence that on the very day, on the very moment of his death, all disease simply up and vanished.

There was peace on Earth for a brief time, until one day, the diseases came back. However, these were not the diseases we had known and all come to detest. These were new, merciless ailments that none could cure or alleviate. Unheard of genetic conditions and mutations ravaged the world, and strange things were happening to the DNA of infants around the globe. Genetic instability destroyed the lives of many, and turned ordinary humans and animals into other strange creatures.

Not long after the assassination of Dr. Ryu and shortly before my imprisonment here in Eidolon, scientists were able to identify the cause of the so called "mutations." The most prominent of these mutations stemmed from a disease known as the Crystalline Virus. This virus caused molecular instability in the afflicted, which in turn led to a host of other problems. Those with the disease were marked as Faders. Other mutations were caused by the Capacious Virus which caused an enlargement of small portions of the brain that usually remained indistinguishable from the rest of it. People affected by the enlargements were marked as Psychics, those who could manipulate matter with the power of their mind alone.

People feared these mutations, and a legion of bounty hunters began to spring up in every city, hired to take down these mutations without any regard for the lives they were eradicating. Humans that had not been affected by any abnormalities turned on the ones who had been cursed with genetic differences. Because of their fear of *getting infected, they could not risk being around those with the strange illness. Hundreds of thousands of people and animals alike lived in fear of the "normal" ones because of something they themselves had no power over.*

Their only hope is now a legend that has been passed down for generations, long before the collapse and longer still before Dr. Ryu's death.

The Legend of the Twilight Dragon was one that all of their kind knew. It was all they had to hold onto. In that legend, it told of how the Twilight Dragon came to be, and how to ultimately destroy it.

Long ago, all the maladies of the world were released from a "box" by a woman named Pandora. Mankind suffered these maladies for many, many generations. While humanity struggled, the darkness that was released out of her box began to coalesce to form something far greater than any of the things initially released from it. What was born from the evil came to be known as the Twilight Dragon, that which would bring the dusk of life to humanity. The dragon's body was made up of fleeting souls, and it fed on the sins of those closest to it. Its very breath oozed disease and suffering.

The legend tells of a group of people called the Kinship of the Twilight Moon, who found the Twilight Dragon and defeated it with a crystal sword forged out of water, seemingly destroying the maladies of the world in a final gruesome battle. However, the world was not without sin, and the remains of the Twilight Dragon fed off of those sins, restoring itself slowly to its former power. It was eventually able to rejuvenate itself, and with it came newer and even deadlier diseases. The maladies spread like wildfire, leaving no part of the world untouched. This cycle has repeated itself many times over, according to the tale.

Now and again, the Old Ones, known as the Eidoliths, would send a group of chosen people to slay the Twilight Dragon to rid the world of the current maladies, but the dragon would always come back and bring the corruption anew. It never failed. And each time

13

it came back, the horrors of the past would be eradicated, but new ones would be established in their place. Its most recent regeneration had brought on the two diseases I have previously mentioned, the Capacious virus and the Crystalline virus. All who had been affected were either killed by prejudice or died from the disease itself.

A hundred, hundred years have gone by since this revelation.

But now, the people are beginning to talk of another coming of the heroes that defeated the Twilight Dragon before, who would defeat it once more, perhaps for a final time. When they come at last, the dawn of a new world will rise, and life will be restored to its former glory.

The tale instructed the afflicted to seek out the legendary Twilight Dragon once more and destroy it, releasing a reversal of the virus. This would cause the genes of the future generations never to become subject to the cruelties of the present. They could save themselves and their children to come, and that gave them hope. But their task would not be so simple, as the quest for the Twilight Dragon was one shrouded in myth, mystery, and the looming possibility that it was all just a fairytale told to make us hopeful.

If they were to fail, they would be subject to the same sad fate as the rest of humanity...a cruel and unmemorable death.

Theirs would be a tale of acceptance in a time of fear and distrust, and the struggle against an adversary nearly as old as time itself. They will soon embark on this journey to try and fulfill the prophecy, for the better or the worse of the world. Chosen by destiny and by blood to defeat the legendary Twilight Dragon, a source of terrible suffering and disease, they are the only ones who can bring an end to the injustice and stand up to the fabled beast.

But it is too late for me now. I have been sentenced to death on the morrow for charges of murder. I cannot claim to be innocent of my crime. My beloved Grian, you must find the Kinship, no matter the cost. You must put an end to this madness before it is too late. Eden's Promise shall not be forsaken.

14

I write this now in hope that perhaps, when this world finally sees the edge of night and meets the dawn, our struggles will not have been forgotten.

Signed

Dr. Adam Ryu Jr.

Grian no longer held possession of the original letter. She had sealed it shut and left it with her son before abandoning him in the other world...abandoning him to the people of Earth. As the eldest daughter of the Fianna and their leader, she could not afford to keep the child of a convicted murderer, a man who had killed one of the last of the Old Ones, no less. But rather than leave her son to die as was the proper custom, she took him to the other world herself so that he could be hidden away, safe from the wrath of the Fianna.

It broke her heart to look upon her lover's grave, to look back on the brilliant man that she had lost to the law. Yet she had to remain strong. She was the law now, and without that law her people would fall victim to the chaos that had already enveloped the land.

Grian stood up from the ground. She had dallied here in the gardens long enough. Her brothers would be waiting for her in the hall. They had to have come back from scouting by now.

"Goodbye, my love. Farewell to you," she whispered to the wind before turning around and leaving.

Chapter Three
Blood and Exile

~~~

"Hello, Aillen!" called the boy. His voice shocked Áine back into the waking world. The Halfie realized that she had fallen asleep on the boy's shoulder as they travelled, and she silently cursed herself for being so lax. He had indeed brought her to his hideout, but she had not seen where it was, or how to get here, or even where the exit was. She would not be able to find her way back home easily.

"Welcome back, Fennen," greeted the man that the boy had called Aillen. "How goes your travels?"

Áine stilled her breath. Perhaps at long last she would find out the reason why these filthy creatures had been intruding in her forest.

"Ah, not so well, my brother." So they were brothers. "The White Forest of Eldra grows thicker with mist every day. It is getting more and more difficult to navigate the dense woods. The wicked Sídhe are more common now than the living. I have found nothing of use there. Even the wildlife seems to have abandoned all hope and vanished from the land."

The one called Aillen shook his head solemnly. "We must get to the center of that forest, Fennen. Now that the Fey King is dead, we must find our sister and bring her home."

"But Aillen, what if she, too, has already departed from the woods?"

16

"If her reputation is anything to go by, I would not believe such a thing. Rumor tells that she is almost as bad as the Sídhe, driving out humans and killing them when she can, protecting those silly dead trees with tooth and nail. She is the perfect huntress."

"I think she'd sooner kill us than help us, my brother."

"I think not, Fennen. The Twilight Dragon has done her far more ill than it has to us. She will accept our terms. With Grian now having taken the vows, she can no longer be sent through the pool by the Eidolith Stone. We have no choice now. We must find her at all costs."

"Were they...talking about me?" Áine thought to herself in her own language.

"For the sake of the Fianna and the Mac Crae, I know. Do not worry, Aillen. I will find her and put an end to it."

"Mac Crae?" she thought to herself. That had been her mother's family name. These two human boys were...they were... Her thoughts became befuddled. Her head began to swim and all she could see was red.

That was when she snapped. These two boys were the kin of her disgusting mother. The mother who, after seducing her father and giving birth to her, abandoned her and left her to her fate. The mother who sullied her heritage with her dirty human blood, leaving Áine as nothing more than a bastard Halfie without a claim to the true Tuatha de Danann power. As Áine's rage consumed her, her firefly glamour melted away, and she stood there before the two brothers, nails bared and heart hardened. They were both taken aback by the Halfie's sudden appearance, but that did not stop her from unleashing all of her murderous fury on them.

Fennen tried to unsheathe his sword as Áine leapt onto him, clawing at his face with her nails and screaming at him in unintelligible nonsense. Blood soaked her fingers and seeped under her sharp nails as his terror and pain-filled cries filled her ears, nearly blocking out her own rage-fueled screaming.

Aillen pulled her off of his younger brother, gripping her hard enough by the arms to leave severe bruises. Áine struggled against him for a brief while, but it was no use. He overpowered the girl quite easily.

Fennen stood back up and touched his blood-streaked face with his gloved hand. If he lived, Áine's fingers would no doubt leave horrible scars where they had caught at his soft young flesh. "Bitch..." he muttered half to himself.

"Fennen, that's her! That's Áine Nic Maoilriain!" shouted Aillen.

Áine jerked to one side, hoping to catch Aillen off balance, but all it resulted in was him releasing one of her arms and slapping her smartly across the face. "Be still!" This was not a wise move on his part, as it only served to further infuriate her, and freed up one of her arms, which she quickly used to secure Aillen's sword from his own scabbard.

"*An bhfuil tu damhsa liom?*" she growled at him, asking him to dance. Of course, without his sword he had best have good footwork to avoid being cut to pieces by Áine's deadly "dancing". She swung at him quickly, but purposefully missed to give him warning. He leapt back and grabbed a shield from the wall. She swung down hard, clanging the sword against his metal defense. A loud clang resounded throughout the hall.

Their deadly dance continued for some time, Áine's feral strikes nicking Aillen's sleeves or his hair every now and then, perhaps a shallow slice on the face, but never attacking anywhere vital. His strong, defensive stance faltered now and again, at which points he took the opportunity to attack her or dodge out of the way of her blade.

His brother, Fennen, tried to intercept the battle more than once, but Áine soon stopped his foolish advances with quick slashes to the wrists and shins. When that led to him throwing small things at her, she picked them up and threw them back with her spare hand, scoring a lucky hit and blinding him in one of his eyes. When even that did not stop him, she spun quickly around and gutted the already heavily wounded boy. Blood soaked his sleeves and stained his shirt, and his face was a disaster. He would bleed to death soon; there was no doubt of that. His attacks ceased not long thereafter.

"You are the Halfie Áine, aren't you?" asked Aillen. "You are the one we have been searching for!"

She did not dignify him with a spoken response, she only slashed at his legs, cutting down his knee in the process. He gasped and winced as he fell to the ground, but his gaze did not falter, nor did his tone of voice.

"Daughter of the Fey King, protector of the White Wood. The perfect huntress."

Áine stabbed him again, this time twisting the blade into his thigh, left undefended by the shield that now covered his arms and chest. He cried out, but still he would not stop egging her on.

"Youngest daughter of the Mac Crae clan, my own sister. And yet you would do such things to me?"

He had gone too far. Her brothers and sisters were all dead, taken by the Plague of Twilight, consumed by the Crystalline Virus. They had already left her alone. This human and his brother could not be Áine's. Even if they were the descendents of her filthy mother, they were no kin of Áine's. They cared nothing for her until the death of her perfect and benevolent father. They did not care that their mother had left her to die in that forest, all alone, until the Fey King came and took her in. They did not even care about her birth status until she was the very last of her kind.

And so, she slit his throat, spilling his blood down his shield.

As his eyes rolled up and his blood dripped down, Áine's rage calmed, and was replaced with something far more horrifying. She came to her senses at last, and became utterly terrified. What had she done? She had killed again, blackening her heart once more. She began to weep.

"*Cuir sin sios!*" shouted a new voice. "Drop it, I say!"

The voice startled Áine so much that she did just that. The sword fell to the ground with a clank, and her entire body began to tremble. She had killed before, on quite a few occasions, but never had it been this bloody. Never had she toyed with her victims before this fight. She had always been merciful with her quick and clean kills, unwilling to sully her home with the blood of mortals. But this... What she had done...was evil. And here was a witness to her crimes.

As she stood there, her hands and feet covered in the blood of her own kin, the horror at what she had just done overcame her. Her tears were no longer those born of rage, but of deep disgust and self loathing.

"*Cad is ainm duit?*" Áine asked the newcomer quietly, still trembling from the massacre. The older woman was everything that Áine was not. Her black hair was shorn short, cropped close to her head as a boy's would be, in stark contrast to Áine's long, wavy, sand-colored hair. Where Áine's face was like a soft, rounded heart, hers was long and angular, with high cheekbones and a chin that tapered to a point. She was dressed in full silver plate armor and a black cape to match her midnight hair, where Áine wore nothing more than strips of loose white cloth that served only to cover up her lady parts. She must have been at least twenty or thirty years older than the blood-covered waif that was Áine.

"Did you mean to ask me my name?" demanded the woman in the common tongue. "If you are going to speak to me, do so in the common tongue, girl. I know you understand it."

Áine struggled at first. She hadn't ever spoken the common tongue outside of her lessons. It had always seemed below her, too bland and lifeless compared to her own language to ever let herself speak it. But now she felt too dirty and wicked to let the elegant and beautiful words of her people roll forth from her lips any longer. She should not have even asked the girl's name in her own tongue. She had sullied the beauty of the speech with her wickedness.

"Wench! Did you not hear me?" demanded the girl when Áine did not respond. "I am Grian Nic Crae, warrior of the Fianna, and eldest daughter and commander of the Mac Crae clan. You would do well not to cross me any further than your bloody act has already done."

Finally, Áine managed to get her voice working again, but all she could manage was a simple word. "Why...?"

Grian's expression softened. "Why indeed, Áine?"

"You...know who I am?" the Halfie asked, struggling with the feel of the language as it crossed her lips.

"My brothers and I have been searching for you for the past two years; I would certainly hope that we recognized you after all that time. You are the last living connection to the Seelie Court, and being a descendant of a matriarch of the Crae clan makes you a political force to be reckoned with. But that is not why we sought you out."

"I want nothing to do with politics," Áine spat. "I only wanted you all to stay out of my home."

"Your home is dead now. The White Wood has long since ceased to grow, petrified by the curse of the Twilight Dragon."

"I spit on the Twilight Dragon."

"Then you are as careless as you are bloodthirsty."

"I didn't mean to kill them!"

"Your actions speak otherwise."

"You know nothing! Leave me to my White Wood, and never return! I care not for human life; I wish only to be left in peace!"

"Even the wildlife which once roamed through the thickets and trees dare not to venture forth into its perilous depths, heavy with choking mist and rife with Sídhe. And yet you wish to return to that cursed land?"

"As long as I live, I will not allow it to be tainted by mortal humans, whether it is clinging to life or already in the thralls of death."

"But you would allow it to be tainted by the immortal, when you yourself are not?"

Grian's question cut her deep. What she was saying was all true. Though Áine claimed not to be mortal, her mortal heritage stripped her of the longevity and eternal life that would have been her birthright, had both her parents been Fey. While she hunted down and slaughtered any human who dared set foot in the White

21

Forest of Eldra, she did nothing to hinder the rising population of undead Sídhe or protect the forest from withering away. She had been nothing more than an angry, grief-stricken child.

"If you wish to atone for your grim deeds, I can lead you to a place where you may undertake such a task, though I cannot help you along the way," she said, as if answering the painful thoughts in Áine's heart that she had not yet even put to words in her own head.

Áine nodded, desperate to find something, anything, that could wash the blood from her trembling hands.

"So it is agreed. Come, child, let me bind your eyes. After today's bloodshed, I do not think that we can afford to have you find your way back here and do such a thing again." Grian tore a piece of the tablecloth off. Though the piece she tore was clean, the rest was soaked with blood, so it would have to be replaced anyways. Áine silently complied, closing her eyes and lifting her face up so Grian could more easily tie the cloth around her eyes.

The deed was done.

And so, despite her desolate appearance and crimson-stained fingers, Grian took the Halfie's hand and began to lead her out of the Mac Crae hideout. "And Áine, should you choose to take up this task when the time comes...*tada gan iarracht. Ni neart go cur le cheile.*" Hearing her own language was somehow comforting to Áine, though she did not understand why this human girl, sister or not, was even making an effort to bring her comfort after what she had done.

The two girls walked in silence towards their new destination for a long, long time. It seemed like years to Áine, though no doubt it was only a few hours.

When at last they arrived, Grian removed Áine's blindfold and took hold of her hand once more.

Áine opened her eyes and gasped. She gazed at the towering pillar that overlooked the shining pool at her feet. It was old, far older than Áine's great, great grandfather's palace, and likely older than the forest itself. Indeed, it had appeared as though the very trees themselves, petrified as they are now, had grown around it and birthed a shimmering pool to serve as a sacred mirror for its beautiful stone face, carved with all sorts of crests and creatures. Etched into its surface was a poem written in the common tongue.

Songs of ancient prophecies
Of Twilights gone and past
Will call to only those they see
The final days will come to pass

The Child of a Songsmith
Two Artificial Beings
Descendant of the Eidoliths
A Psychic that needs freeing
A Faerie maiden from the Wild
A lass who cannot cry
And lest ye not forget the child
Who shall join them from the Sky

What fades today, what fades tonight
The dragon falls, the fallen rise
Our blinded ways are brought to light
And those who die will live their lives

The Kinship of the Twilight Moon
Bound by their blood and by their fate
Shall whet their blade by Light of Lune
And save these worlds 'fore 'tis too late

After reading the tablet, she now understood the words that Grian had spoken to her. She had said that nothing is done without effort, and there is no strength without unity. This prophecy, hidden in her own home, only served to enforce Grian's gentle warning.

"What is this place?" asked Áine. Clearly, it was somewhere within the White Woods, though not in a place she had ever ventured to before.

"This is the Eidolith Stone, with which the Old Ones share their name. It is an enchanted stone carved long ago by the mighty and mysterious Eidolith race, created not long after the Twilight Dragon was first born many, many centuries ago. Its words are magic, the likes of which no human can dare to touch."

"Is this why you brought me here? Because I am not human?"

Grian nodded. "Do you see that shimmering pool there? It is the only known remaining portal to the Other World, the realm that the Eidoliths escaped to long ago when the Twilight Dragon came and threatened their existence. But they grew careless and did not bother to close up the portal from the other side. When the Twilight Dragon split itself in two, part of it followed them through. The Fianna that my clan fights for have been working towards the goal of destroying the part of the Twilight Dragon that remains in Eidolon. What I now task you with is travelling to the Other World, sealing the gate behind you, and slaying the Twilight Dragon from the other side.

"But I must warn you, once such a thing is done, you cannot return to this world. Under no circumstances should you open another gate to this world. Do you understand, Áine?"

Áine nodded, wrapping her mind around all of this. "Why do you need me?"

"As one of the last known survivors with Faerie blood, you are the only one we have found who can use that pool to travel to the Other World."

"You mean...a human cannot pass through?" asked Áine.

"No, we cannot," replied Grian.

"So I am the only one..."

"Yes, Áine."

"You put too much faith in me."

"You put too little faith in yourself."

"Why do you still pretend to care for me?" demanded Áine. "I killed your younger brothers...*my own brothers*. I...toyed with them, I slaughtered them...and I have killed others before them..."

24

At this, Grian pulled Áine close and embraced her. It was...filled with love. "What you have done was a wicked thing indeed, little sister, and it cannot be forgiven so easily. But I should know as well as any what the Berserker's Blood does to a person. I am Feral, as you are, Halfie."

"Do not call me that, human."

"You mean Halfie."

Áine was taken aback. "What? You...?"

Grian nodded. "Do you think your father was the only Faerie to lie with a mortal woman?"

"But we share the same mother..."

At that, Grian burst into laughter.

"I do not understand...what is it that you find so funny?"

"Our mother was a harlot, Áine. I, too, have Faerie Blood running through my veins. Unlike you, however, I chose to embrace my mortal side while you have renounced yours. I can no more hate you than I can be human."

"Then why can't you use this portal?" asked Áine, pulling away from her half-sister. "You are Faerie-kin!"

"My duties lie here, with my mortal clan. And that prophecy is a duality. There are no Faeries we can trust, none even that we can contact, on the other side of that portal, in that other world. You have not been bound to a Kinship as of yet. That is the true reason we had hoped to find you...to send you through and gather the Kinship of the Twilight Moon on the other side of the portal. Some feared that your bloodlust was incurable, but I think that you were just afraid. You won't be killing any more humans, will you?"

Áine looked away, unwilling to meet her half-sister's eyes. But she honestly did wish to atone. Grian had spoken truly. Áine would kill no more humans. "What must I do?" she asked Grian.

"You must never again take a life, for every soul you sever from its body is snatched up by the Twilight Dragon, caught in Liminality, the World Between Worlds. Every soul that dwells there adds strength to the might of the Beast, and when the threshold overflows, the two halves of the Twilight Dragon will reunite at last, and doom us all."

"That part of the Legend is nothing but Myth! Even without my crimes, there must have been countless deaths since the severing of the Twilight Dragon!" cried Áine. "How has Liminality not burst at the seams by now?"

"Only murder and ill intent sends a soul into the clutches of the Beast."

Áine raised an eyebrow at her half-sister. "How do you know all of this? These are secrets of the Old Ones, the Eidoliths. Few were permitted to know such things. I knew bits and pieces, few of which are things you have told me, much of which I learned from the days before the death of my Great Father, but how did you come to know these things?"

Grian touched the stone, and it glowed faintly. "I have been to Liminality myself, Áine, many suns and moons in the past, when I first tried to travel between the worlds. I nearly drowned myself trying to reach the bottom of that pool there. It was there that I met with the Unicorn."

Áine's jaw dropped. Unicorns did not merely "meet" with people. They seldom even came to Faeries. Their magic was the purest and strongest of all creation. They were the first creatures blessed by the Eidoliths, given eternal life and power over creation. Only the Eidoliths themselves shared that power, not even the Faeries were granted such a thing, though they were given eternal life. If a Unicorn touched another living being, its blessing would be given, its pure everlasting life siphoned into the blessed, its magic passed into the human, animal, or Faerie. It could heal all wounds, cleanse all corruption, even truly bring a soul back from death, though it could not grant immortality. If any other creature even dared catch a glimpse of the mighty and majestic Unicorns, their hearts would overflow and they would become awestruck. Unicorns were not meant for mortals.

"What...happened?" Áine asked, though she was almost afraid to learn.

"He took the form of a beautiful young boy with wings as white as pearls, and hair like the silver white Sands of Saldasir. He called himself Lune."

Lune! That was the name of the Unicorn who had blessed the Prophecy of the Twilight Moon, the very Son of the Moon himself. Every man, woman, and child in Eidolon, human and Faerie alike, knew of Lune. The Bearer of Light, the Walker of White, the King beneath the Moon. He was the one who would be the judge at the final battle against the Twilight Dragon, who had once been his brother, bearing witness to the battle of the Kinship of the Twilight Moon. Lune himself would bless their blades with his magic.

But he had been slain, long ago, by the Agents of the Twilight Dragon, the cursed Sídhe who feared their Lord's defeat. Lune's blood was spilt, and he was forever doomed to wander through the threshold of Liminality. It was said he would stay there until the day the lost Daughter of Pandora awakened at last as a member of the Kinship and returned to her home. Only then would Lune once more be reborn.

Áine remembered the songs well.

This was the Unicorn that Grian had met?

"He took my hand and told me of my fate, and he told me of yours. Two sisters, bound to walk the same path, though in worlds far apart.

"I asked if he was really the Lune we heard spoken of in Legend, and he merely laughed. It was one of the most innocent, pure, and wonderful things I had ever heard in my life. Like silver bells. Then he said that the Sídhe's mistake was spilling his blood, for because such an act had been carried out, he could now watch over the both of us, from his vantage point in Liminality. He truly was the Lune of Legend.

"When at last my astonishment faded, I asked where I was, and he explained that I had merely taken a wrong turn. He led me out of the light and back to Eidolon, where I began my search for my fellow brothers and sisters, my own Kinship of the Twilight Moon."

She took hold of Áine's hand and led it to touch the stone as well. It had the same reaction as it had for Grian. "It seems as though the Old Ones have approved of you. Your path has been laid before you now."

Áine looked up at her half-sister. Long had she believed that all other Faeries had died out, but now, she had finally found another. True, Grian was a Halfie as she was, but Áine no longer felt alone. She did not want to leave as soon as she had found true family once more. She wished that her fear and grief had not gotten the best of her. She wished with all of her heart that every drop of human blood she had spilled would return to the bodies and lives of the people she slaughtered. She had ruined everything. "Grian..." she began quietly, but her half-sister interrupted her.

"Here is where we part ways. You can either rise to challenge your fate, go through that portal and close it behind you to help our cause and avenge your people, or you can stay here in your dead forest and remain as the loneliest Halfie for the rest of your life. Either way, we shall never meet again. The choice is your own. I leave you to your decision. Though our time together was short, and not met in the best of circumstances, I am grateful that I met you, Áine. Farewell, little sister." With that, she released her hand and disappeared back into the mists.

When the last silhouette of Grian disappeared behind the petrified trees, Áine sat down by the pool and buried her face in her hands. The path she would walk at first seemed like a weak attempt at redemption for the horrible crimes she had committed. There had been many Kinships throughout the ages, repeating the cycle again and again. No matter what, it would be reborn. Even if she did succeed. How would that right her wrongs? Slaying the Twilight Dragon was something many brave heroes had done in the past. They were valiant, courageous folk, filled with magic and wisdom.

Áine was naught but a murderous waif, deluded by her own self-proclaimed right to the White Wood. Her crimes haunted her, her loneliness made her sick to her stomach, and many times she contemplated ending her own life right there and then. Someone else could take up this path. Someone worthy.

Not her.

Certainly not her.

As she sat there at the foot of the stone tablet, her own hate-filled actions haunted her every thought. The words of the prophecy mocked her, tormented her. How could they possibly be true in light of all she had done?

But in the end, she realized that...it *had* to be her.

As Grian had said, Áine was believed to be the one of the last people alive in all of Eidolon who had Faerie blood flowing through their veins. She was the only one who could go to the other world and find the descendants of the Eidoliths who had escaped to Earth so many years ago. This lake was a one-way portal, the likes of which could only be used by those with magical heritage. Not many now could claim that right. It was the last true right she had.

Hope began to bubble up inside of her once more. This task would not only allow her to redeem herself for the lives she took by saving the lives of countless others, but it would allow her to properly avenge the death of her family and the fall of the White Wood. She decided that she would renounce her life as last of the Faeries and at last embrace the human side of herself. She would take the name McCrae, the way her human surname would be said in the common tongue, and renounce the name Nic Maoilriain. She lifted her face up to the treetops, smiled, and let herself fall into the cool water by her feet.

Áine would at last rise to meet Destiny.

Chapter Four
Soul and Soil

~~~

Grian knelt before the corpses of her brothers. Dark blood soaked the wooden floor beneath them, stained the torn table cloth, and splattered the walls where they had fallen.

She...may have overdone it a bit. She hadn't expected for Áine to go Feral like that. Though perhaps it was better that way. There was no possibility that Fennen and Aillen could be mistaken for still being alive. Such carnage was precisely what Grian needed to give Áine that last push. However, this mess was not going to be fun to clean up.

Perhaps she'd have the children help her later. The little ones were always eager to get on Grian's good side, with her generous rewards of honey cakes and letting them steal sips from her wine at supper. She was a woman with conquests not only on the field of battle by the banner of the Fianna she so honorably served, but also in the hearts of the little ones who would bear the future of her clan on their shoulders. The least she could do for them was spoil them a little since she was away so often, making her something of a "favorite aunt" amongst the younger ones.

Besides, they would have to get used to the sight of blood sooner or later. They were the children of warriors.

She sighed a great sigh before standing up and clapping her hands twice. "Come on, you two, stand up," she commanded. "Or did my little sister deliver that much of a beating to you?"

On command, the two young men stood up, rubbing their aches and wiping the blood from their faces. As they brought their hands away, there wasn't a scratch on them. Their wounds were no more. There never had been, and never would be, scars upon their perfect faces. All that remained to signify that there had been a fight at all was their torn clothes, and the blood that spattered the room they stood in. "Come on, Grian, couldn't let us rest a little longer?" complained Fennen. "We don't get the opportunity that often."

"You didn't really look all that comfortable. Now come on, we've got work to do," replied Grian. She put her helmet back on and turned to walk out the doorway. When she realized that the boys were not following her, she stopped at once, and her voice grew cold. "Don't make me say it twice."

Grumbling, Fennen and Aillen followed their sister as she passed through the threshold.

"What has become of the Maoilriain child?" asked Aillen.

"I have sent her through the portal, to Earth, as the Fianna have instructed me to do. She will cause us no more trouble here, and will not interfere with our clan's work any longer."

"Are you certain that was such a wise thing to do, Grian?" questioned Fennen. "She could have aided us. She had Faerie blood, like you..."

"That's right, like me. The prophecy only needs one Faerie Maiden from the Wild. And that role has already been filled here. We have neither care nor use for her here, and she will aid us far better from her place on Earth."

"But Grian, she was so young, so confused..." said Aillen.

"What if she were to go Feral again in the other world? Would that not be detrimental to our cause? You should have gone in her place, Grian. At least then we could have kept an eye on her. You we can trust. Áine is a wild card," added Fennen.

Grian laughed, interrupting him. "She was wild and vicious. You should have seen the mess she made of you two!"

"You forget that it was all part of the plan, Grian," Aillen countered fiercely. "We are not as weak as we appeared. You underestimate us, and that is not wise."

"Who are you to tell me what is unwise, Aillen? You who bow your will to me and to the Fianna who gave you life and purpose?"

"She would not have left a scratch on us if not for the Will of the Fianna."

"But we don't have a scratch..." Fennen blurted.

"That's right. Nor shall you ever. For Golems do not bleed."

Chapter Five
Fins and Tales

~~~

It was early morning, with the sun only just having started to peek over the horizon. The trees glistened with their morning dew, reflecting tiny sparkling rainbows off of their golden leaves. It was early autumn, and the trees had just begun to change their colors. Few had yet to fall, carpeting the wet, muddy ground in their yearly coat of reds and browns.

Two young women by the names of Áine McCrae and Leilani Moanna sat by the bank of a lake, watching the scenery. It had been almost two years now that the girls had met and made this magical place their home, adventuring together, singing together, and sharing their company; though neither had ever revealed much more of themselves to one another than their names. That wasn't to say that they weren't close, as they had been one another's only companions for a very long time, it was just that their memories were too painful to share. Neither of the girls were human, and neither wanted to relive the pain of how such things had come to be.

But Áine had wasted too much time already running away from her path and avoiding telling the truth to Leilani. She was afraid that she would think her story crazy, as she had been warned that people of Earth were quite skeptical of anything except for that which they had seen for their own eyes. Such was the burden of having been born without the blessing of Magic.

Yet Leilani, too, had the gift of Magic. Áine had sensed the potential to wield it within her from the moment they first met, and as soon as she had her safe and sound, she had begun to awaken her potential. She gave to her the gift of Faerie blessing, sacrificing half of her own potential to awaken that of her friend's. After all that had happened to the poor girl, she deserved to have a fantasy or two come true. And easing the pain of her friend helped ease the pain of her own guilt.

Even now, Leilani was quite the budding Spell Weaver. She could open simple portals, cast short-term underwater-breathing spells, and even create barriers with the waters of the lake she called home. She could even tap into the deep magic potency of Pearls, True Magic. Few Spell Weavers, no matter how powerful they were, could tap into True Magic, and yet Leilani could. Perhaps there was a chance that all of this would soften her reaction to the tale that Áine had no choice but to tell her. It was one of the reasons she had delayed so long.

"Leilani," she began. "There is something that I must tell you. I have already waited far too long."

Leilani looked over to her companion. "You know you can trust me, Áine. You have been my only friend these past years, I would not abandon you." The words that the young maiden spoke were true. Even the clothes that Áine wore were once Leilani's, given to her when the strange lady had appeared to her, nearly naked, at the time of her brave rescue. Leilani no longer had any use for them, now that she was what she was.

Leilani had dark tanned skin and appeared as if she had Hawaiian features. She had long black hair that shone a shade of blue in the dim morning light, and was held away from her scarred face by strands of pink and white pearls and faded blue silk ribbons. In addition to the pearls and ribbons, there were a few shells that she was wearing as hair-clips above her left ear. The only real clothing she wore was a silky blue tube top, though truth be told, she needed nothing else.

She looked like she was around the age of eighteen or nineteen; not quite in her twenties yet not quite out of her teens. Deep, pale scars covered her back, streaking down from the base of her neck in

34

grotesque vertical patterns. Her legs were replaced by one long, gray tail with a dorsal fin sticking out from the back. In fact, it looked more like the tale of a dolphin rather than a fish, especially since it had no scales.

"I know, my friend, but still my past has frightened me too much to go on. Now, though...now I must press on. And you must come with me."

Leilani wanted to laugh, but resisted doing so. She fully understood how hard it was for her friend to speak about, well, anything really. In all of this time, she only truly knew one thing about Áine – she had saved her life, and for that, she would be eternally grateful. Instead, she just glanced down at her lower body, where instead of legs, she possessed a leathery grey tail and some fins to go along with it.

The gesture was not lost on Áine. She smiled. "You will not need legs to walk alongside me. We shall use the pearls."

"But Áine, you told me that we were never to use them. Not until the day..."

"That day has come, Leilani. They are beginning to gather at last. He is coming."

"Who is coming?" asked Leilani. She was beginning to become quite confused.

Áine looked at her with eyes filled with longing. She took a deep breath and let out a great sigh before going on. She held a pearl up high and blew on it. Waves of pale rainbow light burst forth from the tiny orb and shrouded them in its soft warmth. Leilani took that as her cue, she waved her fingers in a quick pattern, appearing to spell something out. When her motions were complete, the light now showed a number of faces in quick succession.

First there was Áine herself, diving into a shallow pool beneath a tall stone. Then there was Leilani, being unbound from a table...a memory she was already all too familiar with. Next followed a sweet young face, with bright blue eyes and blonde hair near as white as snow, known to most of the modern world as Prince Anton of New France. Neither of the young women had personally met him before, but they knew him by sight quite well enough. Then came a number of young men and women who neither of them recognized, but both felt a strange familiarity with. A golden haired teen with hopelessness in her chocolate eyes. A small child with a braided crown of dark hair perched atop her pale head. A dirty faced youth with fire in her eyes and wind in her dull black hair. The Peach...and the Cat...

When their faces had all been revealed, the vision rippled and began to fade away. Finally, the image ceased, and Leilani let out a breath she had not realized that she had been holding.

"Who are these people, Áine? What did that vision mean?"

"The child of a Songsmith, two artificial beings, descendant of the Eidoliths, a Psychic that needs freeing, A Faerie maiden from the Wild, A lass who cannot cry, and lest ye not forget the child, who shall join them from the sky."

"That old Eidolith prophecy?" asked Leilani.

"It is time I told you the truth, my friend, as I should have told you long ago when first we met. I am from a world as different from this one is as night is today. I am from a place where magic is real, and spirits roam free, deadly and tangible. It was the birth place of the Gods of Old. But I can never go back."

Leilani put her hand on Áine's shoulder.

"Too long have I kept these things hidden from you. Now I must tell you of why I came here, and why I saved you two long years ago. You must believe what I say. For the fate of the very world depends on it."

Leilani nodded, and thus began Áine's tale.

~~~

"So...this prophecy...you believe that I am part of it? I have heard tales of the Twilight Dragon, but I had never really believed in them."

Áine pinched Leilani's arm.

36

"Ow! What was that for?" she asked, rubbing her sore spot.

"I believe that you may be the maid who cannot cry."

"Pinching me isn't going to prove anything. I've had much worse..." she said as she lightly stroked her tail.

"I know, I was merely trying to make a point. You don't have tear ducts, Leilani, I've noticed. Aside from nullifying your pain, it's one of the reasons why you don't like staying out of the water. Your eyes get dry, and you look uncomfortable when you blink. You can't cry."

Leilani answered in silence. Áine must have had excellent vision to have noticed such a thing. Well, she was half-Faerie...maybe that had something to do with it. Back then, when she had been...no, she wouldn't think about such dark times. Well, they had sealed up her tear ducts. Her eyes got very dry very quickly, and when she wanted to cry all that happened was that she got a very runny nose.

"You must speak of this to no one," Áine ordered Leilani.

The finned girl nodded. "I understand. Even when we do find the others, I do not think it would be wise to tell them of these things right away. I know you and trust you...you did save my life after all. But to strangers, I think this would be too much."

Áine hugged the finned girl. "Thank you, Leilani. I shall not soon forget your kindness."

"Don't worry about it," replied Leilani. "Though, you never answered my question. Who is coming?"

"One of the people mentioned in the prophecy. When I touched the stone, images of their passing were burned into my mind. What I showed you just now through the power of that pearl was what I saw when I first touched the stone. Being born of Faerie blood, I can sense their presence, as their lives have been linked to my own through our collective fates. I felt him coming just now."

"I see." Leilani laid back on the damp dirt and looked up at the pale sky. "When will he arrive?"

"Tomorrow night."

"Does he know we're here?"

"Doubtful."

"What would you have me do, Áine?"

Áine was quiet for a while as she thought. It would be hard enough to explain her own presence, let alone that of a finned girl. And she didn't know how the Prince would react. The easiest option would be for Leilani to let Áine handle this on her own. "Go to Atlantis. It is safe there, and we will not have to worry about explaining your fins in addition to explaining the prophecy when he arrives."

"I understand." Leilani took hold of Áine's hand and gave her quite a serious look. "Don't scare him away, Áine. We need him. It will be nice to have a new friend." And with that, she dove into the lake, down, down, down, and never resurfaced.

Chapter Six
Ice and Water

~~~

This was it. Today was the day. The day that young Anton would finally go out and begin his pilgrimage. No longer would he be tied to the title of Prince Anton Christophe LaCiel of New France. Now he would simply be Sir Anton, and he would embark on a journey to become a true Spell Weaver, as his mother and uncle had before him.

It was a rare and great honor to be a Spell Weaver, for no mortals could cast magic in their own right. One's bloodline had to have been blessed by a true magical being in order to be granted access to a select set of spells, which were only faint echoes of true magic. Yet it was a great gift all the same, one that Anton would not squander, one that he would use to help people in whatever way he could.

"Here are your new garments," Anton's father said as he handed him a bundle of delicate looking clothing. "Take them with peace, and wear them with grace. They are not as fragile as they appear, just like you." He smiled at his son with pride. "My son, a strapping young lad of nineteen. How time flies!" It was hard for the King to believe that his little Anton was about to go into the world on his own. But it had to be done. Without the rare magical blessing that the late Queen, and by inheritance, her son, possessed, the world would continue its decent into lifeless decay. "My dear Prince...you are all grown up now. How your mother would have loved to see this day."

Anton smiled back at him. It would be months, maybe even years before the young Prince would see his father again. His loving, benevolent father, King Damien.

Prince Anton took a look at the garments that his father had handed to him. Amongst them was a short, fitted, cream colored tunic; a dark blue hooded robe to keep him warm, a light blue vest lavishly adorned with snowy embroidery and two slits along the shoulder blades; thick tan boots; and a long silver rope meant to be tied at his waist. Although his hands would most certainly be concealed beneath the long baggy sleeves of the robe, a pair of embroidered, cream colored, fingerless gloves was included in the pile. This was the customary garb for a travelling Spell Weaver-in-training, though Anton had picked out the colors himself.

"Are you sure you're ready, my son?"

"Ready as I'll ever be, *père*."

"This is your first time going so far from home. You be careful now, *oui*?"

"*Oui, père*. I have gone out twice before, I can be trusted with this. I can do it."

"I know you can," said King Damien as he touched his son's face gently. "*Je t'aime*, my son, and be safe."

"I will. I promise."

With that, his step-mother Queen Emeraude's handmaidens escorted Anton out of the Throne Room so that he could prepare himself for the long journey ahead.

The Prince sat at his bed for a long time, taking in his surroundings and absorbing them like a sponge so the feeling of home would last for as long as possible. He would miss the boyish blue bedroom here, decorated in all things he now thought to be too childish for him to have much care for any longer. Toy planes, enchanted blocks, his modest collection of wooden cars and wind chimes... Those days were over now, though. There would be no more time to hold his old teddy bears and toys to his chest and pretend to have grand balls and order them around like the King he so wanted to be, no time for secret make-believe worlds of wonder and magic. Now he had to use real magic to fix that which had already begun to be drained from the lifeless world he was about to set off into. It made him sad, in a way, but also excited. This was his chance to change the world, to make his mark. To live.

"Genevieve, I am ready to go," Anton said firmly after he had finally finished preparing himself. His step-mother's handmaiden nodded respectfully and led the Prince into the unassuming car that would take him to the city limits, where he would set foot in the dead wilderness at last.

The car ride was long and uneventful, though he savored every moment of it. They were the last precious few he was going to have of his old life. There wasn't going to be another chance for him to ride in a car again, let alone a limo, for a long, long time...drinking hot tea and enjoying the cool breeze of the built-in air conditioner.

Anton's reminiscing was cut short, however, when the car finally came to a stop. "Here is where we part ways, Prince Anton," said the chauffer. He did not even turn to look at him as he opened the limo door for him, his head bowed down in respect. "I wish you luck in your travels."

"Thank you, sir," Anton replied with a not-so-graceful bow. He had never been very good at those. "The sentiment is much appreciated." And with a tip of his hat, the door was shut behind him, and the car drove off into the distance. Anton was on his own.

~~~

It had been many weeks now since Sir Anton first stepped out of that limo and began his pilgrimage, and already he was becoming used to his new way of life. Today he found himself standing in a great, empty plain, his newest charge. The crispness of the cool autumn morning settled in all around him. There was no sign of any color anywhere. Even the reddish colors of the earth so natural for autumn were nowhere to be seen. Everything that he could see was either the dead-brown of the blades of grass or the muddy-brown of the soil beneath it all. Even the sky was a desolate, dusty-brown

41

color. He seriously stuck out like a sore-thumb in all of this brown-ness.

But then again, that was why he was here in the first place...

"Ugh, there's nothing but brown, brown, brown and more brown! Not even a decent brown, like the color of a lively tree trunk! Just muddy, murky, dusty, sickly, disgusting brown!" Anton shook his head in disgust. "A most displeasing color!" his short, silvery hair blew in the dry, dusty wind as the Prince preached to himself, crossing his arms across his chest and making an angry face at his surroundings. He knew it was childish, but he couldn't help it. This was his own way of rebelling against it all.

In the past few years, it had recently become necessary for Spell Weavers like Anton to go and repair what had been destroyed by what was known only as the Plague of Twilight. Wherever it struck, it sucked the life out of everything. That was why everything was so brown. Nothing had life in it anymore. It was rumored that this Plague of Twilight was just another malevolent force caused by the Twilight Dragon, which was undoubtedly how it got its name. Now he and other Spell Weavers like him had to breathe life back into the dead lands. Anton himself did not believe in the dragon, but he certainly believed that something evil was afoot for such awful things to be happening.

"This simply won't do. What has happened? I know for a fact that autumn has more than just dusty brown everywhere you look! And I definitely know that not everything suddenly dies at once the moment the cold breeze comes along! Ugh..." He had always had a habit of talking to himself out loud, being an only child and being alone for most of the time. It was just a way to break the silence, to be honest, and to reaffirm his own thoughts by hearing them spoken, even if there was no one else there to hear him speak.

Anton took a quick look around, just to make sure that he wasn't simply imagining this. This was the third time that he had been called upon this month alone to fix the unnatural bleakness of the landscape. And on top of that, the other two times had been before he was meant to go out and use his magic in the first place.

The world was most certainly getting worse if the plague was beginning to spread so frequent and fast.

Everywhere he looked was definitely brown. No matter how far he walked, that was the only color to be seen. He walked further and further along until he found tall grass...which, by the way, was still brown. Anton burrowed his way through the grass until he came to a clearing.

"Ugh, it's still all brown!" He looked into the shallow pool of water. "This is brown too? I've just about had enough of this hideous color! But that's why I was summoned here, I suppose, so I can't complain. These people sure do need to elaborate more on their job descriptions," the Prince complained almost cheerfully to himself.

Anton quickly dusted himself off and clapped his hands twice to scatter the dust from his gloves. He took a staff from inside of his robe's sleeve that was about four inches shorter than his arm. It had a blue and gold handle etched with snowflake designs, not unlike the patterns in his gloves, and it had long, silver strings of beads dangling near the top. At the head of the staff, there rested a beautiful silver Celtic knot carve-out that featured delicate carvings within the silver metal itself.

Anton raised the staff high in the air, waved it around in a complicated pattern in the sky, and cried out, "*Flocon orage!*" What he had just said was an ancient French incantation passed down by his birth mother's side of the family for generations. It literally meant, "Snowflake storm," but for some unknown reason, it would not work for anyone without that family's bloodline or in any other language. Such is the mystery of the Spell Weavers' birthright.

Within moments, a huge blizzard formed up...but there was not a cloud in sight. This was specialty snow, a physical manifestation of Anton's will. Within the very flakes contained particles of his own life energy, energy used to heal and fix. After a few minutes, the entire plain was covered in almost two-feet of snow. Even the shallow pool had frozen over with ice. Flecks of silver powder could be seen drifting blissfully through the air. And yet altogether, it was not unbearably cold.

While the snow and ice was blowing all around, he danced around in a very flowing, ritualistic manner. The longer he danced the snow flake storm dance, the longer the snow would fall. Anton danced and danced until every inch of the land was frozen over. He then stood in one place and looked at the landscape that he had changed.

Now instead of dusty brown, blues and whites were the only colors in sight. "That should just about do it."

The Prince took three steps back, and then twirled his staff around once in a three-hundred-and-sixty degree motion in the air. He thudded it into the snow. A huge ice-blue ripple formed around the base of the staff and rapidly expanded. Everywhere the ripple passed, the snow and ice melted away, leaving lush green grass that sparkled in the sunlight with fresh dew. Tiny multi-colored flowers sprung up everywhere. The sky became the clearest blue that anyone could possibly see, with tiny blooms of clouds speckling the sky every now and then in the far west. The water became crystal-clear, and lilies even began to grow on it. It was now spring in autumn; not exactly the way it should be, but just the way he liked it. And besides, in only a few hours, the landscape would hyper-accelerate itself into the proper season anyways. This brief spring was only meant to rejuvenate the soil for the true spring in the coming year.

With a satisfactory and almost prideful grin on his face, Anton slid his staff back into his sleeve. He inhaled deeply, enjoying the sweet aroma of fresh air rather than the disease inducing air that was formerly present within the previously desolate plain.

Life was there again, and it was wonderful to behold.

"That takes care of that! I suppose my work here is done." And with those words, he walked right out of the plain.

As Anton walked, he began to think aloud to himself, as he often did. Silence unnerved him, and as he had no travelling companions to talk to, he simply took to speaking his thoughts aloud.

"First, I must head up to north again to get that next spell from my uncle. Then I can head out east from the main palace to go and take care of that other Call I was instructed to take. While I'm at it, I can go get more supplies back on the mainland, since by then I will no doubt have exhausted what my father gave me to start out with."

He walked and walked, but when a three way split came about in the road, he hesitated. He blinked at the intersection as if he had come to a sudden realization of something crucial yet forgotten.

"Um...now which path should I take?" he asked himself aloud as he gazed upon the signs. One way was the way he needed to go, in the direction of his Uncle's manor, and the other way was simply an unnecessary detour.

A strange tugging sensation suddenly washed over the young Prince. He felt as though he wanted to take that unnecessary detour. No, he didn't merely "want" to. It grew and grew until the want became a need inside of him. "I am on a bit of a schedule...but...I suppose that it can't hurt to go on a little adventure. But just a little one!" He tacked on at the end of his sentence as a little bit of self-scolding.

Anton took a deep breath and then rolled back his long, baggy sleeves. Then he twirled around twice with his arms outstretched and his face to the sky, and when he stopped spinning, his hand pointed in the direction of the road that led away from where his uncle lived. He already knew which one led to his uncle's land, but he deliberately went the wrong way. It was as if some foreign yet internal voice was propelling him to go against his right mind.

"It's just a silly little detour, I'm not doing anything wrong," he kept telling himself as he walked along his newly chosen path.

The path that the Prince had chosen was wide and open at first, but then, as he traveled farther along it, it began to have undergrowth appear around the edges. Rats scurried along the dusty walkway. Then brambles inched closer and closer to the center of the now twisting path. This was more than bizarre, as in modern day

45

New France, the brambles and unkempt pathways were unheard of and kept under high maintenance. "Why is this road so disorderly?" He thought to himself that as soon as he got through, he would send an order for the road-workers to clean up and fix this road immediately. Anton could just barely pass through; there was so much foliage in his way.

"I won't turn back now," he said to himself. "I'm sure I'll end up somewhere soon enough."

Anton kept on traveling down the now uncertain path, until darkness had fallen and a sliver of the silver moon had risen. It was a welcome sight compared to his fears of a pitch black sky, as last night there had been no moon at all. He silently thanked the heavens that there was at least a slight bit of silver light to help him on his way in this intimidating darkness.

As he pushed himself further and further, however, even the tiny light of the sliver of moon could not penetrate through the thick branches and tree tops. The road was now entirely encased in brambles and outgrown branches that appeared as if they were black in color. And worse yet, they seemed to be whispering vile things to one another in a language that he could neither understand nor even knew if he was really hearing to begin with. Was he going mad?

"What are you trying to tell me?" he cried aloud. "Let me pass, please!" He was getting angry.

But he was not worried or even the least bit frightened. Anton was only losing his patience, which, for one who was raised as a Prince and trained to be able to have unyielding patience, he unfortunately had very little to speak of.

He took out his staff once more, and cried out, "*Neigeux haleine!*" This was the second spell that he knew, this one literally meaning, "Snowy breath." He grabbed his staff from both sides with both of his hands and dipped and pushed it forward. He ducked down and swung his body back as he said this. Within mere moments, a frigid wind began to blow from behind his and push forward with unimaginable strength.

The Prince could hold his ground since it was his own spell and the magical wind was forbidden to touch him, but the branches that had been clawing at him had no choice but to pull back. They were being blown out of the way, and then frozen in place.

As soon as the wind died down, Anton replaced the staff in his sleeve and continued on his way. He walked down the path as fast as he could to get out of the dreadful area. He then took out his staff once more and twirled it in the motion of the infinity symbol, and then slammed the head of the staff into the ground, causing a blue ripple to emanate from it. The ice melted off of the branches, and they slowly resumed their original positions.

And so, he continued down his newly cleared path, not bothering to take in any of his surroundings; not that he could have seen them even if he had tried to in that eerie darkness. Coming this way was a mistake. He just wanted to get this silly little detour over with and get to wherever this road would take him so that he could hurry up and be on his way to see his uncle. And perhaps to get some rest while he was at it.

.

Chapter Seven
Fate and Fireflies

~~~

Anton eventually wound up at a great lake covered in a thick veil of mist, clouding all sight of the surface of the water, with the full moon shining brightly overhead. He was greatly puzzled, as he distinctly remembered that just earlier that night, not five minutes prior, the moon had only been a sliver. Had he just imagined it being so slim? Or was he now imagining the moon in all of its pure, silvery beauty? Anton couldn't decide which moon had been the real moon. They both had been so real.

Soft, silver moonlight caressed the slight ripples below the mist on the water's delicate surface, though thick mist obscured his vision. The wind sang a near silent lullaby as the grains of sand along the water's edge danced with its melody known only to the earth.

He could hear faint music - human made music, as if from a stringed instrument - from somewhere. It drew him into the icy blue water. A shiver ran up his back as he sank into the frigid tide. To Anton's surprise, it wasn't more than waist deep. He waded closer and closer to the music until he could tell what the instrument was...a violin. "It has to be close to here," Anton said to himself. "It's getting louder."

As he waded through the water, his eyes became clouded over with calm, and he eventually lost all interest in doing anything else. He didn't care that his body was becoming numb from the chill of the frigid waters, and he didn't care that he was getting himself soaked. He didn't care that it would take hours for his robes and boots to dry out even after he got out of the water. He didn't care that he would probably get a case of the chills because of his carelessness. He just kept moving forward, closer and closer; as close as he could manage to get to the beautiful music emanating from the center of the lake.

Swoosh, wish, shwoom... The ripples carried him in deeper. "It's so enchanting...so soothing..." Anton whispered to himself. He spun around twice to make sure that it wasn't coming from behind him. The last thing that he wanted to do was to head away from the source of the music. But it seemed like it was all around him now, and it was getting harder and harder for the Prince to determine where exactly it was coming from.

As Anton waded deeper into the water, he began to notice fireflies hovering about over the water. The deeper he moved in, the thicker the concentration of the little flickering bugs. On and off, their lights waved in and out of sight, ebbing and flowing like the tide of the water. They seemed to be dancing to the music of the violin.

"That's strange," he said to himself. "I suppose the little things like pretty music too." Anton kept on wading further into the lake. At least he had his heading again. All he would have to do was watch for where the fireflies clustered in larger groups.

As he grew closer to the source of the music, Anton began to hear a young woman's singing voice. It rang with a motherly air, despite the fact that it sounded like it belonged to someone so young. The voice could not have belonged to anyone out of their late teens.

He could hear the words more clearly now.

Counting the tears of the crystal blue waters
Rolling into the dark depths of time
Rumbling and raining their loneliness and despair
All in the waters, the waters of time

49

He wandered deeper and deeper into the water. Nothing could stop his entranced hunt for the mysterious and enchanting music.

Come see the crystalline memories of angels
Flitting away to begin Heaven's climb
Fluttering and waving away evil in the air
All can be seen in the waters of time

Don't turn back, don't turn back
Until you've looked deep in your heart
Don't look back, don't look back
Until you've seen the way

The cool water lapsed around Anton's body, soaking his clothes from the waist down, but he still didn't care.

Lifting away all the drapery of the night
Showing the light that banishes crime
Twisting and turning its way there and everywhere
Lead us into the waters of time

At long last, he took a few more steps until he finally saw a figure, standing waist-deep in water.

What the Prince encountered was a young woman dressed in a soft-pink, sleeveless turtle-neck sweater and a long, white, flowing sarong. Her neck was adorned with a crystal-chained necklace with a pewter crescent moon on it. Where the sarong parted, a peek of navy-blue shorts could be seen. She had long, dull, sand-colored blonde hair that must have reached to at least her waist, but it was hard to tell as it was blowing around in the cool wind. Judging by the curvature in her bangs and in the drier parts of her hair, it was slightly curly. The beautiful young woman was standing waist deep at the center of the lake with her eyes closed shut, playing a violin and singing.

Don't turn back, don't turn back
Until you've looked deep in your heart
Don't look back, don't look back
Until you've seen the way

Anton's heart stopped. He had never believed in love at first sight, but now he had his doubts. She possessed bewitching beauty and an enchanted voice. There was nothing plain or ordinary about her. Even her wavy, sand colored hair had personality. Her image was the very meaning of loveliness.

Fireflies danced around the mysterious girl as if she was their keeper and queen. The soft music that serenaded from the strings of the violin seemed to call to the little flickering lights that glowed all around them. Her voice rang clearly in harmony with the instrument's music. It was as if the fireflies, too, were singing softly alongside the serene hum of the violin.

The young woman playing the violin, as if she had become suddenly aware of Anton's presence, immediately turned around and stopped playing her instrument.

Anton jumped. He hadn't expected the young woman to turn around.

"Greetings, Sir Anton Christophe LaCiel, Prince of New France. The son of King Damien and Princess Emeraude, I do believe. Or is Emeraude queen now? I may have missed that news, as I've been here for some time now..."

The Prince interrupted the young woman's monologue with, "Yes, my step-mother is queen now."

The woman paid little heed to the interruption, and continued her speech without missing a beat. "Yes, you should know what it is I speak of. You are the Prince on a Pilgrimage."

"Wait...what?" Anton replied. "You...know what I am?"

"Who doesn't?" she replied softly as a little firefly landed on the dainty tip of her perfect nose. She smiled even softer than her reply, blinking once ever so slowly. The firefly flew off as she took a breath.

"You have a point...but how did you know that I was coming?" Anton tucked a strand of his short hair behind his ear.

"My friend's magic told me that you would come here tonight. She, too, is a Spell Weaver, as you are, though her powers are limited to the Sight and Sound, where yours can affect the physical world. A rare gift indeed." Then, quieter and almost to herself, she mused, "I must wonder, was it the Winged Ones who blessed your bloodline?"

Anton gulped. It was widely known that no human could cast magic. Could not cast true magic, anyhow. There was but a single way that a mortal could even be granted access to magic's echo – to be blessed by Faerie, Haneshiro, or Eidolith hand. Once touched, the bloodline of the blessed would pass down access to the spells for as long as the bloodline went on, no matter how diluted it became.

There was an old poem they used to say about it.

By Fey Touch, sight
By Sky Touch, might
By True Touch, shadow, soul and light

When Áine had mentioned the Winged Ones, she must have been alluding to the Haneshiro. He started to fidget in his boots. She couldn't possibly have known that...she couldn't... He tried to calm himself. There were, after all, more methods than one to bless a bloodline...

Áine had spoken truly, however. It had been the Haneshiro who had blessed his line. Faeries could not gift powers that could physically manifest without significant outside interference, and no human had been blessed by the Old Ones, the Eidoliths, since before The Collapse.

"We have been waiting for you," said the young woman. She let her violin rest on her chest. "This path is what you thought was merely a detour, am I wrong? Well, the path you have chosen will lead you on the greatest journey of your life. Bigger, even, than your pilgrimage, though I promise that will not end here either," she finished in a soft voice that spoke just above a whisper.

"Who are you? What do you know about my pilgrimage?" Anton's breath caught in his chest. There was something unnatural about this young woman, although he couldn't quite pinpoint what.

"I am the last of the Tuatha de Danann. My name is Áine... McCrae, and I am pleased to make your acquaintance." She gave the Prince a warm, soft smile – the kind of smile that a mother would give her child. Though Anton had never met his birth mother and had only been away from his step mother for a short time, the pangs of missing them both stung his heart as Áine's smile graced him.

It was eerie. He couldn't quite decide whether or not to trust her just yet, though the calming and motherly aura about her was certainly throwing Anton for a loop. He had been taught that Faeries were tricksters, though not generally malevolent. This seemed far too complex to be a simple prank, but...what was he to do?

"How come I was drawn to this lake? I was supposed to head up to the mainland and meet up with my uncle..." Anton began to think back to the split in the road, and how he had deliberately chosen the wrong path.

"To teach you your next spell, I know," Áine said calmly. "Yet what drew you here was nothing but your fate." Anton didn't quite know what to say to this, as he had never believed in fate or destiny or any of that nonsense. He was trying to understand what on earth was going on. And so, he responded with only silence and a blank stare.

Áine was the first to break the silence. "Sir Anton?"

"But how did you...?"

"I told you, I'm a Tuatha de Danann, a Faerie. I know things that no mortal could."

"Áine, what do the Faeries see in me that isn't in anyone else?"

"Not the Faeries, as few have interest in mortal affairs, but the Eidoliths themselves who whispered their prophecies on the wind. You carry the blood of the greatest Snow Queen the world has ever seen, the one who sang her spells with the very wind that the Eidoliths themselves once shared their spells with. You carry a great power within you. And your soul is connected to those who will purge the world of all of this misery once and for all."

"What are you talking about?"

"The Twilight Dragon. Surely you have heard of it. The very purpose of your pilgrimage is to alleviate the pain of the scars its Plague has wrought."

Anton paused for a moment. Áine had said "Twilight Dragon." He knew of the legend, but had never actually taken it seriously. The people called what he fought against the Plague of Twilight, but there was never any evidence that this creature was what caused it. It had only gotten its name from the ancient fable. But now he was curious. "What exactly is the Twilight Dragon, Áine?"

Áine looked down into the water and into her reflection, as if to ask it for guidance, or perhaps to stall to come up with an answer. "I do not know. No one knows. Some say it is a real dragon, some say it is a parasite that eats away at the heart of humanity, and others still do not even believe it exists. Some tell that it is the embodiment of the combined evil that was released from Pandora's Box so long ago. It is a child's Faerie tale, and a harbinger of destruction. But for those willing to defy their fate, the Twilight Dragon is a beacon of hope, for if they can purge the world of that monstrosity, they can put an end to the madness."

"I do not believe in fate," replied Anton.

"Whether you believe in fate or not, that does not change the fact that destiny has its own way of fulfilling itself. Somewhere deep down within yourself, you knew that something was calling you here. That call...the very call that brought you here to this lake...*that* was destiny. That call was your path to defy your fate."

"Defy it or follow it? Which is it that you are trying to tell me? And what is it that we are *destined* to do?" Anton asked sarcastically.

"We must find them, and help them fight."

"Help who? Are there more Spell Weavers like me out there helping to heal this world?"

"Not quite. There are others, and they will help us heal this world, but only one other is a Spell Weaver like yourself. Yet it will not be so simple to gather us all together. We are scattered to the wind, many having been thrust into great peril. And one is more crucial to us than all the rest. Without her, we are lost, though it is doubtful even she knows of her own importance in the prophecies. And it is imperative that we save her before her execution at dusk tomorrow."

Anton blanched. "Who?"

"Her name is Orienne Andraste. She and her younger sister, Melaenie, are the last remaining of the Andraste line. They are the heirs to the Legacy of the Twilight Dragon. The last of the true Eidoliths. I'm supposed to go with you to fulfill a task...to protect the last of the Andraste line that is being hunted down." She smiled in such a way that it seemed surreal. She had that kind of ability, which not many others did. This almost made it seem like magic to Anton. It was a kind of magic that even he did not possess. He decided that he was going to believe Áine's claim to being a Faerie.

"But they'll be dead if we don't come to their rescue. The poor things...little do they know that this world needs them more than they need us. Isn't that a shame...the Earth is that desperate as to need to choose people on the brink of death to be her saviors?"

"Destined ones? Death? What are you talking about?" Anton took a step back from Áine. At age nineteen, death was not exactly something he was ready to come face-to-face with just yet, and a sense of dread was slowly beginning to overcome him. No, he wasn't going to trust this woman.

"They are kindred souls with a power they are unable to control."

"And how does that make them destined ones?"

"It doesn't. It just complicates their struggle. But they are the only ones with a strong enough will to change the course of humanity, and their own fate. It is their birthright as well as this strength that makes them the chosen ones. And they need our help."

"Why us?"

"I do not know. But some force outside of our own power brought us together and told the fireflies of what was to come. That is enough of a reason for me to stand up and break the chains of fate."

"But I thought you said that fate had a way of fulfilling itself. Now you tell me that those who wish to defy it are the only ones who can stop the vicious cycle? Which is it that you wish me to believe?" Anton asked accusingly.

"Nay, I said that only about destiny. This world and everything in it, and the path of the universe as a whole: *that* is destiny. It can be thwarted or upheld, but it is the will of the universe, which always strives to support life.

"Now, the fate of an individual, that is a different matter entirely. Whether or not an individual defies their fate or not can never impact the greater path of destiny. If one simply leads their life calmly along the path of their fate, nothing would ever change. It is only through those who deviate from the path, as you have, that the road to destiny can be traversed. Fate is a thing to be defied, while destiny is a thing to be embraced. If no one was to take a stand, the universe would crumble, stuck in stagnancy. This is the way of things.

"Though...rest assured; nothing is final or absolute. There *is* free will. If there wasn't, fate would not be so strong of a prison. It is your choice whether or not to break free from it." The way she said this made her sound like an oracle. "Did you ever wonder why the prophets of yore kept their heroes shrouded so vaguely? It was so that many could rise to the challenge, not sealing the destiny of the world on the chance that a single person remained unaware of their chains of fate, or perhaps unwilling or unable to break them."

"How do you know all of this?"

"Like I said, I am a Faerie. I am one of those who were born with a fate imprinted upon me by the Twilight Dragon itself.

Though I personally was not affected, the Plague of Twilight stole away the lives of my family and friends, and left me all alone. I swore vengeance all those years ago. I chose to break free of the dark chains of fate it bound me in and rise to fight the fabled beast."

"So...fate is a bad thing?" Anton asked. With every further statement, she only made the young Prince's head spin more. It was a bit hard to follow, admittedly. It wasn't completely due to his air headedness.

"Not...necessarily. Sometimes it is good, sometimes it is bad, but at least it is a thing of stability. Yet with only stability, no change can come, and what this world needs right now is change. We cannot afford to be bound to our fate now." Áine suddenly changed the calm expression on her face into one of fear and urgency. "Their voices are calling out to us, even now. Can you hear them?" she asked the Prince.

"The other chosen ones?" Anton asked quietly, timidly almost. Áine's sudden swing was startling, and made his heart skip.

For a few minutes everything had gone silent and still. There was no wind; there were no crickets or katydids, and not even the slightest ripple in the water to break the stagnancy. The fireflies stopped mid flight and hovered motionlessly in the air, softly blinking on and off in the soft light of the moon. Anton closed his eyes and tried to concentrate. Áine lifted her arms out of the water and held them at either sides of Anton's face. She let go of her violin, causing it to float on the water's surface. She began to channel her power through the Prince' mind, and for a moment he struggled with whether or not he should let her.

In the end...Anton decided to revoke his former judgment. Perhaps he would trust the Faerie. For now.

Anton completely let his guard down, and he suddenly began to feel an unusual warmth flow down his spine. Everything went black. Though his skin still felt cold from the icy water, his heart began to well up with a strange, yet comforting heat. His ears began to ring before he began to hear the voice of a young girl that echoed itself until it sounded like a thousand voices at once.

57

But amidst all of that, he was able to focus on the face of a terrified young woman. She could not have been much younger than he was. Hair fair as gold, long and shining that hung just below her shoulder blades. Her face was puffy, tear-stained, and dirty, but even her sorrow could not hide her beauty. He was overcome with the desire to wipe away her tears and comfort her, to rescue her, as a brother would for a little sister. He didn't care that he had never met her before, he felt... connected to her.

Áine slowly brought her hands back down to the water and away from Anton's face. The voices quieted in his head, and his vision came back. The image of Orienne Andraste no longer burned in his mind. He felt himself beginning to cool down a little again. The iciness of the cold autumn lake returned to lap around his body. It was in that moment Anton realized that from this point onwards; his "fate" had changed. He felt it in the core of his soul that Áine was going to be, for better or for worse, his partner from here on out, and perhaps the first of many companions. When Áine's powers had coursed through his mind, it was not only that one young girl's voice, though hers had been the loudest. He had felt many others; many who he had never met, but now knew he would meet soon. Ones he would have to help. And he knew at last that his decision to trust Áine had been the right one.

"Áine, are those really the cries of the ones being hunted?" the Prince asked her innocently. "She...was so scared."

"Yes... But you could only hear one?"

"No, I heard many others, but none as strongly as the one you call Orienne."

"This is bad. It means she has fallen into greater danger than I had anticipated. She is not dead. But if we don't hurry, she soon will be!"

"Then there isn't a moment to lose."

"You're absolutely right," she said, before planting a delicate kiss upon his lips. His lungs suddenly felt much more powerful, as if he could blow down a brick house with a single breath. It was intoxicating. "I cast a Faerie spell on you. You should be able to hold your breath much longer now. It's quite a fair ways to our destination."

Anton was speechless. Did she...really just kiss him? His heart was all aflutter. Perhaps it was just an effect of the spell, but he didn't want to let go of the feeling. It was wonderful. Like flying.

"Come, follow me, Sir Anton." Áine dove into the water, holding her violin in one hand and her bow in the other as she disappeared into blue mist. Anton was still a little confused, but he knew that he had no other choice but to swim after the Faerie if he wanted to find out what was going on here. Aside from that, he truly did feel as if something was pulling him toward the enigmatic violinist. He removed the staff from his sleeve, clutching it in one hand as he took a deep breath, and dove headfirst after Áine.

They swam through the cold waters, going deeper and deeper until they could see a golden city in ruins. It was covered in a pale, rainbow colored force field. Just as Anton was about to run out of breath, the two entered through the force field. Anton was surprised to find that the ancient city he had seen only moments before was really just a gigantic air pocket, which (from a distance) was just an elaborate hallucination. Inside of the multi-colored force field was just an empty, desolate place with a lot of chunks of gray rock lying around. The fine sand that covered the bottom of the lake had been condensed into a rough and ugly stone-floor in this area.

"Sir Anton?" asked Áine after the two of them were safely inside of the bubble.

"Hey, Áine," the Prince interrupted after he had managed to catch his breath, ignoring the Faerie's question. "You can just call me Anton. You don't have to use formalities with me if we're going to be saving the world together and all that jazz. You've got to be older than me anyways, aren't you? Don't Faeries live to be thousands of years old or something?"

"I'm quite young, actually," replied Áine. "I'm only eighteen."

"But you're still a Faerie, so really, I'm the one who should be paying you respect with formalities." He took her hand and kissed it.

She laughed a twinkling Faeries' laugh, but it was only meant to be a kindly gesture. "Don't be silly, you're a Prince for goodness sake. Even those who are older than you are supposed to call you by your proper name." Áine didn't bother to mention that she, too, was technically royalty, and a Princess in her own right...but that title had long been buried, and she no longer felt the right to have it.

"Just do me a favor and simply call me Anton, would you?"

"Alright then, Anton."

"Much better."

"Do you know what this place is, Anton?" Áine inquired, making sure just to use his first name without any titles. She hoped that the person she was destined to journey with would at least have a sense of humor or imagination.

"An old, rocky place at the bottom of a lake surrounded by a mysterious yet beautiful and strange hallucination-inducing shiny and multi-colored force field that looks as if the inside of it were rampaged by angry demolitionists?"

Áine stared in awe at the young Prince, raising an eyebrow in inquiry. "Angry...demolitionists?" When she was hoping for humor, she was expecting something along the lines of sarcasm, and when she was hoping for imagination, she expected some kind of fantasy related story, not some really random stuff that was probably just blurted out on the spur of the moment.

"Sorry," Anton muttered after he noticed that Áine was giving him weird looks. "I get carried away sometimes. I can't help it." He began nervously tapping his foot on the ground. He didn't like it when he ended up embarrassing himself without meaning to.

"No, Anton..." Áine breathed, more patient than most would have been with the silly boy. "Would you like a second guess, or should I just save ourselves the trouble and just tell you myself?" Áine sighed, and Anton could tell that she was trying to mask her annoyance.

The Prince was about to take another swing at the answer, but the look on Áine's face convinced him otherwise. Instead, he sheepishly grinned and said, "Maybe...you should just tell me."

Áine put her hand to her forehead and took a deep breath, then exhaled slowly. "This is what we call Atlantis."

"Um...*we*?"

"She and I." She pointed towards a finned girl just outside the rainbow-colored barrier. The odd-looking finned girl was smiling happily as she swished back and forth in the water.

The girl swam through the barrier and ended up flopping down onto the hard ground. "*Aloha*! I'm so glad to have finally met you, Prince Anton LaCiel!" she squealed as she waved hello. She turned to Áine. "The one who was coming was Prince Anton, of all people! I can't believe it! I mean, I know I saw, but...wow!" though she sounded far more excited than she probably should have been. "I've always been a huge fan. You're a very talented Spell Weaver for your age." She spoke with a slight Hawaiian accent that seemed to give the echo of her voice an air of joy. Her accent truly matched her appearance. At least, it matched the upper half of her appearance. "I'm a Spell Weaver too, you know."

Anton had never met another Spell Weaver before. His heart was filled with excitement at the prospect. Perhaps this aquatic lady would be able to teach him a thing or two, if their blessings happened to be compatible. If not, he was thrilled all the same.

Áine turned towards the Prince. "Anton, I'd like you to meet my friend Leilani Moanna, the guardian and sole resident of Atlantis and this lake."

Leilani exclaimed, "We're going to have the adventure of a lifetime, aren't we?"

Chapter Eight
Cage and Contemplation

~~~

Orienne Andraste now sat captive in a prison built specially for her kind, and her sister had been left for dead. "Oh God...I was such a foolish, stupid idiot..."

Orienne and her sister, Melaenie, had been running low on supplies again. They had been living alone together for quite some time now, ever since the death of their mother. They needed to go out, something they only did when it was absolutely crucial to the siblings' survival. Orienne had had a bad feeling about something that entire day, though. She wasn't that willing to let her little sister out of the house, or even go out to the market on her own. She didn't want to risk exposure, that day of all days. She tried to tell Melaenie not to go, but she convinced her to let her take a trip to the market. Orienne gave in to her little sister's request, one of the biggest mistakes she had ever made in her life.

While walking out the door, Melaenie caught her foot on the porch step and *faded* before she fell. As it just so happened, there were people walking by their house at that particular point in time. Why they had been wandering so deep in the woods the sisters shall never know, but nevertheless, they were there. They saw Melaenie fade, and they began to shout. She then turned and from her shock and utter despair at someone having seen her fade, she began to cry. The people then began running towards the Andraste's house.

Orienne quickly picked Melaenie up off of the ground, and the two of them began running through the house, grabbing anything lightweight that they could carry.

"Orienne!" she cried. "I'm so sorry! It was an accident! Now we have to run," she pleaded. "I'm so sorry!" She began crying harder and holding onto her sister's hand.

They were going to leave anyways; it's just that we weren't planning on leaving so soon. And they weren't planning on being chased out, for that matter, either. For goodness sake, we didn't even have time to take any provisions or belongings with them, save for the clothes on their backs and a single knitted blanket. Orienne briefly comforted her sister before she said, "You're right. We have to go. And we have to go now."

Just then, the sisters heard angry banging at the front door. They could hear their hateful screams and accusations ring throughout the house. "Melaenie, go out the back door. I'll push stuff in front of the front door to buy us some time. I'll be right with you, I promise."

With that, little Melaenie ran off to the back door and began making her way through the woods behind their house. Meanwhile, Orienne sprinted to the front door and locked every latch as fast as her fumbling hands would allow, and kicked the table in front of it for good measure. When everything was securely locked, she dashed out the back door and into the woods after her little sister.

The leaves shook vigorously in the cold, autumn wind. Nightfall loomed all around them, its airy voice calling out to them in the darkness. There was no moon and there were no stars to light their path, assuming that they were even on a path to begin with. Orienne was beginning to doubt herself on this imaginary road that seemed only to lead straight into more terror.

The sky was blanketed by a black sheet with a hint of crimson touch. This night would be long and terrible for both of the sisters, as Orienne had feared from the very beginning. Long, claw-like limbs attached to tall, twisted tree trunks curved their way into the path before them, hindering their already slowed movement. Small twigs crackled and snapped beneath their feet as they ran through the brush and bramble that covered the ground. With every slight sound, the sisters grew even more afraid, for *they* were close behind them, seemingly ever-present.

Orienne and Melaenie ran for quite some time, doubling back and taking unusual turns in an attempt to throw off their pursuers. It soon became too dark in the dense forest, and they decided to risk taking a short break there in a murky patch of closely grown trees. That was another huge mistake. They soon heard someone's urgent footsteps coming closer towards them. It had to be the hunters. The sisters got up and began running again. There would be no time to rest.

"I think they went this way!" called a man's voice.

"They went through here!" cried another. These calls were subsequently followed by a loud siren and a light flashing in the sisters' direction, dangerously close to their true location.

Orienne panicked. There was no way this could ever turn out well. She picked her little sister up in her arms and dashed off in another direction. Hopefully this way wouldn't lead to another flashing light and give them away.

Orienne and Melaenie at last came upon a place where they could rest...or so it had seemed. What they had discovered was a rather thick bush that would easily conceal two small children, or one average sized adult. However, as only one of the two sisters were a small child, the other would not be so lucky. Orienne would have to leave her precious, innocent sister behind if they were to have any hope of surviving through the night. Melaenie needed the rest far more that she did, and she would need to go on ahead to find help for them anyways. That is, if anyone in their right mind would be willing to help the two of those...*things*...

"Orienne!" wailed Melaenie. "Don't go!" She had dark black hair that was as cold and piercing as onyx, and midnight-blue eyes. She was wearing a small lavender colored dress that was delicately decorated with blue flowers and green embroidery. She wore tight black leggings beneath the dress that served to cover her legs. Her hair was pulled back into two braids that had been tied together in the back of her head as if to crown her. She was only twelve years old, not even a teenager yet. She definitely took after their father, at least in outward appearances...that damn bastard... Orienne had always been grateful that she had not taken after his personality as well as his looks.

"Be still! Do you want them to find us?" the elder sister quickly snapped back at Melaenie, her face etched with worry.

"No, but..." replied Melaenie. Her face was filled with fear, and it hurt Orienne to look at her.

"Then do as I say!" Time was running out, and she had to get her to cooperate. This was the only way...

"But you *promised*!" argued Melaenie.

"Forget about that, now! I can't keep it forever, especially if by doing so we may both end up dead!"

"Don't talk like that, sister!"

"It's only true, now please, stay here. Be still. And be silent." Orienne tried to pull away from her, but to no avail. She clung to her like a leech.

"No, stay!"

"They will find us for sure if you don't let me go right now!"

"Sister, please stay with me! Please!"

Melaenie grabbed onto her short scarlet dress with her tiny hands, pleading as hard as she could for her big sister to stay. Orienne couldn't let them be found, though, so she couldn't give into her begging.

"Even if they find you, they would be easy on you. You're still young. But if they find me with you, they will kill us both. I'm too old for their silly games of innocence. Do you understand me?" Orienne whispered frantically. She didn't truly believe what she was saying, but she had to tell her sister anything to get her to let her leave. There was little time left now, and it was quickly slipping through their fingers. She had to get away from her sister before *they* caught up with them.

Melaenie looked at her with pleading, tearful eyes. It broke Orienne's heart to pieces. "Orienne..."

"Hush, now, you don't need me. Mom taught you a little bit of Karate before she died, and I'm sure you can use that to defend yourself, if you run into any trouble."

"Orienne, I'm twelve...no amount of Karate could help me fight off a group of adults..."

"Try, my dear little sister. Please, try..."

"But..."

"I'm sorry Melaenie, but I must find help...anywhere. I cannot take the risk of the two of us running through a dense forest with *them* hot on our trail. Then *they* really will find us," the elder sister whispered hastily. "I'll come back for you, I promise."

Orienne kissed her little sister's forehead as if she believed that everything would go exactly as planned, that the two of them would find the easiest possible way out of their undesirable situation. She prayed that things would fall that way, but in her heart she had an uneasy feeling that they wouldn't. Nothing ever went perfectly as planned...

Her sister stared at her, tears spilling from her big, blue eyes. It was in that moment that Orienne questioned her decision. How could she leave a helpless twelve-year-old all alone in the forest? She must be a terrible person to look up to... But she knew that they needed help, and they weren't going to get it just by sitting there or by wandering around in the dark. How hard was it to see a blonde teenager wearing a red dress running around with her younger sister in the woods? Despite short dresses being the current fashion, they weren't exactly ideal articles of clothing to be worn when running through the woods. Especially with their powers acting up since they were so flustered. And especially since they had *them* hot on their trail, not even so much as a few feet behind them...

Orienne hastily bundled Melaenie in the one extra blanket that she had managed to grab from the house during their hasty departure, and then quickly walked off deeper into the woods, leaving her younger sister behind. Could she really so much older than her? She was almost six years her senior...and had half the courage that she did. She was so scared, but she let Orienne leave her there in the end... She felt like she was a horrible person. She kept trying to tell herself that it wasn't abandonment, it was protection! But how would she be protecting Melaenie by leaving her to be found by the ones who were hunting them? "I...I had sentenced her to death."

She couldn't believe how crazy she had been; leaving her little sister like that and running stupidly, desperately, to find help that she knew wouldn't be there. Who would help someone like her, honestly? Especially since most people just try to kill her kind? Orienne knew that things wouldn't go smoothly, but she just couldn't bring herself to trust her primary instincts. Something inside of her was pushing her to try anything, even if deep inside she knew the odds were against her. But why did she have to be so stupid like that? All she was doing was pushing herself backwards in futility. All she really managed to do was worsen the situation for both her and her little sister.

Twice while Orienne was running away she tripped over a rock or tree root of some sort. The laces of her knee-length boots kept getting caught by the brambles of the woods time and time again. Once, she scraped her face, from below her ear to her collar-bone. Blood trickled down her neck and stained the collar of her dress. But she thought nothing of her pain, for she knew that what her sister was going through was much worse, without doubt. She could not let even one selfish thought into her head while she knew that the life of her last remaining family member was at stake. She had already lost one sibling to their hate; she couldn't possibly lose another without going mad.

She had to stay focused at all costs.

Then came the scream.

They had found her little sister.

Orienne panicked. All she could think of was running for her life until her legs could run no more, hiding out for the night and finding help in the morning. All she could do was pray for the best, and hopefully that would be enough.

But she knew in her heart that it wasn't. Praying was never enough.

In her panicked state of mind, she hardly noticed that she had run headfirst right into one of the people who had been chasing down her and her sister. And then...then she faded from the shock. She went right through him and toppled face-first into the ground. She was absolutely covered in grass and dirt. She was a complete wreck.

The man was un-amused. He grabbed Orienne by the hair and started to drag the poor girl through the woods. She kicked and screamed, wailing for her sister, crying out for help, wishing for anyone, anything, to suddenly appear and help her. Her screams echoed between the trees in vain. The man hit her in the back of the head with a blunt object she could not see, and her world went black.

When she came to, she found herself in a small cell-like room with no doors except for a hole in the ceiling that was covered with a trap-door. There was nothing but a pasty green gymnast floor-mat and a really dusty, broken mirror in the room. There was a small puddle of water in the far left corner, and broken glass around it. It seemed as if the last Fader who had been in this room had put up a fight before their untimely death. There were hints of blood on the broken glass, and even some in the water. There was a single, rotting dresser, with old potato sacks hanging from the half-open drawers.

"How random..." she said to herself. "Why potato sacks?"

Next to the rotting dresser, a blue, ceramic vase was knocked over but not broken; the dry, lifeless forget-me-nots still resting in their cracked confinement...their grave. It must have contained some hidden meaning at one point, but Orienne had too much swirling through her mind to look for it at the moment. Potato sacks...forget-me-nots...and rotting wood...it all seemed so familiar.

Had this perhaps happened once before? Had she once seen this before?

Orienne sat there on the floor for a long, long while, until she could see the first light of the morning sun peek at her through the cracks in the trap door in the ceiling. It was almost as if the light was taunting her.

That's what she was hearing in her head. She must have been going crazy with everything that was pushing and shoving its way through her thoughts. "But I suppose that's what I deserve for abandoning Melaenie... Damn it all..."

This had all happened because the Andraste sisters were both Faders. It is a strange genetic condition; caused by a virus most commonly known as Crystalline Virus that appears in infants shortly after birth. This virus acts in such a way that it temporarily dissolves the bonds of atoms within the body, causing it to "fade." When fading occurs, they become almost like ghosts. They appear to be see-through or transparent, though they are still quite visible to the human eye.

The fading reaction is greatly sped up by the release of hormones within the body, which results in many Faders "fading" whenever they feel strong emotions such as fear, love, nervousness, or excitement. Many Faders begin to fade more often as they reach their teenage years, or if they had a particularly traumatic childhood. Due to the intense prejudice against them, unfortunately that was the case for a vast majority of people like Orienne and Melaenie. Beatings, parental abandonment, loneliness, open hostility...these things were not unfamiliar to their kind.

Except that the only things they can actually fade through are organic matter such as plants, animals, or even people. They could fade through structures made of wood, but nothing made of metal, cement, or any other material made by man. Unfortunately, this meant that there was no way to use their powers to their advantage. They could never escape from places where Fader Haters hold them captive. They could never escape from someone wearing gloves made out of synthetic material. What was the good of it if they couldn't even use it to keep on living?

For some reason, a lot of people dislike Faders, even though they think and feel exactly like normal human beings, not to mention act like normal human beings, and were even born to normal human beings. Those kinds of people will go through any lengths to get rid of them...to kill every last one of them.

Think of it this way: people went around hating people because they had the cold, and killed them off just because they didn't want to catch it as well. Sure, what the Faders had wasn't exactly the primitive disease of the common cold, but it basically followed the same principles. They had no right to hate the afflicted.

No one wanted to be afflicted with the condition of Faders, because they all die before they reach the age of twenty, whether it is from the Fader Haters or from their unstable atomic makeup. It was pretty common knowledge that dying from losing yourself was a very painful way to go, and you'd rather be getting your limbs torn off by rabid beasts and have your body burned in a searing inferno at the same time as having your head smashed off after frost bite than die by losing yourself.

This is one of the main reasons why many Faders give in to the Fader Haters long before their time.

At least they dispose of them in a much less painful manner. Orienne herself didn't have much longer to live out her own life, having just recently turned nineteen. But she had vowed never to give into the hatred, and she refused to look away from the path of justice. Long ago, she had sworn that she would find a way to stop this curse even if it turned out to be the death of her.

Her mother had once told her about the condition after her brother had died. Though Orienne and her siblings had been Faders since birth, they never really knew what dangers it held for them.

In her youth, her mother had been friends with a young boy who died from losing himself. She hadn't even known that he was a Fader, since he kept it so tightly under wraps, and rightly so. But even so, that did not save him from his awful fate. She told Orienne that he was in so much pain that he couldn't even scream out in agony; all he could do was throw himself about in an attempt to replace his current pain with a different, less searing one and stare wide-eyed at his surroundings with his mouth gaping open in torment. And all the while he was see-through and no one could hold him in an attempt to comfort him. She always told her children that her deepest regret was that she could not comfort her friend in his greatest hour of need. Even now, thinking back to it made Orienne wish that none of this ever had to happen to anyone, especially someone so young. Especially to a young boy she had never even known, yet felt so close to...

After a few more hours of sitting alone in the room, Orienne began to get distressed. She knew that *they* would kill her soon, just like her brother before her, and countless other people who had suffered the very same fate. If she couldn't get out, if she couldn't escape, she would soon be joining the others. "I'm not ready to die yet! Oh, dear brother! Protect me from what fate may befall me yet!"

And that's when it hit her. The potato sacks were what they found *his* body in when they first discovered that he was dead. The forget-me-not petals were strewn across his pale, lifeless face, and their aroma surrounded his motionless body. Splinters of rotting wood were found deep under his nail beds, as if he had been scratching at rotted wood. A shiver was sent down her spine as she remembered that terrifying image from so long ago. Was this where he, too, had been held captive so many years ago?

Orienne shrank to her knees and screamed as the terror from that day rushed through her with a horrible, aching speed. She was going to die here, the same as her brother, alone, terrified, and hopeless. And this time, there was no one left to look for her or mourn my passing after the deed was done.

The night came without mercy, blacking out any light that would have let its way in through the sole window, and she was left to sink into a dark and restless sleep.

71

Chapter Nine
Madness and Memories

~~~

Ophir...Ophir is dead. He was murdered. The bad people did it, the bad people killed him. No, Ophir, come back! Don't go, don't go! Mama, his body is gone, where did it go? I think they took it...they couldn't even let us give him a proper burial! They couldn't even let us put him to rest! No, they had to take his body, too... Ophir! Why did they have to kill you?

Orienne's horrific memories could not hold her exhausted mind in its nightmarish clutches for long. She awoke, teary eyed and groggy, from things she had wished to un-see since the day they were engraved in her mind. But though her body was awake, her nightmares still clung tightly to her mind.

It was hard for her to believe that they were all once the big, happy Andraste family.

When Orienne and Melaenie had found their brother Ophir's body on their doorstep on that fateful day, they had all been devastated. They went inside to tell their mother and father about it, but when they went back outside, the potato sack was empty. They hadn't even heard anyone or anything come to the porch to take his body away, but it was gone nonetheless. Orienne remembered being so angry at the Fader Haters. Hadn't they ruined enough? Hadn't they done enough harm? They didn't even have the decency to let his family burry him after his brutal, heartless murder. He was only a child, for heaven's sake.

Willing herself out of her memories, Orienne finally decided to get up and walk around in the little confined space that she was in to shake off the terrible feeling that was quickly filling her entire body. She needed to calm herself down before she died from her own fear.

She walked directly over to the puddle of water with the blood spatters. She thought that she saw two tiny figures that looked like people - and what appeared to be a mermaid with the most beautiful pearl and shell adorned hair and dolphin-like tail - swimming up through it. "That's weird..."

She rubbed her eyes and looked back into the puddle. There was nothing there. Orienne assumed that she had merely been hallucinating from fear, still caught between her grim reality and her terrifying memories. Unwilling to stay near the puddle any longer for fear of further visions, she walked over to the drawer that was holding the empty potato sacks...or seemingly empty, anyways. The potato sacks actually turned out to have objects in them. Not potatoes, but they held picture frames and lockets within the sacks.

The first sack that Orienne opened had a bunch of photos of what she could only assume to be Faders that had been imprisoned here before. She sorted through countless photographs and lockets before I pulled out a picture of Ophir, her brother...her *twin* brother. He was Orienne's beloved twin brother, and a Fader just like her. He and Orienne were mirror images of each other back then. They even had the same haircut; it was rather short back then.

She still couldn't believe that they had taken his life at such a young age. She remembered how Mother used to cry herself to sleep after that. To add insult to injury, her father left them not long after. Orienne remembered overhearing as he told their mother that his only son was gone and that his presence was no longer necessary. She remembered his words very vividly. "My only son is dead. I see no reason for me to remain here any longer. I only see it as a waste of my time."

She remembered her mother begging and pleading for him to stay, and that they could try to have another son together. He didn't

73

listen. He walked out the door that night with a single suitcase full of all of his belongings, and he left. He never returned.

It just made Orienne sick every time she thought about it.

Now that she looked back at it, though, she couldn't see how her mother could have ever loved him in the first place. But...she knew that she did. Somewhere along the lines, he must have fooled her heart.

Melaenie, who was a very small child at the time, was deeply distressed by their mother's uneasiness. Though Orienne and their mother tried their best to keep the true horrors of her brother's death from her, she was not so young and so blind as to go without noticing her mother's growing neurosis. Their mother became so protective of her two remaining children that she wouldn't even let them leave the house unless it was absolutely necessary. Since her children were also Faders, she didn't want to take the risk that another one of them would fall victim to the hands of those paranoid murders.

In the time after Ophir's death and the departure of their father, Melaenie took to learning all sorts of foreign languages. What better use for her time, she said, than studying the beautiful languages of the world? Their mother would go out and buy her all sorts of books in different languages, both novels and study-books. Melaenie reveled in them, and quickly learned all that the books had to teach her. The bookshelves in her room were overflowing with these kinds of books, and what wasn't on the shelves was stacked up in medium-sized piles a few feet high around the room. She became mildly proficient in German and French as well as in her native tongue, English. In regards to any other languages, she couldn't stick with one long enough to learn more than basic words, phrases, and grammar in order to become truly fluent, but she definitely knew her way around languages. Orienne had tried to help her with her studies, but the elder sister simply did not have the knack for learning languages that Melaenie did. Orienne had always envied her little sister for possessing such ability.

Around two years after the death of Ophir, Melaenie once told Orienne that she was going to run away from the house, just for one night, because she missed the outdoors so much. She made Orienne promise not to tell their mother about her plan, because she was going insane with no contact with the outside world and knew that their mother would stop her. Orienne, fully understanding how it felt for such a little girl to be caged up in a bedroom with nothing but books to let her escape, felt sympathetic for her caged soul and let her go. How was she to know the tragedy that would soon befall them both because of her clouded decision?

Within a few minutes of the time their mother was supposed to tuck the little one into bed, she began furiously searching the house for Melaenie. She began throwing cushions at walls, and knocking over her priceless pottery, only to have half of the collection smashed to pieces and the other half to be rescued by Orienne by sliding and catching them with the cushions her mother had already thrown. She was still unwilling to tell about where Melaenie had gone, fearing that she would do something drastic if she knew, something more drastic that she was already doing. Orienne quickly got to work at pretending to search for her little sister.

Their mother soon worked her way to the kitchen, and that's when things got really out of control. "Melaenie! Melaenie, where are you?" she kept on shouting, over and over again. She picked up the silverware and tossed it to the side. Forks and spoons scattered everywhere, making the kitchen floor a hazardous place to walk bare-foot, or even with slippers on. Broken glass was strewn across the tile, and their mother was still running around frantically, regardless of the way that the glass was cutting up her feet and making them bleed. Then she began to frantically pull out her hair. Locks of short golden curls fell silently to the floor as her mother sobbed furiously.

Orienne struggled to bring herself to tell her mother now, she looked so distraught. She was frightened by her crazed performance to the point of immobility and almost to the point of being speechless.

Regardless, the elder sister pushed herself and walked over to her mother, hot tears forming in her own eyes, her muscles tense with fear. She inched across the hazardous kitchen floor, careful not to step on the forks or broken glass. Orienne opened her mouth to tell her, but then she grabbed the kitchen knives and threw them at the wall. Orienne was so frightened that she dashed out of the room without telling her of Melaenie's whereabouts. There she hid in her bedroom, waiting for her mother's fearsome cries of anguish to cease.

She opened the window and called out to her sister. Melaenie was nowhere in sight, though, and it was far too dark out to go search for her. She began to get worried that perhaps she really *had* been taken. What had she done?

But then she saw a little light come from the garden. Melaenie's head popped up above the little fence, and instantly turned her head and looked at her sister.

"Mama is in trouble?" she asked. A terrified look appeared on her face, and then she ran towards the wall of the house that led to the bedroom. She furiously climbed up the vine-covered wall and back into the house. Orienne grabbed her arms and hoisted her through the open window. "Mama!" cried Melaenie. "Mama, please don't cry anymore, I'm here!"

The sisters burst through the bedroom door hand-in-hand as they called out to her. The two of them dashed down the hallway, their thoughts riddled with uncertainty, and then they stopped dead in their tracks. By then, their mother's wails had stopped. An air of misery had filled the room. They warily made their way into the kitchen, afraid of what their mother had done to make her stop crying.

The floor was covered in blood, forks, knives, spoons, broken dishes, their mother's beautiful golden hair, and the cupboard doors ripped off of their hinges. Everything including the kitchen sick was torn from its rightful place and scattered throughout the kitchen. The table was broken, its four legs splintered off in all corners of the room. Chips of wood could be seen everywhere, sticking out of the walls, splintered drawers and cupboards...just everywhere. Had she really expected to find Melaenie hidden inside the wooden table? Their mother had drowned herself in the sink, her arms bloody from scratching herself and her head close to bald because of ripping her hair out. There were even wooden splinters all jammed under her finger nails and around her hands, probably from throwing and clawing at the table and cupboards. To say the least, her children were horrified, and emotionally scarred for life. Orienne had known that the pressure had been building up for her mother, she really had, but she never imagined that she could be hurt *that* badly by Melaenie's little disappearance act.

After that, everything was pretty much a blur. Orienne and Melaenie remembered crying for a long, long time. They weren't crying just for their mother, but they were crying for themselves as well. They no longer had anyone to take care of them.

Their brother was dead.

Their mother was dead.

Their father had walked out on them, and even if he hadn't, it wasn't as if he cared enough about the girls to take care of them in the first place.

Two young girls, Faders no less, left alone in the world, with thousands, possibly even millions, of people who hated them, not to mention all of the people who actively hunted down their kind and were actually willing to act on their murderous impulses. Orienne and Melaenie already knew that it was only a matter of time until they, too, would be discovered and killed. It seemed as if there was no escape, and no end to the hell they had found themselves in.

The sisters buried their mother's body in the backyard late at night when they knew that no one would be watching the house.

The two of them blamed themselves six ways 'til sunset, but deep down they knew that there was nothing they could have done. They were so young, and the tragedy was inevitable in the end. All of their mother's sorrows had piled up, and she had no way to release or ease the pressure. All of her tragedies...Ophir dying, her husband leaving, Melaenie escaping in the middle of the night,

Orienne saying nothing, and seeing what she had done to her home...and to herself. Their late mother had never been particularly adept at handling pressure, but since all of her support beams had been knocked down, almost simultaneously, she was forced to hold the roof up on her own. And she couldn't handle the weight.

They had driven their mother to suicide, and they would have to live with that guilt for the rest of their lives. The question was, could they survive their trials long enough to do even that?

Orienne and Melaenie tried their best to survive in the house for a while after that, living off of the stores in the basement and whatever they could pick up from the market using their meager funds from selling their books and belongings. That is, until those people saw the sisters by chance that day and chased them out of their own home. And that's when they ran away and ended up lost in the middle of the woods, and stuck in their current predicament.

Orienne could only wonder as she drifted off to sleep for the second time that night while she was trapped in that awful place. It had been two days now. Her executioners would not bother to keep her alive in there, wretched and starving, for much longer.

Chapter Ten
Freedom and Fellowship

~~~

Orienne was startled from her dreams once more as she heard a loud splashing sound and a few gasps for air. She turned around, and saw two soaking wet people leaning out of the puddle in the ground. She hadn't thought the puddle was all that deep, so she was rather confused at this sudden appearance. In fact, Orienne had even checked for the depth of the puddle with her own two hands when the vision struck her before, and her fingers had caressed the floor.

"*Bonjour*, my lady. My name is Sir Anton LaCiel, Prince of New France," greeted the boy with the short, silver-blonde hair. He took hold of her hand and kissed it gently.

She blushed at the very notion of his chivalry. She didn't know why, but her heart was beating so fast. Was she really developing a crush on this handsome stranger?

If Orienne had been paying even the slightest attention to the world outside since the death of her brother, she would have known who he was, and that he was a powerful Spell Weaver who was helping to drive back the Plague of Twilight. Instead, she stared at him blankly, marveling at his accent and strange appearance. She hadn't seen a boy since the death of Ophir and departure of her father. She was taken aback at his strikingly good looks, though she didn't allow it to distract her for too long.

"My name is Áine McCrae," breathed the one with the long, sand-colored hair.

Shortly after the two pulled themselves out of the puddle, another girl arose. This one had a black coloring to her hair and Hawaiian features in her face, and her skin was quite tan. "*Aloha*, Fader! You are Orienne Andraste, correct? We've come to rescue you!"

Orienne was awestruck, and her only response was a confused nod of the head.

The two people who had emerged from the puddle grabbed onto Orienne's arms. They pulled her towards the little puddle of water and proceeded to jump in.

"Sorry to cut the introductions short, but we must get out of here," said Áine. It was strange how that even in that rushed tone, her voice calmed Orienne's nerves. It was so motherly, something she hadn't heard in a long, long time.

"Hold your breath," the Prince said. Before Orienne had time to realize what was happening, they all thrust themselves into the puddle, and were completely immersed in crystal clear water. It was then that Orienne noticed the black haired girl's strange fins. Confusion struck her once more, but so much strangeness had enveloped her life in these past few days that at this point she was willing to take it all at face value. Regardless, the four people were deep beneath the floorboards now, and Orienne would never have to look at that horrible place ever again.

They swam deeper and deeper in to the chilled water, and it seemed that they were the only living creatures under there. That's when Orienne noticed a rather large multi-colored force field at the very bottom, which marked their near arrival at "Atlantis". Inside of the barrier dome, it looked as if a beautiful, golden, underwater city was concealed beneath it. Orienne almost gasped in awe at the sheer scale and beauty of it all, and certainly would have if she had not been so deep underwater.

They finally arrived, and when they passed through the colorful force field, the image of the golden city disappeared and revealed what was really there - just a few large chunks of cement and old, broken pieces of things. Piles of rubble stood on the edges of the force field that could have easily been watchtowers when they were in their prime. Orienne sighed out loud.

"What's the matter?" asked Anton, cocking his head slightly at Orienne's disappointment.

"I suppose that I had over-excited myself a bit much." Something in her gut had been telling her that it was too good to be true.

"Oh, I'm so sorry about that," replied the finned girl. "The barrier is kind of an illusion that is generated by the pearls. It has that effect on people. I think that it's generating an image of the past, but that's just my own opinion. Who knows why it really looks like that from the outside?"

"Who are you?" Orienne asked, her disenchantment wearing off.

"My name is Leilani Moanna, and before you ask, no, I am not a mermaid. I'm still one hundred percent genuine human...I think. It doesn't matter anyways."

Orienne could tell that she was thinking really hard about something...or maybe not. It was sometimes hard to tell because Leilani made weird expressions with her face that symbolized things other than what she was thinking about. Like when she was confused she looked really happy, and when she was sad, she looked confused, and when she was angry she looked sad. Orienne didn't know if it was just her or if there was seriously wrong with the way she thought expressions were supposed to appear, though she immediately felt guilty about it afterwards. How was she to know that Leilani's expressions stemmed from the same incident that turned her into the creature she was now?

"So that explains your appearance. But why didn't you leave the...um...puddle, or whatever it was, back when we were inside of the prison?"

"That is because you can only get back to this place if someone keeps a connection to the portal in Atlantis..."

"You're kidding...Atlantis?"

81

"Oh, it's not really Atlantis. At least, we don't think it's really Atlantis. It's more likely some old city or some such that sank beneath the lake. Really, we're beneath the French District of New Europe."

"We're in France?" Orienne asked.

"Per say," answered Áine. "The waters around us are indeed part of what flows beneath the surface of a lake in New France, but to tell the complete truth this abandoned city was never part of France's boarders."

"I see..." Orienne said, not completely understanding what Áine was telling her. "Well if it's not France, and it's not the New States...how did we all get here?"

"As for how I personally got here, Áine rescued me and brought me here. Using a pearl from the lakebed, she was able to create a portal to find me and bring me here, not unlike the portal we used to find you. I've been here ever since. And now you're here too! One big, happy family!" exclaimed Leilani.

Family...that word made Orienne want to burst into tears. Her family was gone. And now these strangers were treating her more kindly than even her own father had in the past, though guilt still filled her about her failure to protect Melaenie and her mother. In an attempt to distract herself from her sorrow, she turned to asking more questions.

"So, you used magic?"

"Just a little. Though I am technically a Spell Weaver, what I know is self-taught, and I don't know any real spells that work along the lines of my blessing. Even Áine knows more magic than me, but that's because she's a Faerie. The Prince here is the real Spell Weaver, not me." She pointed towards the handsome boy with the fancy robes.

"What magic you *do* see is what I have been able to gather from these pearls." She pointed at the pearls she wore all over her body and the pearls that made up the circumference of the bubble of Atlantis.

"Then...Áine," Orienne began, turning towards the sandy-haired woman. "How did you get here?"

"That is a story for another time, and another place," she said. The motherly tone of her voice was gone, in an instant replaced by a dark and foreboding half-whisper, solid and heavy as lead. Her words sounded final. None of them dared ask her further, though Leilani already knew the truth.

"Oh, come on Leilani, I'm only a Spell Weaver in training. I only know a little bit of magic, not nearly enough to call myself a Spell Weaver," mumbled the silvery haired boy, trying to turn the conversation away from Áine's unexpected darkness.

"The pearls can do more than just create a barrier, or open portals," she continued. "They hold some of the world's oldest, purest magic within them. It was through these pearls that I could see you. Most humans have lost the ability, but those with magic in their blood have regained this power that we once shared with every other living creature on Earth."

"Oh," Orienne said. She never would have guessed that pearls could be so powerful. "Why have you been looking for me?"

"We were meant to free you and gather the others to seek out the Twilight Dragon. Only together will the Kinship of the Twilight Moon have the power to defeat it," answered Áine.

"You said Twilight Dragon..." Orienne gasped, her heart starting to race. Were the stories true, then? "The legend..."

The Kinship of the Twilight Moon
Bound by their blood and by their fate
Shall whet their blades by Light of Lune
And save these worlds 'fore 'tis too late

"It is all true."

Orienne was ecstatic. Frightened, yet overjoyed. If the legends of the Twilight Dragon were true, then there was hope yet. "Áine?" she asked. She remembered the long, wavy-haired one introducing herself with that name, but she asked just to be sure. They had been in such a rush; she didn't quite have time to memorize their quickly stated names.

"I think a fresh introduction is in order, don't you think?" asked Áine after Orienne had addressed her.

Then the short-silver-blonde haired boy walked forwards, smiling sweetly as he did so. "As I have said before, I am Sir Anton LaCiel, Prince of New France and a Spell Weaver-in-training, son of Queen Emeraude and King Damien. You can just call me Anton, though." He smiled at her and did a deep and graceful bow that Orienne was sure only cultured boys could pull off. But then he tripped and landed face first on the dusty floor. When he got up, his face was covered in dust, but he smiled a goofy smile and all of them giggled. He brushed off the dust as best as he could. It was a friendly gesture, and just the kind of thing that they needed in order to loosen up a bit.

"It's a pleasure to meet you, Leilani, Áine, and Anton. As you all apparently know already, my name is Orienne Andraste," Orienne replied.

"Come now, you must be hungry after all that," said Anton, handing Orienne a thick cut hunk of bread with a generous slice of cheese on it. He had pulled it out of a sack that was sitting in the corner of two overturned pillars.

"Yes, thank you," Orienne said, hungrily and gratefully taking the food that was offered to her. She had indeed, been starving.

"I've got just enough for everyone," added Anton. "Let's dig in," he said as he handed a slice to everyone.

Over their meager meal of bread and cheese, Orienne explained to them everything that had happened to her thus far, and by the end of the ordeal she could say that they were thoroughly upset and that they felt horribly about her unfortunate experiences with Fader Haters. It appeared as thought they were not at all too fond of the whole extreme anti-Fader thing either. Orienne felt relieved to have met such understanding and accepting people. For the first time in her entire life, she felt safe. Safe and sound...while who knows what was happening to her little sister.

At that thought, her heart sank.

Orienne knew that Melaenie had been discovered in the woods during their attempted escape, but she didn't know what had become of her, or where she may have been taken.

As if reading Orienne's restless thoughts, Áine spoke up. "The other Fader girl, Melaenie...yes, I think I know what has become of her. She is currently being taken to the south-eastern region of New Egypt."

"How did she get there?" Orienne exclaimed. "We were all the way in the New States!"

"Private airplanes, love. It's been almost two days since she was taken, I think that is plenty of time for all of that travelling. Shall we go?"

They all nodded hastily in agreement. If what Áine had explained was true, then the fate of the world was intertwined with Orienne's and her sister's, whatever they would be. They had a duty as fellow members of the Kinship of the Twilight Moon to rescue Melaenie, no matter the cost.

And besides, what kind of heartless bastard honestly needed an excuse to rescue their younger sibling?

Chapter Eleven
Sand and Sister

~~~

"Leave me alone, you stupid jerk!" screamed Melaenie as she kicked and punched the man who was carrying her deeper and deeper into the desserts of New Egypt. Her once soft hair was wild in her face as she was shaken around, bobbing up and down in her position from when he threw her hastily over his shoulder and carried her off.

This was the not the man that had found her hidden in the brush, but the Bounty Hunter that the group of Fader Haters had traded her to for a hefty sum of money. He was not the one who had dragged her kicking and screaming out of the greenery, but he was the one who would lead her into Hell itself. Melaenie wasn't stupid. She knew what happened to people like her when people like him got hold of Faders. Despite all of her efforts and struggling, one small girl was no match for this muscular menace of the desert. Even one who knew Karate.

The man was very dark skinned from intense exposure to the sun, and he was very muscular. His eyes were dark and held a thick sense of hostility within them which could be sensed even behind his large, dark sunglasses. His thin, chapped lips curved into a demonic half-smile. A tattoo of the eye of Horus was needled in on the back of his head. He was bald, and had silver body jewelry running down from underneath his eyelids to his pants line. He had five silver eyebrow piercings above his right eye. He wore beige cargo shorts that stopped right below the knee and were so baggy on his body that you could probably shove a baby elephant into them and no one would ever even notice. His feet were clad in simple brown reed and papyrus sandals. He wasn't dressed at all like a professionally employed Bounty Hunter, which probably meant he was merely a Freelancer. That only made him all the more dangerous.

"Cretin! You're such a stupid man!" screeched Melaenie. "And you smell awful, too! Let go of me now, or I'll be forced to scream random insults at you in languages your tiny little mind can't even comprehend! And maybe if you're lucky, I'll avoid using profanity!" she continued as she delivered a particularly powerful kick into the man's side. Unfortunately, it had no effect.

"Shut your mouth, if a stupid Fader like you knows what's good for you!" The man smacked her, not even wincing from her barrage of kicks and punches. This caused her to fade right through him. Times like this made her wish that she could fade voluntarily. At least that would be useful. She took this opportunity to run away from the startled man.

"Stop! Fader! Somebody, stop her!" he screamed out after her.

Melaenie dashed through the desert at lightning speed, being careful not to sink into the sand holes or trip and fall into the dunes. Then, just as suddenly as the black haired youth had taken off, she stopped dead in her tracks, and fear overcame her.

"Oh no...did I just...?" she looked up at the expansive city that stretched before her eyes that she hadn't noticed in her panicked sprint from the man. "I went the wrong way!"

What Melaenie was standing in front of was the very place no Fader in their right mind wanted to end up...in the south-eastern region of New Egypt, the Fader Hater capital of the world. She was already sweating from running, but now a cold sweat overcame her, quickly replacing her heat with a disturbing and unwelcome chill.

Soon, from a mixture of Melaenie's uneasy tears and droplets of sweat, there was just enough moisture in the sand for a portal to be opened. The others had been watching her from the pearls the whole time, and now was their chance. They didn't waste a moment for fear that the small puddle would quickly evaporate into the hot desert air. Leilani pushed them up; giving them the extra boost that they needed in order to reach the surface in the necessary time-frame.

Immediately, Anton, Áine and Orienne pulled themselves through the tiny puddle and stood next to Melaenie. However, the tiny puddle of moisture quickly evaporated in to the hot desert air, just as they had foreseen, and their only means of escape was lost. Since the only one who could activate the portal was whoever was in Atlantis, which for the time being was only Leilani, and they needed water to gate through, the Prince and the girls were now trapped right alongside Orienne's sister, Melaenie, with a Freelancing Bounty Hunter who was already hard at work raising Hell hot on their trails.

"How did you get here, Orienne?" asked Melaenie. She looked at the Prince and the two young women, all dripping wet, with a strange mix of both relief and confusion.

"We used a special water portal," replied Áine. She smiled at Melaenie's startled little face in an attempt to make her smile, too. All she could manage, though, was a weak fidget of the corners of her mouth.

"Who are they?" asked Melaenie, turning to face Orienne.

"These people?" Orienne replied. She looked over at the others, who nodded at her, as if telling her that it was okay for her to talk about them.

"Oh, they're good people. They rescued me from the Fader prison. You'll get used to them." Orienne pointed first to Áine, who was still carrying that violin of hers. The bow was tucked between the sweater tied around her waist and her sleeveless pink turtleneck. "That is Áine. She's a really good at playing music. And she's a Faerie."

"Wow, a real Faerie?" exclaimed Melaenie enthusiastically. She smiled, excitement filling her at the very idea that she'd met a real-life Faerie. She'd read plenty of stories about them, and had always been a believer.

Then Orienne pointed to Anton, who was twirling his elaborately decorated staff and dancing around in circles like he was some kind of exotic dancer. He was busy casting a spell that would hide them from view for a short time. "That's Anton, a Prince from New France. He can use magic. He's really funny and nice, and I'm sure you'll get along with him."

Melaenie nodded at Orienne in response. "A real Prince!" she squealed. She gave an admiring smile in Anton's direction, who returned the gesture with a bright, enthusiastic smile of his own.

"They're friends. You can trust the both of them."

Unfortunately, their peace was short-lived. Right after the introductions, a large jeep pulled up right behind them and honked loudly, startling all of them. Anton's spell faltered, Melaenie and Orienne both faded, and the man driving the jeep yelled out, "I've found you, you dirty Faders! Damn vermin, polluting the humans with your vile disease!" He seemed to hiss on the word "disease." He continued his poisonous talk. "Now be good little girls and boys and come along quietly, unless you want to get run over in the sand!"

Áine, Anton, Melaenie and Orienne didn't bother to have a second thought as they took off running through the sand. They realized that they had nowhere to go except for into the south-eastern region of New Egypt. So, into the fray they leapt.

The jeep was hot on their trails as they dashed through the streets of New Egypt. The only thing slowing it down were Anton's barrage of ice spells, but even that was only slowing it down a tiny bit, and they were running short on energy and breath. The sand wasn't helping them get around any faster, either. They went as fast as they could possibly manage past the shops, past the wild dogs, and past the civilians, who at this point were also running and screaming at the tops of their lungs.

"Faders, run everyone!" the people screamed out every which way. Baskets full of old fruits, rotten vegetables, and stale bread ended up being tossed in their direction...at least until the crowd saw that Prince Anton was running not far behind them. Much to their surprise, the people stopped hurling random objects of little value at them and retreated into their homes or shops. Just then it dawned on the others that it would be a very good thing to have the Prince traveling with them. After all, who would possibly want to be on the French government's bad side unless they had a serious death wish? They had Spell Weavers in their midst.

Just when the four of them were about to collapse from exhaustion and Anton ran out of the excess energy he needed in order to call upon his icy-powers, the jeep suddenly stopped in its tracks with a loud screech. For what seemed like an eternity to the group, but was more likely only a few seconds, it seemed as if time had stopped.

The jeep was surrounded in rippling air waves for about a half-second, and then it flew backwards and crashed into a nearby building, sending pieces of the vehicle and building flying in every direction except for towards them. The entire vicinity burst into flames as the oil from the engine ignited on impact with the building. Fire and ash billowed into the air, but it was covered in a shield of invisible energy. They could see the smoke and flames press against the invisible force field. Without air, the fire died away, and without a place to go, the ash simply floated back towards the ground.

"I believe it would be safe to say that the man who was driving that vehicle is most certainly dead..." Áine said in a half-whisper. She was certainly correct. If he hadn't, they would have had to redefine their understanding of natural human mortality.

After the dust and smoke cleared, they could see a figure. Within a few moments, it was clear that someone was standing directly in front of them. At first, they were afraid that it might just *be* that man in the jeep, and he had been extremely lucky. Or made a deal with the Devil or something. However, upon closer inspection as the figure began to walk towards them, they felt relief wash over them as they realized that this was, thankfully, not the case.

A young girl was the one who stood in front of them, with a dirt-streaked face and extremely long jet black hair that reached down to her knees, though it would probably be even longer than that if it were to be combed out straight. It was tangled and wind-strewn with frayed curls that danced randomly in the rest of her straight-as-a-board hair. Despite the dirt, adorable rosy-cheeks still managed to glow through. She wore an old olive-green sailor style girls' school uniform, with long black leggings and dark-green shoes. She was as pale as a ghost beneath the grime, and she held a half-eaten jelly donut in her left hand. Despite her attire, she sure didn't appear to have any Asian features whatsoever save for her jet-black hair. In fact, she looked as if she was of European descent. Irish or Scottish even, if the depictions of different nationalities in Melaenie's Foreign Language books were accurate in the slightest. She only held her attention on the four others for a moment, before she abruptly turned around and began screaming what sounded like extremely profane words in another language at the dead man in the van that had been reduced to mere scrap-metal. According to Melaenie, it sounded like some kind of Gaelic. Áine's face visibly lit up at the sound of the young girl's words, something which shocked all of them.

"Now stay out of my alley, you scum!" she yelled at the corpse in the overturned hunk of metal and leather that was once a jeep. Her voice rang with a light Irish accent. Finally, it seemed as though she was through with her cussing in her foreign language. The four all stared at her with wide eyes. She turned back and looked at them with a weird expression on her face. "Excuse me, but I believe I just saved your sorry arses."

An unnatural wind blew around her, and with it carried a metal name-tag on a chain. At that point, they knew that she was a Psychic, and a skilled one at that. There was no other way that a little girl such as herself could have moved that jeep like that (what with the vortex of air and all) unless she possessed the unnaturally enhanced powers of the mind.

And suddenly, Orienne became frightened. She wasn't stupid; she knew what Psychics were capable of doing. If they felt like it, a Psychic with well-developed powers could single-handedly wipe out a hundred people with little more than a single thought. They were probably the only people with powers that humans actually had reason to be afraid of, not that she justified such prejudice. Regardless, she couldn't help feeling a little bit of that prejudiced fear of the teenaged Psychic herself right then, and she was ashamed.

Orienne fumbled around with the name tag that had blown towards them and into her hands for a few seconds until she could decipher some of the writing on it. "Keaira Aleshire?" (Mind you, she pronounced it entirely wrong). Let's just say a certain bratty teenager wouldn't be too happy with them in the following moments to come...

Chapter Twelve
Clues and Runaways

~~~

"Aye, you lout could never get it right! Kee-EYE-rah! My goodness, and you looked like such an intelligent bunch, too. Guess it serves me right for perceiving people before I even get to know them. I suppose that I'll just be on my way now. *Slán.*" She turned on her heel and began to walk away from them, with her dirty little nose snobbishly stuck up in the air.

Áine would not let Keaira go so easily, especially after hearing her speak in her own native tongue. "*Stad!*" she cried out. All stopped and turned to look at her, Keaira included.

"*An bhfuil Gaeilge agat?*" asked Keaira.

"*Tuigim,*" replied Áine. She looked as if she were about to cry tears of joy.

"*Cé as thú?*"

"*Is as* Eidolon *dom.*"

At the mention of that word, Eidolon, even the Psychic looked frightened. Her grin melted off into nothing short of shock and horror. She quickly turned tail and began to flee.

"Wait!" Orienne cried. Despite her initial fear, she knew that they needed all the help they could get, and a Psychic would be the perfect addition to the Kinship of the Twilight Moon. And...the prophecy...

A Psychic who needs freeing...

93

"Aye, what do you want?" she groaned sarcastically. "Leave me be! I want nothing to do with Faeries and Sorcery. Don't think I don't know what you are. I may have saved you all from an untimely death, but do not take that as a sign of my friendship!"

"Why don't you come along with us? I mean, it's not like you have anywhere else to go."

"And you just assume that because I hang around in an alley way I don't have anywhere else to go? I don't even know you. Why don't the rest of you tell me who the hell you all are and then maybe I'll consider it?" she spat at them.

"Sir Anton LaCiel, at your service," answered the Prince, performing his trademark bow.

"I am Melaenie Andraste."

"My name is Orienne Andraste."

"And I am Áine McCrae," added their beautiful Faerie friend.

Keaira grinned mischievously at them and then raised the donut to her lips as if she was going to take another bite out of it. "I'll think about it," she said before opening her mouth wide and taking a huge chunk out of the donut in a single chomp. A few crumbs tumbled from her lips as she chewed, falling like glazed snowflakes on the hot, sandy ground. "Why don't we go speak in a more private area?" asked the young Psychic, looking back and forth like a guilty thief.

They willingly complied. Keaira led them to an alley that looked like it could have been someone's make-shift home, perhaps her own.

"Do you live here?" asked Melaenie, obvious bewilderment in her voice.

"You have a problem with it?" snapped Keaira. "In case you people didn't notice the dirt and the old Japanese girls' military uniform, I'm an uncontrolled Psychic orphan on the run."

"Why are you on the run?" inquired Melaenie.

"Because, little girl, I ran away from that lousy orphanage in New Japan." Keaira said this as she flicked a stray midnight-black strand of hair away from her face. "Such a lousy place to keep such brilliant minds. A shame, really." She crossed her arms in front of her chest and rolled her eyes.

"Why did you do that? Run away, I mean...and how did you manage to get all the way down here to New Egypt?" asked Orienne. The Andrastes were curious as ever.

"Their food was nasty. All they served was oatmeal. The same kind, every day. Watered down, cold, plain oatmeal with the occasional dash of bitter-sweet syrup. Day in and day out, morning, noon and night, nothing but. I guess that the people running the place thought that's all we Psychics needed. Any more brain food and our minds just might burst from the pressure." She said the last part in a very cynical, mocking way.

"Wait just a second, you ran away because of the food they served? Not because they treated you like criminals? Sorry for being blunt, but isn't that kind of a stupid reason to risk your life to run away from there?" asked Anton.

"Well, there was that too, but why make a fuss over the obvious...hey, wait a minute! Don't interrupt me while I'm speaking, Prince!" snapped Keaira. "Just because you're royalty doesn't make you any more important than me!"

"Well, actually," began Anton.

"I'm not counting government positions. I'm talking about our general humanity," snapped Keaira.

"Okay, okay," replied Anton, taking a step back.

"Besides," continued Keaira. "My best friend, he...he was tested on a lot. It hurt me too much, in more ways than you can imagine, for me to just sit there and let that happen. I would have taken him with me, but there wasn't enough time..."

As Keaira said that part, Áine eyed her in a way that couldn't quite be described. It was almost like Keaira's words were a riddle, and Áine's eyes were trying to unravel the mysteries of that riddle. Though, that's not exactly what her eyes gave away. There was a slight hint that she had already guessed what that meant, though she wasn't entirely sure. Orienne heard her say under her breath, "Other."

Orienne didn't have a clue what that word meant at the time, so she brushed it away without a second thought, eager to hear the rest of Keaira's story.

"What happened next?" asked Anton.

"Fine, your majesty," replied Keaira as she performed a mock curtsy. "I was in an orphanage for Psychics, since many Psychics lose their parents at young ages. When we are infants, our powers are unrefined and out-of-control. Many Psychic babies usually end up...killing their parents...by complete accident, and then we are taken to that stupid place up in New Japan."

There was a little bit of an awkward silence that hung in the air all around them after she confessed this. Psychic children accidentally killing their parents because of their uncontrolled powers? No wonder people were so afraid of them that normal people felt they had to be locked away in a God Forsaken institution.

"Do I frighten you?" Keaira asked in response to the silence.

"No," said Orienne. "I thought so at first, but now I know better. Just because something is scary does not give someone the right to lock that something away. Especially if that something is really someone, and if that someone is a human being. And...if the reason they are feared is only because of an accident. Is murder the only way we humans know how to fix our problems?"

"Killing another human being, even if it is only by accident, is no small matter, Orienne Andraste," responded Keaira. "They are right to fear us, but not right to treat us so."

"I'm so sorry, Keaira. I had no idea that life was so traumatic for a Psychic.," Anton proclaimed, and then slapped his fist into his palm, a new look of determination on his face. "I promise that when I come of age and become eligible to run for King of my country, I will stop children from New France from going there, and hopefully influence the rest of the world to do the same," Anton announced dreamily. "I will not rest until justice is found!"

"Trust the little Prince to be so naive," said Keaira, brushing Anton's comment aside as if it meant nothing, even though it truly was an act of kindness on his part. "May I continue?"

"Sorry, go on..." apologized Anton.

"Anyways, about how I ended up here... I was born in New Ireland. My parents loved me dearly, and used to tell me all sorts of tales of faeries and the like. Gaelic was my native language, though it is a dying one in this dying world. When I was about six years old, I...I accidentally..." She paused to take a deep breath. They waited anxiously to hear what she had done. Finally, after what seemed like an eternity, she clenched her fists and began her story anew. "Back at the orphanage for Psychics, my only comfort was my best friend in the whole world, although his Psychic powers didn't even come close to mine." Keaira made a gesture to show her...rather petit muscular physique. It was quite comical, actually.

"My friend told me that in certain parts of Africa, Psychics were not confined to such cruel places. They were far more preoccupied with Faders than our kind there. He was a wee lad who was also from New Ireland. His name was Gaignun. He told me that he and the other Psychics would help me get out and be free if I promised to go back one day and free them all. So, Gaignun and a group of the more controlled Psychics all set up an elaborate plan along with the other lesser Psychics who were willing to lend a helping mind to get me out of there. It...worked." She took another deep breath as she looked up to the sky. "Wow, it's hard to believe that I was in that horrible place for eight whole years before I was able to get out..."

That made Keaira around fourteen years old, since she had been there for eight years after her arrest when she was six years old. At this point everyone was sitting around in a semi-circle on the ground like it was story time. As she spoke, it was as if she took herself back to her past, and all of the listeners were travelling back in time with her as observers.

"That was the day. The day I was going to get out of that horrible place. No more nasty food, no more living in a cold, dark

97

cell, no more torture, no more experimentation. No more having to watch him suffer over and over again, and feeling every moment of pain as intensely as he did, despite the fact that it was not my body that had electricity and poison coursing through it.

"Damn them all. Those inhumane monsters... Enslaving us, testing on us, criminalizing us...all because of what we had been born as: Psychics. Were we not just as human as they thought they were?

"Heh. No. We were more human than them. Their treatment of us was nothing short of monstrous.

"I and other Psychics like me were victims of a mutation let lose by the infamous and legendary Plague of the Twilight Dragon. The mutations we suffered from were caused by the Capacious Virus, which meant that we weren't monsters, we were just ill! We needed help, needed some kind of treatment, not torture. But to them it didn't matter. These unnatural brain enlargements caused by our illness enhanced different Psyonic aspects of the mind, such as telekinesis or telepathy. We could manipulate matter with the power of our mind alone. Some could even see slight traces of the future before it even occurred.

"When a child is born as a Psychic, they have little to no control over their mind. What infant does? As a result, great tragedies tend to happen around us. Many of us end up killing our parents and nearby persons by complete accident from the littlest things, including a burst of laughter, a fit of crying, or even trying to reach for a hand to hold. It's no wonder people fear us, but I don't think that's any reason for them to do to us what they do. It's not like we wanted to kill the people we love. It's not like we weren't all devastated after these uncontrollable accidents.

"I am one such Psychic who killed my parents in this way. I was only six years old at the time, but I don't remember who they were, or how it happened, all I know is that it must have, or I would not have been taken to this orphanage for Psychics in the first place. The shock of killing my own parents must have been so traumatic for me at such a young age that I repressed the memories."

As they listened to Keaira's story, Orienne couldn't help but sympathize with her a little. She knew the pain of being responsible for the death of her own mother. But Keaira...she couldn't even remember her mother's face. She had to live knowing that she did such irreversible damage that the images of her mother and father were erased from her own mind. That was something more painful than even Orienne could have dealt with. At least Orienne had her mother's face to hold onto in her mind, and in her heart, and she didn't care enough about her father to really give a damn that she barely remembered him.

"But that day...that was the day when I would finally be able to leave all of it behind me.

"It was pitch black outside. Not even a hint of the moon or the stars were there to ease our nerves. Granted, this was probably better, as it was harder to take care of that kind of light for this kind of secretive operation. Down below, the floodlights were on, meant to detect any potential escapees. But one of the other Psychics, Arielle, who had the power to bend light with her mind, was already working on taking care of those.

"'Keaira,' called a voice from behind me. It was Gaignun, my best friend. 'Are you absolutely one hundred percent ready? You've got the plan down?' he asked, trying not to sound too worried about me.

"'Yeah, Gaignun. I'm ready, I've got it,' I replied after taking a deep breath. I could handle myself just fine...though I had to admit, it was more than a wee bit scary having to go off on my own.

"As my powers involved using telekinesis as an offensive force, it wouldn't be hard to fight back if need be. My only issue was that, as much as I hated to admit it, I didn't have complete control over my powers, and the last thing I wanted to do was to accidentally kill someone by losing control. That would not make a very good case for the Psychics, to say the least. At least, that was the case when Gaignun wasn't around. When he was with me, I never had any problems focusing my energy. Most people simply attributed this to being because he was my friend, but I knew better. I knew who he was to me. 'You sure you can't come with me?'

"'Well...' he started, but he was suddenly cut off.

"'He can't go with you,' said Mateus, another one of the Psychic boys. Mateus was a pyrokinetic who could manipulate fire. He wasn't very good at it, but I bet if he had just had a little bit of training, he'd be quite a formidable force. Unfortunately, he was also a jerk. 'He's here for insurance.'

"'Insurance?" I demanded. 'What the hell are you talking about?'

"'We can't have you abandoning all of us after we're going to go through all of this trouble to get you out of here to get help.'

"'Shut up,' I huffed angrily. 'Yeah, right, like I would just abandon you guys. We're like family.'

"'Well, just in case. We all know you won't abandon your little boyfriend.'

"'He's not my boyfriend!'

"Everyone briefly laughed after my quick denial before returning to the seriousness of the situation. They were all helping me to escape. Everyone had been planning an escape for years, but we knew that only one or two of us could get out at a time. On top of that, we also knew that this was probably a one-time deal. Every single breach in security that we were about to make would be quickly remedied for good afterwards. The people in these facilities didn't make the same mistake twice. Not now, not ever.

"As I was classified as one of the most powerful Psychics in the entire facility, most of us simply agreed that I was the one who was going to get out – on one condition...I would have to go back to rescue the rest of them. I could have easily brought one other Psychic with me in my escape...my Other, but in order to be used as a bargaining chip for me to have to come back, Gaignun was not allowed to come with me."

"What's an Other?" asked Melaenie.

Keaira turned to face the little Fader, putting her hands on her knees as she leaned over to look her in the eye. "An Other is a very special person, wee lass. Every Psychic has one, though not every Psychic is lucky enough to find theirs. They're like best friends, except we're connected through our minds as well as our hearts. Gaignun...was mine."

Melaenie nodded in understanding. Her sister, Orienne, had known about Others for a long time, since many romance novels compare being in love to finding your Other, but she knew that it wasn't quite the same. Lovers couldn't physically feel what the other felt, couldn't speak to each other by projecting their thoughts into the other's mind, couldn't just *know*. Others could.

"Go on," Áine urged. Áine also knew of Others, though her knowledge came from being part Faerie. Psychics weren't the only ones with Others, though being a Halfie, Áine was not entitled to one as her late Faerie kin had been.

"Ah, yes, um... As I was saying, there was no way I could coordinate movements efficiently enough with anyone else, so I was stuck going it alone. I shuddered at the thought.

"'Keaira, it's okay,' said Gaignun as he gave me one last hug. 'I can handle anything they throw at me.'

"'Liar! When I'm here with you, you can barely take it. You forget that I can feel it; too...you're my Other, Gaignun. You can't fool me."

"'I can take it. I promise. I'll do good. I swear I'll do good, Keaira."

"'You'll do *well*, you mean,' I corrected him matter-of-factly.

"'Grammar whore,' he retorted.

"'Illiterate moron,' I joked back. As strange as this might sound, these insults were normal for us. Yes, the two of us regularly threw around insults as terms of endearment. So we were a little strange, what else was new?

"I hugged him back tightly, trying my hardest not to cry. Even if I did get out, and this whole thing was successful, where was I going to find anyone willing to help a bunch of Psychics escape from the orphanage? Without someone to help me, there was no way that I could return here and rescue the others. It might be months, even years before I found anyone who would help us. It might even be forever.

"Because life isn't always like they tell in fairytales. People don't always kiss in the rain. Love doesn't conquer all. Bad guys do get rewarded, and good guys don't always win. The hero doesn't always get the girl, and the not-so-helpless damsel-in-distress doesn't always get rescued by her knight in shining armor by the end of her story...and I should know. I've had to live that kind of story for as long as I can remember."

Again, the prophecy made its way into their minds again.

A Psychic that needs freeing...

Maybe Keaira herself had escaped from her prison, but there were countless other Psychics still trapped there. And her Other. If that was anything to go by, only part of Keaira had escaped that day. The rest of her was still trapped in that orphanage, and she needed to get out. If they truly were meant to fulfill this prophecy, then perhaps the Psychic Orphanage in New Japan was where they needed to make their next heading. They knew where they had to go next...and it was all thanks to this young girl.

"Keaira," Orienne began.

"Yes?" Keaira asked in response.

"We will help you rescue them."

"You'll...what?" she asked, wide-eyed and breathless.

"We'll what?" asked Áine. She had done enough rescuing in her lifetime, between Leilani, Orienne, and now Melaenie. She didn't think she'd be able to save an entire facility's worth of psychics as well. But she had sworn...

"Áine, you know the prophecy as well as any of us," said Anton. "You were singing it yourself just last night."

"Prophecy?" asked Keaira. "Are you speaking about the Twilight Dragon?"

"Yes," Áine answered.

"You mean...it's real?" she asked. "It's not just a Faerie tale meant to give us hope? It's not just a lie told by the Eidolith extremists?"

"We don't know for sure, but we're willing to believe it. It's the only hope we have. And now, because of you, we have our next heading," Orienne responded.

"Orienne is right," said Áine. She was remembering the vision that she and Leilani had invoked not all that long ago. Keaira had, in fact, been a part of it. "I can't believe I didn't see it. I knew there was a reason why our roads would cross paths here... Keaira, you are one of us. We will do all we can to rescue the other Psychics."

Keaira began to tear up at what they had promised to her. She fell to her knees, smiling and sobbing her heart out. "I...I thought I would never see them again! I thought... No one...no one would be crazy enough to help a dangerous person like me free other dangerous people...and now...now... You guys are crazy..." Her voice was cut off by her own sobs. Melaenie and Áine walked over to her to hug and comfort her.

Orienne was right, she may have been a little rude and rough around the edges, but she was one of them, part of the Kinship of the Twilight Moon. She needed them as much as they needed her. From that moment forward, they would welcome her with open arms.

When she had finished crying, she asked them to take her with them, and there wasn't a veto amongst the lot. She began to lead them out of the alley in the safest, most hidden way she knew, and as they travelled, she continued to tell them her tale.

"I had begun to despair at the thought of never seeing my best friend in the entire world ever again. 'I guess this is goodbye, huh?' I remember asking him.

"'Don't worry, Keaira, we'll see each other again.'

"'But...'

"'I believe in you,' he said as he smiled sadly.

"'We all believe in you,' added Arielle. 'You'll find someone, and you'll rescue us all.'

103

"'Yeah, what she said,' laughed Mateus, trying unsuccessfully to ease some of the tension in the room. 'You can do it.'

"'Alright...'

"'Now get out there and show them what it means to mess with the Little Dark One,' finished Gaignun.

"With that, Mateus took Gaignun and the two of them headed back to the cells to start gathering everyone else. Arielle stayed with me in order to take care of any interfering light sources we might come across.

"It wasn't long before the two boys returned, with sixteen other Psychics in tow, each one with the power of telekinesis. 'Let's do this,' said one of the girls in the crowd.

"And the rest, as they say, is history.

"I was out.

"I was free.

"So," Keaira continued. "After my great escape, the Head Mistress sent some of the guards to come chasing after me. I was always kept under high surveillance because of the level of my powers, which is almost the strongest of Psychic energy."

When she saw the look of unease in their eyes, she quickly added, "Oh, but don't worry about that, I'm in complete control over it."

They all stared at her as if they were expecting her to go off at any moment. Could they really trust that a fourteen year old had complete control over her Psychic powers? It seemed like they were playing with a ticking time bomb, and judging by the girl's personality, she had a short-fuse in more ways than one. They let her go on with her story, however.

"I got as far as the Sea of Japan, and then I was forced to find a way to get out of the country. I found an old cubic zirconium ring on the ground near the airport, and I attempted to pass it off as real gold and diamonds. It worked, and I earned myself a ticket to New Egypt in a first-class seat. It was the first flight available, and I needed to get out as fast as possible. No one suspected what I was up to, or so I had thought."

Keaira paused to make sure that all of them were still paying attention to her story and then took another bite out of the donut in her hands.

"As soon as the plane reached my destination, I was stopped by the man I had sold the ring to. He had gotten the ring checked out at a jewelers' shop at the airport, and discovered that it was not made of real gold or real diamonds. He had the security guards chase me through the city demanding that I repay the vast amount of money I owed him. Yeah right, not even in his dreams would I do that. Well, anyways, I ran and ran and ran until someone grabbed my sleeve and pulled me into this very alley."

This time it was the resident Prince who interrupted. "Oh, who was it? Was it a handsome young man, or perhaps a friend of yours? Oh, wait; maybe it was another one of those security guards! No, no, I know, it was your guardian angel descended down from heaven to save you from those bad, bad men! No, no, wait a minute! It was your long lost sister, but then after she helped you she did some weird kind of super-jump out of sight and you never ever saw her again but now you're searching desperately for her so that you can find the answers to your oh so mysterious past!" said Anton. When Keaira gave him a look that could scare a crying baby into silence, Anton cringed back. "Sorry, so sorry. Please continue."

"I had originally planned to make it through New Egypt as fast as possible without being found out, but my plans were changed when that lad pulled me into this alley. I knew then that I had to stay here until something big happened...something that would set my destiny in motion."

Áine visibly raised her eyebrow at the mention of "destiny." Orienne had already been filled in on the same information that Áine had supplied to Anton about the semantics of fate and destiny, so it was easy enough to pick up this key word when the young psychic had said it.

"But what about the boy?" asked Melaenie.

"As I was saying, I was pulled into this very alley by a completely random person. It was a really good-looking lad...and now that I think of it, he looked kind of like Blondie here in the red dress, only more like a boy and with shorter hair. He told me he was on the run and that I could hide out with him here in this alley for as long as I wanted."

"Wait a minute," Orienne stammered nervously. "He looked like me?"

"Yes, yes, why?" Keaira replied. Her patience was wearing thin, but Orienne was willing to push her luck to find out if the boy she spoke of was indeed her brother, long thought to be dead. For the first time in years, she felt a glimmer of hope in her heart. Maybe Ophir really was still alive, and the disappearance of his body so many years ago was merely because he ran away and went into hiding. It was far-fetched, but with all of the craziness that she had been witness to these past few days, anything seemed possible.

"Was he a Fader?"

"As a matter of fact, he was. Why?"

"Orienne, do you think...?" began Melaenie.

"Where is he now?!" Orienne interrupted. She began to get a cold sweat. It couldn't be...could her twin brother...was he alive? Maybe it was just a coincidence...but she couldn't resist temptation, she just had to know if the boy that Keaira was talking about was her beloved brother, Ophir.

"He left not long ago. In fact, he left just minutes before you and those other girls came screaming your heads off through this alley with that stupid jeep hot on your heels. Said he couldn't be seen by who was chasing you." Keaira looked at Orienne as if she had suddenly grown three heads. "It's no small wonder, with all of the attention you lot attract."

"Tell me what his name was!" Orienne nearly screamed as she tackled Keaira to the ground by complete accident. Even Melaenie was frightened by her sister's uncharacteristic behavior.

"I don't know! Now get off! You're hurting me!" and Keaira threw her off with a wave of Psychic energy, and Orienne faded. This time, it was Orienne who everyone was staring at. Was the one who saved Keaira Orienne's brother? She might never know, but it was a rather awkward situation. She couldn't believe how she'd just behaved...it was like an undisciplined child. She was scared of herself now; she couldn't believe how far she had gone. Tears started to form in her eyes, but she quickly wiped them away so as not to seem too emotionally unstable to the others. "Are you quite finished?"

"No...I mean, yes, I mean...I'm...I'm sorry. I don't know what came over me." Orienne mentally slapped herself.

"Anyways," she continued, uncrossing her arms and resting her hands on her hips. "He told me that he had escaped from a Fader prison about four years ago and had been running from country to country ever since. He told me that he had faked his death so that he could look for the Twilight Dragon and stop anything like what happened to him from happening to anyone else. He said the lives of his sisters depended on it. If you ask me though, he was a little crazy. Anyways, using the skills he had learned in his travels, he taught me all about living in hiding in this very alley. In time, this place became my home. Then that jeep came and I blew it up and met you all. And thus, my story ends." As she finished, she did a little bow as if she had just preformed an epic Shakespearian play all by herself.

"It just has to be Ophir, I know it!" Orienne thought to herself. "But why would he leave so suddenly...and right at the moment we all arrived? And why would he go around without a name?"

"Where are you guys headed to, anyways?" asked Keaira.

"Like we said before, we're going to find the Twilight Dragon and defeat it once and for all. We need all the help we can get," said Áine. "*Ni neart go cur le cheile.*"

"Specifically, we are going to my uncle's place in New France. I've got to pick up a spell, and I'm sure he'll be able to provide us with some hospitality," added Anton.

After they purchased their supplies, (Prince Anton went in by himself to avoid any problems) they all decided to set up a picnic just outside the city limits, since it was a nice day and no one was on their trail for the time being. Keaira made sure of that, and Anton did not hesitate to recast his shrouding spells.

When everyone was off ahead of Keaira and Orienne, with Keaira way behind so she could easily catch anyone who was tracking them, Orienne heard her call out. "Hey, you!"

"What is it?" Orienne asked. "Is something the matter?"

"No, no one is following us or anything. But I have something for you."

"What?"

"You appeared to be very interested in the boy in my story. You wouldn't happen to be...one of his sisters, would you?"

"I'm not entirely sure, but I think so. If you had given me a name, I could have said so, but you said you didn't know so..."

"I lied," she told her quietly. "What did you expect? When you jumped me like that you completely caught me off guard. If you had frightened me enough, I could have easily killed you, do you realize that?"

"I'm sorry," Orienne replied.

"Oh well, it's not like it matters now. His name was Ophir."

"That's him! That's my brother!" Orienne's heart suddenly began to well up with the happiest feeling she had had since...since so long ago, she could not even remember the last time that she had felt that happy.

"He told me that if I ever met his sisters, I was to give this to them." She handed Orienne a crumpled piece of paper with quickly scribbled writing on it. "It's like he knew that you were coming." It read:

Orienne, I know you are out there somewhere. I'm sorry for faking my death, and I am even sorrier for being unable to see you now. It has been a long four years without you, Mother, or our little sister, but it must be a little longer still before we can be reunited. I worry as to why either of you would be so far from home, but I must implore you to return there as soon as you are able. It is not safe out here. You must trust me. Go back home. I don't want you or

108

Melaenie to get hurt. It's why I left in the first place. Please,
Orienne, just go home.

   With love always, your brother, Ophir

So now she knew for sure. The boy Keaira spoke of was indeed Ophir. Orienne felt so relieved that her beloved brother was still alive and well, somewhere out there in the world. She thanked Keaira and then ran off to catch up with the others, and to tell Melaenie of the wonderful news. However, the cryptic message he had written did unnerve her a little.

When they had finally decided on a good place to rest, Áine, Anton, Melaenie, Keaira and Orienne all set up their little picnic. It was a nice change of pace for them, this nice, leisurely meal. Everything had been so rushed of late, and little food, if any, had been available to the girls. This picnic was a little slice of heaven.

Even though all of this adventuring business was a lot to take in, they could get used to it. For the first time in their lives, they had friends, they didn't have to hide away in the woods or by the lake anymore, and at last they were free. And best of all, they were learning so much. They had discovered that there was still hope, and Ophir was out there somewhere, helping them in his own mysterious way.

Chapter Thirteen
Moon and Sun

~~~

As they traveled through the desert together, the sun beat down on them, glaring into their eyes and scorching their skin with its unforgiving heat. None of them were very tan, Keaira being the palest of the bunch, and they burned quite easily. But they did not let this get their spirits down. No, they were far too preoccupied with their newfound sense of freedom, heavy burdens having been lifted from all of their shoulders.

But no matter the heat or exhaustion that touched their bodies, it did not touch their hearts, and they did not travel in silence.

"Hey Áine, you're a Faerie. What's your story about the Twilight Dragon? I'm curious."

"I'm only a Halfie, Keaira."

"Halfie, whatever. Doesn't change anything. You're from another world, Áine! Don't you understand how exotic that is to us Earthlings?"

"I couldn't care less, actually. And my past is something I'd rather not talk about."

"I wasn't asking about your past, I was asking about the Twilight Dragon. People here in Earth have lots of legends about it. No one really knows what it is, or even if it exists. But you, you're a Faerie – er, well – Halfie. You come from a different culture, a different world entirely. Surely you've got a different side of the story to present."

"I'm rather interested in hearing something about that, too," added Prince Anton, cutting into their banter and clearing away some of the tension while he was at it. "My people say that it had something to do with that old Greek myth about Pandora's Box."

"It was no myth. Pandora truly existed, though the stories have been far exaggerated."

"Did she actually have anything to do with the Twilight Dragon?" asked Orienne, her interest in the subject equally piqued.

"Truthfully, yes, though she only released it. She had no hand in creating the beast."

"Who created it? Or what?" asked Keaira.

"Ah, well you see, we don't really know for sure. But still, we do have our own stories."

"Well let's hear them!" Anton requested playfully, trying not to seem too intrusive as he scampered up closer to her.

"Alright, alright," Áine smiled, laughing at Anton's antics. And...was that a blush that Orienne spotted on Áine's cheeks, or merely another sunburn? She couldn't tell for sure, though it did not stop her heart from pulsing blood thickened with jealousy.

Regardless, the tale began.

"Long, long ago, there were two spirits who created the universe. After many millenniums of work, the two had finally created a world that could sustain life. However, the planet had two overlapping worlds on it, pinned to separate planes of reality.

"Unwilling to scrap their most delicate work, they knew that in order for the two worlds to coexist and give rise to life, a sacrifice would have to be made. To better aid in the growth of their worlds, the two spirits decided to take root in the bodies of light that would lend strength to their young creation.

"One became the Moon, who decided to watch over the spirit world that overlapped Earth, unseen and full of magic. The other became the Sun, who claimed rule over the Earthly realm, full of life and truth. To keep the balance, souls from each realm would cycle into one another after every death.

"Things went well enough for a long time. However, one day while the Moon was looking down over the Sun's domain, she saw that the creatures there were troubled. The balance of life had been thrown off somehow. Souls from Earth were too afraid to go to her Spirit Realm, and so they did all they could to seek immortality or live as long as they could. They huddled alone, afraid of the dark, afraid of harm, afraid to even live their own lives for fear that their lives would end. She took pity on the creatures and their fear, and decided to send them a creature of her own, to help ease the transition between the two realms.

"She sent a moonstone plummeting to Earth from her place on the moon. Where the stone fell, there lay a being who had no name, no memories, and no fear or evil in his heart. He was different from the creatures all around him. Pure white and wild as the wind, with a single horn spiraling out from his beautiful head, he was perfect.

"The Unicorn was what she called him.

"The spirit of the moon had meant for him to bring peace and love to the corrupted world below, and at first the Unicorn took joyful pride in his task. But as time went on, it became apparent that the other creatures were jealous of his purity and wanted nothing to do with him. They shunned him, and called him 'One Horn' or 'White Beast.' They were even afraid of his horn, despite that it was incapable of even so much as drawing blood, and so they tried again and again to break it off. The evil in their own hearts made it impossible for them to even look at him sometimes. And so, he became very lonely.

"One day he looked up to the moon, where he knew his mother still lived, and asked her for her help. He was desperate to find some form of companionship, and to help those he had been sent here to help. Yet he knew he was unwanted, hated even. And so, the Spirit of the Moon answered his plea. If the creatures of Earth did not want him, she would send him somewhere else. She opened up a door to another world for him to walk through, and told him that all would be well. No longer would her precious Unicorn wander the

Earth in vain, but run free in Eidolon, in her domain of spirits and dreams where he would live forever under her gentle gaze.

"However, the creatures of the Earth would not allow their toy to escape so easily. They overheard the Unicorn's plea to the Moon, and planned to sabotage his journey to Eidolon. Just as he walked through the gate, they gathered around it and smashed it to pieces. The gate crumbled around him and became closed off while he was still in the threshold. A piece of the gate fell down onto the Unicorn and broke his horn clean off.

"The Unicorn was sent spiraling into a deep rage, one that had never been known before, and one that would never be known since. The pain of his horn forcefully being broken from him, the crushing grief at the thought of betrayal, the drowning waves loneliness that the other creatures and now even his own mother had sent washing over him...it was all too much for a being of such purity to take in. Filled with such hatred, he was purified all over again; only now, he had become a being of pure evil.

"That was the day he fell from grace. The Spirit of the Moon had not meant for such a thing to happen, but what was done was done. The damage was irreversible. And he never stopped blaming her. He broke off their friendship that day, and turned away from her, his heart full of hate.

"For years afterwards, he only further altered himself, frustrated as he was stuck between planes of different dimensions. He was everywhere and nowhere all at once, and only his memories of imagined betrayal stayed with him. Piece by piece, he changed his body parts into those of other creatures until he became something new entirely. And every time he changed himself, his madness and hatred for the Spirit of the Moon grew.

"As hatred consumed his heart, parts of it began to crystallize and fall from him as physical representation of what had once made him whole. His love was gone and he became as greedy and selfish as a full-grown dragon. Finally, as he decided that using his magic for chaos and destruction was far superior than using it to uphold the harmony he was once a part of, he shed away his true self. From his vantage point in Liminality, where he could see all that transpired in both worlds, he fed the fire of his hatred and bided his time for the day he could escape and enact his revenge.

"He devised a plan that would turn the Spirit of the Moon against her brother, the Spirit of the Sun, thereby destroying that which destroyed him and "truly" setting him free. He reveled in twisting the moon's light and the sun's light into something more magically powerful than either were alone, thus creating the twilight. It was thus how he came to be known as the Twilight Dragon.

"From this twilight, he was able to pull stray souls from Eidolon through the cracks in the gate to Liminality and corrupt them to suit his own design. These were the first Sídhe, the wicked Fey that killed for pleasure and lived their lives of undeath for the sole purpose of empowering their lord creator, the Twilight Dragon.

"And yet, when he shed away his former self, the Fragments of the Twilight Moon were created. Shed from the heart of the worlds first Unicorn, who in turn became the first Twilight Dragon, was pure solidified will of the Spirit of the Moon. He had unwittingly created the tools that would lead to his own defeat.

"The Spirit of the Moon had not yet given up on the creatures in her brother's realm, however. She sent a second moonstone plummeting to the Earth, and this time she gave her Unicorn son a True Name, a gift that would make his magic far stronger and more stable than that of his brother. She called him Lune, the Bearer of Light, the Walker of White, the King beneath the Moon.

"Lune was different in many ways from his lost elder brother. Though his heart and soul were as pure as the moonlight that gave him life, he was neither naive nor weak willed. He cast his magic wherever he stepped, healing the land and easing away pain from all who gazed upon him.

"Slowly but surely, the fear of death and journeying to the other world all but vanished from the creatures who lived in the Spirit of the Sun's domain. They no longer lived their lives in hiding, and they grew to love and respect Lune. Many were ashamed of the way they had treated his brother, though none, not even Lune or the Spirit of the Moon herself, knew what had become of him after he became trapped in Liminality. Yet now that Lune's mission had been accomplished, he no longer needed to remain on Earth. This was the world where magic could not flourish, where immortal beings such as he could not walk forever. His true home was in Eidolon, with his mother and the spirits he was meant to guide after death.

"And so, the Spirit of the Moon opened up a second gate. The Twilight Dragon took this opportunity to release the Sídhe into both worlds of Earth and Eidolon to act as a distraction while he, himself escaped from the threshold between worlds so that he might take revenge on those who had wronged him. The Sídhe seized Lune before he even had time to react, and they tore him into a thousand, thousand pieces. The Spirit of the Moon cried out as she watched helplessly as the Sídhe murdered her beloved son. Now both of her children had been lost to Evil.

"When Lune was dead, and his pure blood had stained the ground in the world between worlds, the Twilight Dragon thought himself to be unstoppable. He walked among the creatures of the land, whispering hateful and distrusting words into one another's ears. To some, he claimed that the Spirit of the Sun was overconfident, overbearing, and wanted to impose his will on all who lived in his domain. He was a tyrant, obsessed with control. To others, he claimed that the Spirit of the Moon was a deceiver, a trickster, and a villain. She soothed only to seduce, and her dominion over the night made her untrustworthy. He turned the creatures against their protectors, and against one another. He mused and manipulated until at last, such dissent had arisen in them that they did not hesitate to begin the very first civil war.

"When at last the Spirits had discovered what the Twilight Dragon had done, it was too late. The fighting had already begun. Though they were powerless to stop the battles, they had not yet given up hope. Rumors had begun to spread of a mystical power source left behind by a mysterious being, that when used could

115

restore balance and harmony to the world. When they realized that what they spoke of must have been the remnants of the first Unicorn's heart, their own hearts were filled with sorrow. But now that they knew what exactly this power was, they did not hesitate to go out and search for it.

"And so, the two Spirits left their homes in the Moon and the Sun and embarked on a journey to find the Fragments of the Twilight Moon, a journey that would last for many days and nights. At long last, they found them, however, and used them against the very creature who had created them in the first place. Fitting the pieces together, they forged a magical box that would absorb all negativity into it and lock it away forever. *This* was the villain who had turned them against one another. *This* was the betrayer who had caused them so much pain.

"They tore his body in two and sealed him into this box that would hold him for all eternity. And as soon as the lid closed shut, Lune, whose spirit had lived on in Liminality, poured his will onto the lock, sealing it shut with all of his might.

"But the seal was not as strong as the Spirits would have liked to believe. Though the body of the Twilight Dragon remained imprisoned, his will did not. As his already severed body continued to deteriorate, each and every evil that would ever be was conceived one by one, and trapped in the prison of the box, as his hate-filled soul still called out for the new corruption to join the existing darkness in his heart. Throughout the following years, his voice, though it was very quiet now, would haunt the creatures of both worlds.

"And only the Eidoliths, made in the image of the Spirits of the Moon and Sun, who shared the power to create something from nothing, would be able to stand against it when at last it escaped from its meager prison."

~~~

At some time around midnight, they all stopped to set up camp. There were five of them and only three blankets - the one that Anton had taken on his pilgrimage, the one that Orienne had escaped the house with and wrapped around her little sister, and the one that Ophir had given to Keaira. This may have presented a problem, if Anton hadn't requested that they use his ingenious (yet highly unoriginal) plan to pull names out of a hat (or rather Áine's violin case) on who would share a blanket with whom.

Anton and Áine were the first to be paired up. Melaenie, who was too young and shy to feel comfortable sleeping with strangers and yet felt too old to sleep with her sister, would use the smallest blanket for herself. Another pair ended up being Orienne and Keaira. However, they refused to sleep next to each other. They were simply incompatible with one another.

They argued childishly for some time until the Halfie spoke up.

"What if one of us were to switch places with you?" suggested Áine.

"Áine is right," added Anton. He looked towards Áine with a longing expression as he said the next part. "If it would prevent there from being trouble..."

"Absolutely not," replied Melaenie sternly, not even letting Anton finish. She seemed to already know what he was trying to suggest. Not with her sister! Such indecency!

"Oh, but Melaenie, can we please redraw? Pretty, pretty please?" begged Keaira. She looked at Áine and Anton with big puppy-dog eyes and attempted to do the boo-boo-lip. She was quite skilled at looking unreasonably adorable, which Orienne envied about Keaira. She was such a brat, and yet she was able to appear so innocent.

Melaenie, who had a soft-spot for adorable things, said, "Okay," without another thought. In fact, she even said it with a smile on her face. And so, they put their names back into the violin case and redrew.

The pairings were as such - Anton and Orienne, Áine and Keaira, and Melaenie all by her lonesome.

117

Anton was the only one who seemed let down. Though he had agreed with Áine's suggestion, it wasn't hard to miss his yearning expression as he gazed over at the Faerie longingly, as if s*he* was the one he would rather cuddle up next to. Was it true? Had the Prince who had courted many a maiden fallen for the Halfie? Áine didn't seem to notice the pleading from his sky blue eyes; rather, she simply ignored him as he trudged over to Orienne with their designated blanket.

"I guess that means it's the two of us, right?" Anton asked Orienne as he tucked her in. Orienne nodded shyly. They took their blanket and snuggled in close. When they finally got a chance to lie down, Anton took off his robe to reveal that he had two white wings poking out from his shoulder blades.

Orienne gasped. "You're a Shironohane!"

Shironohane were a race of beings who hailed from a far away world. When they first fell from the sky after The Collapse, people thought they were angels, come to Earth to take them to heaven or share their divine might with the people. When the Shirohane began kidnapping people and demanding tribute after being exiled to their own cities in the sky, people no longer thought so highly of them.

There was an enormous backlash against the Shironohane, causing many of them to flee from Earth or cut their own wings off to blend in with the humans. Those who remained but refused to remove their wings were hunted down and shuttled back up to the few remaining cloud cities that were still aloft in the sky. It was declared that any Shironohane who left their cities were to be given but a single warning, which if unheeded, resulted in a prompt execution.

For Anton, a prince, to be a Shirohane...one who still had his wings, for that matter, it was almost unthinkable. No, it was impossible! How had no one noticed that the French government had been infiltrated by such...such wicked creatures? And how could Anton be one of them? This couldn't be true... Orienne began to shrink back in fear. Suddenly, she wasn't so sure that her desire to sleep next to the boy had been such a wise idea.

118

"I'm only half. My father was one who cut off his wings, and my mother was a human."

"Was?" queried Orienne.

"She died shortly after I was born. Queen Emeraude is my step-mother."

"I'm sorry," replied Orienne.

"Nothing to be sorry for," Anton sighed. "Emeraude has never treated me as anything but a beloved son. She is one of the best mothers any child could ask for. I never knew my birth mother, so I can't say that I miss her."

Anton pulled at the blanket a little and ruffled his wings to get into a more comfortable position. Orienne was so startled that she faded through the blanket. He hadn't known that she was so easily startled, because after she faded, he gasped and tried to stifle a giggle. It was a little awkward for them, with the two of them staring each other down and trying desperately not to laugh. Anton, of course, was the first to crack. He giggled quietly so as not to waken or bother the others. His joyful laughter was contagious, and Orienne soon found herself muffling her own laughter right along with him.

"You okay?" he finally asked her after his laughter seemed to calm down a bit.

"Fine, you?" asked Orienne, still smiling. She began to feel silly for being afraid of Anton. He was nothing but a sweet, kind young man. And she should know better than to be prejudiced against others. After all, she herself had been subject to some truly horrible prejudice for being a Fader.

"Yeah," he replied, smiling back an even larger grin than her own.

They laid back in silence for a short while before Anton spoke up again. "I tried to cut my wings off once. It was a terrifying experience. Blood and feathers everywhere. It was the worst pain I'd ever felt. My father found out and stopped me from finishing the deed. Told me that I should never try to do such a thing again. He didn't want me making the same mistake that he had made just to fit in.

"'They'll kill me,' I said to him. But he held me close and told me that he wanted me to fly."

Orienne was speechless. Why was he telling all of this to her? They barely knew one another. But she...she wanted to know more about him. After all, he had learned her story.

The only difference was that Anton had only told her. None of the others were aware at all.

She finally found her words again. "And did you? Fly, I mean."

"I did, a few times. It was the most wonderful feeling, soaring through the air. I stopped once my father remarried. My step-mother was afraid that someone might discover my secret, and it would cause more controversy and political upheaval than either of my parents were willing to handle. So I continued to hide my wings, and I kept my feet on the ground."

"Why didn't you tell any of us about your wings?"

"People don't very much like Shironohane. It might cause trouble for us if people knew that the King of New France and his son weren't really humans."

"Do you think that Shironohane are the only ones who are hunted? Look around you, Anton; we're all hated by the people. We aren't going to feed you to the wolves."

"I know. Nonetheless, I will tell them all in my own time. You are to keep this as our little secret. Alright?"

Orienne nodded.

After their conversation, the two of them snuggled in more comfortably, ready for sleep. They quickly checked around to see if their little outburst had awoken any of the others. Thankfully, it hadn't, and with that all cleared up and their exhaustion setting in, both of them were out-cold within minutes.

Chapter Fourteen
Magic and Mischief

~~~

The next morning, they all woke up to a shock. At first Orienne was frightened to awaken next to a strange man who was not her brother, but she calmed down as the memories of the previous day came back to her. She smiled, thinking back to the story that Prince Anton had confided in her. Did he really trust her so?

She looked over to the other side of her. There was Melaenie, sleeping quite soundly, curled up in a little ball. That was right, she and her new friends had also rescued Melaenie from the Fader Hater.

So much had happened.

Melaenie had tried to take everything in stride, keeping to herself and clinging to her older sister, and laughing at the others' jokes...it was strange to be surrounded by such kindness.

But the shock that everyone else experienced was far more... "physical" so to speak. Keaira had jumped up, screaming, "No fair, that was *my* piece!" and then she unleashed a psychic wave that sent all of the rest of them flying into the trees, which, of course, was a rude awakening for everyone. Melaenie was flung back into her sister, and she could hear Orienne go "oof" as she slammed into her stomach.

"Sorry, Orienne," Melaenie muttered quickly.

"It's...okay, Melaenie," she replied between gasps. It seemed she had accidentally knocked the wind out of her.

Anton took the moment of confusion as his cue to quickly slip his robe back on, hiding his white wings from view once more.

Keaira fully woke up and asked why everyone was in the trees. The whole time she kept her adorable, fake-innocent smile on. Melaenie, soft as ever, tried to smile happily right alongside the Psychic, humoring her. Her sister had always warned her against getting on people's bad sides, especially if they were more powerful than she was. Keaira was a powerful psychic, and clearly stronger than Melaenie. So she smiled back.

Everyone except for Orienne and Melaenie went over to Keaira and viciously tied her to a tree as Áine dangled a rather large lump of cheese in front of her face. Melaenie quietly wondered to herself where she had suddenly acquired the cheese; as they purposely avoided buying food that easily spoiled in the heat save for the milk that was meant to be a treat yesterday. She also wondered why she was even dangling the piece of cheese in front of her in the first place. And what had happened to her seemingly unending patience, for that matter?

"Ha! What's that supposed to do? I'm a Psychic, in case you've forgotten, I can untie these ropes without moving a single finger!" Keaira laughed in their faces.

"Oh, we haven't forgotten at all!" said Áine vengefully. She tied the lump of cheese to the lowest branch of the tree and began to laugh as if she were an evil maniac. Áine had been the quietest one of the group, the most sensible one of them all...up until now, anyways, so this was rather astonishing for her to be acting this way. It was as if her personality had done a complete one-eighty.

"MUWA-HA-HA-HA-HA!" she cackled.

When Keaira attempted to untie the ropes using Psychic energy, she just couldn't. "What did you do to me, you dumb Faerie freak?!" she screamed. Áine replied with more of her maniacal laughter.

"You're the Psychic, and now you're calling me a freak? Oh, that's rich!" she laughed heartily.

Melaenie watched in silence as Keaira took a closer look at the lump of cheese, and then gasped in utter horror. She seemed to have made some kind of frightening discovery. "No! It couldn't be!"

"What couldn't be?" asked Orienne, as clueless as to what Keaira was so shocked about as her sister was.

This time, it was Anton who spoke up. "She hung a special artifact that hinders the powers of the mind. Those kinds of things are only authorized for Spell Weavers to carry, in case of a psychic related emergency. You may be familiar with the Psychic Wars a few years back. That magical petrified cheese was enchanted by none other than the great wizard Donato-Jacques-Alphonse-Amaure LaCiel IV," explained Anton. "It is a great heirloom of my family, and I must ask...Áine, where did you get my cheese?"

"It was in your satchel!" Áine accused in a rather comical manner, which was followed by even more crazy, evil laughter. She had definitely snapped.

"What were you doing rummaging through my things?" It wasn't hard to see that Anton had let his staff slide out of the hiding place in his sleeve, and he was now clutching it tightly in his hand. He only did that when he wanted to cast a spell.

"Wait a minute," started Keaira. "What kind of name is Donna-Jackie-Alpha-whatcha-ma-who-jama-whatsit?"

"Donato-Jacques-Alphonse-Amaure. It is a highly-respected name that has been passed down on my mother's side for generations! It is bestowed upon the second-born son of..."

"Um, may I please interrupt?" Melaenie asked timidly. Everything went quiet. With all of the ruckus, nobody had even noticed how much they were bothering the littlest member of their growing party.

"Hmm...let me think about that one." Keaira stared off into the distance for a few moments in quiet contemplation. Then she turned to face her again and said, "No."

"Keaira, stop being a brat," retorted Áine, reverting back to her normal self for the most part. "Be nice to the poor child." The maniacal laughter had stopped, and her expression had softened noticeably. "What's the matter, little one?"

"I...um..." Melaenie's mind completely went blank. She couldn't think with all of the focus on her like that, and her head started to spin. "I..."

"Melaenie?" asked her big sister. "Are you alright?"

"I don't feel so good..." was all she managed to say before she collapsed to the ground and vomited. As soon as she realized what had happened, she was overcome with embarrassment and began to cry her eyes out.

"Melaenie!"

Áine and Orienne rushed to her side, ignoring the rude gestures and groans that the tied-up Psychic was making. Her sister put a cool hand against her sweating brow to check for a fever while Áine opened up her violin case and began rummaging around for a small pouch of herbs, most likely what was meant to be a cure for her nausea. "Water..." she began to mutter to herself as she filled up her water skin with the water from the shallow pool at the center of the oasis and mix in the herbs.

"Water!" exclaimed Anton all of a sudden, in response to Áine's mutterings. "Leilani!" He dashed from the side of the palm tree to the shallow pool of water that was just beside them.

Suddenly, the same idea seemed to hit all of their heads at the same time. Áine quickly administered the medicine to Melaenie before Orienne hoisted her onto her back. They all ran over to the tiny fresh-water pond, with Melaenie piggy-backing, and started calling out, "Leilani! Leilani!"

Their calling into the shallow pool of water was not nearly as psychotic as it looked. In fact, it was completely one-hundred percent sane, much to Melaenie's and Keaira's shock and disbelief. Within moments, a finned girl stuck her silvery head out of the water and said, *"Aloha!"* Her perfect voice etched with her Hawaiian accent rang through the air. Melaenie stared in awe, along with Keaira, who had never seen her before.

124

Leilani looked at the two newcomers and said, "Listen, before you even ask me, no, I am not a mermaid. So don't ask. Seriously."

The two of them nodded in synch and let Leilani continue to talk.

"It's a good thing I heard you guys. I've got good news. Áine...I think I've found them. I think I've found the Peach and the Cat."

Áine's jaw dropped and her heart stopped. All knew of the role that Dr. Adam Ryu's creations played in bringing the people out of The Collapse. If Leilani had truly found them...

Without truly meaning to, Melaenie interrupted. "What's going on? How did I get involved in whatever it is that you people are doing?"

"Oh, you mean they haven't told you your mission yet?" asked Leilani sadly.

"I know that you guys are trying to find the Twilight Dragon in order to destroy the Crystalline Virus that is making so many people into Faders."

"So what has you confused, little one?"

"It all seems rather silly to me. I'm not exactly a formidable opponent for a dragon. Especially one that doesn't even exist. Are you sure this isn't crazy talk?" Melaenie asked quietly, trying not to sound too sarcastic for fear of upsetting the strange mer-girl. She didn't know if she wanted to believe all of this. So much had happened in such a short amount of time. The Twilight Dragon had never been anything more than a legend to her, though she was quite familiar with it thanks to her sister telling it to her as a bedtime story when she was young. Well, younger. "What am I even supposed to do against it? Talk it to death?" Melaenie's only legitimate skill was studying languages, which in all honesty didn't seem like it would be that useful in this kind of situation.

"Nonsense!" said Leilani. "You're an Eidolith, there's nothing you can't do. Besides, it's written in Destiny's Stone, kid. So, how does it feel to be one of the heroes that will be responsible for freeing humanity from the big, bad Twilight Dragon?"

"Is what she's saying the truth?" she asked her sister. Orienne smiled and nodded at Melaenie in response.

"The Twilight Dragon is just a child's Faerie tale to give hope to the little Fader children like me! And since when did I agree to any of this?" Melaenie argued, still knee-deep in denial. She was becoming scared again. She feared that she just might vomit again, wasting Áine's precious herbal medicine.

"Since I said so, which would be right about...now. Have fun on your mission girls...and Anton! Little Miss Andraste, if I hear that you haven't been even remotely aiding these young people on their quest, even after all they did to rescue you, I'll hunt you down and put a curse on you. Or have Anton put a curse on you or something." And with that, she dove back into the water.

"Is she really going to curse me?" Melaenie asked.

"No," replied Áine. "She's just trying to be conversational."

"She's not very good at it," Melaenie replied.

"I almost forgot!" Leilani exclaimed as she popped out of the water again. "Here are your communicators. With these, you'll be able to contact me anytime from anyplace." She handed each of them necklace chains with a crescent shaped capsule on it. The crystalline capsule was translucent, and in it was seemingly ordinary water, though it sparkled more vibrantly than any water they had ever seen before.

"We can communicate with these?" asked Melaenie.

"Yeah, this isn't nearly a large enough space of liquid to transport ourselves through to Atlantis," added Anton.

"It's simple, really," began Leilani. "I've discovered a way to communicate using the water from the Lake of Atlantis. Áine helped develop it, too. Inside of those capsules are droplets of water from the lake. All you have to do is say my name, and I can talk to you."

"But then how will we get to Atlantis if all we can do is speak to you?" asked Orienne.

"That's the thing, you can't. It would be a little inconvenient. However, through the use of this special water, my voice can reach you. This way, none of us will have to go through all of the trouble of finding a big enough puddle for me to fit through if you needed to get a hold of me for any reason at all," replied Leilani.

"Besides, look, they're so pretty!" exclaimed Keaira. It was true; the charms took the forms of beautiful, sparkling crescent moons. The crescent moons were a symbol of unity of sorts among them. They were, after all, the Kinship of the Twilight Moon. What better way to represent their bond?

Melaenie looked at the charm in her hand. "Look! They have these strange markings engraved on them, albeit they're really, really tiny and hard to read. Leilani, what language is this?"

"That, my young friend, is the writing of the ancient Eidoliths. In a time when the lake of Atlantis was topped with a great city, there lived a group of people who protected that lake with all of their might. The Andraste bloodline is the last remaining bloodline of that ancient race of people, who claimed to hail from Eidolon itself.

"They infused the waters with their unsurpassed magic, and learned how to use the pearls as ways to channel and store such magic. Their system of writing seemed most fitting for your charms, since the prophecy you all now follow was written by the Eidoliths themselves."

"How in seven hells did you learn all of that?" asked Keaira.

"Years and years living in that lake with nothing better to do, that's what. Áine played her part, too. If she hadn't used her gift to..." she paused and bit her lip, as if she had said too much. "If Áine hadn't taught me the language, I'd have never learned any of this."

Keaira had just managed to get one arm undone from the rope. The little brat was rather resourceful when she had to be. It must have come from all of that experience on the run. Though she was not that physically strong, her will was certainly powerful. Her pushy, bratty exterior was probably only there to guard her spirit from the cruelties of the world... It was too bad that most people

127

would never be willing to find that little lost child hidden beneath the dust and dander of her antagonistic outer self.

"We should have a name for ourselves," said Keaira.

"We already do," replied Áine. "Kinship of the Twilight Moon."

"From the old poem?" asked Melaenie, who proceeded to recite the bit which mentioned the Kinship. "The Kinship of the Twilight Moon, bound by their blood and by their fate, shall whet their blades by Light of Lune, and save these worlds 'fore 'tis too late."

"It's a pretty decent name," said Leilani. "A little bit of a mouthful, but fitting nonetheless. After all, we were named by the prophecy that brought us all together. I think it would be wrong to change it."

Addressing the actual matter at hand, Áine asked, "So, where are we headed to next? Do you have any leads, Leilani?" She finally seemed to be back to her normal self.

They all looked towards the finned girl in the water. She had to have some kind of idea right?

Anton, however, was the one to reply. "We're going to my uncle's place in New France. After that, we can figure out where to go next, but it's rather urgent that we get there."

"Very well then, Prince. Follow me down here, if you'd like to go the fast way. Oh, I almost forgot. The Peach and the Cat should be waiting for you when you arrive. You'll know them when you see them, trust me. Well, they technically won't know you're all coming to them, but you get my point right? It was good that you delayed the trip to see your uncle, Anton, for if you had arrived on schedule, Dr. Ryu's creations would have passed you all by. Oh, yes, and before you depart, please untie Keaira from that tree." She then lifted one of her long, slender arms out of the water and pointed over to Keaira, who was in fact; still secured firmly to the tree with the exception of the single arm she had managed to get loose.

"All right, finally! At least you would have the common sense to make them let me out of this tree! Hey, Anton, you can have your

128

creepy petrified cheese back," she squealed as they were all forced to untie her.

"Well, come on now, don't just stand there!" Leilani waited for Anton to jump in, who was followed by the rest of the group.

Keaira dove in after them last, not completely sure of what was going on. "Ah, what the hell, why not?" she exclaimed, as she dove headfirst into the seemingly shallow pool of iridescent water.

They all followed Leilani to the multi-colored air bubble that was Atlantis, where she briefed them on their mission. If ever they absolutely had to make an escape, they only had to be together to pour out the water in their charms at the same time. There should be enough water in the lot of them to create a one-way gate to Atlantis. It would be simple enough to refill their charms once they made their escape.

As for the immediate plan, they were to stay the night there with Leilani, and store their extra supplies in Atlantis, keeping only a little bit of food and their charms with them just in case of an emergency situation. This little underwater dome was going to be their hub and hideout from now on. It was far safer down there than out in the open where Bounty Hunters and other overbearing authoritative forces lurked.

Anton, Orienne, and Áine immediately set to work at clearing some of the rubble to build a make-shift shelf out of for easier storage access rather than leaving everything just piled up on the ground. Keaira tried to help, too, but it wasn't long before she found out that the barrier around Atlantis worked much in the same way that Anton's enchanted cheese had - her powers were all but useless, and she was far too scrawny to rely on her physical strength.

When all had been said and done, they ate, and laughed, and settled down for the night in their new home.

Chapter Fifteen
The Peach and The Cat

~~~

"Pa...pa..."

"Good. Now, can you open your eyes?"

"Eyes...eyes...yes. I think I can. My eyes are...my visual sensory preceptors. Activating eyesight." She opened her eyes to the world around her for the very first time in a very long time per the request of her Papa. It was an unusual sensation, sight. So much light, so much data input. Simply taking in her surroundings was almost enough to overload her after so many years of resting in sleep mode.

There were seven short, white haired girls garbed in clothing black as pitch standing in the room, staring at her. All were identical, all motionless, expressionless, lifeless. Their eyes alone, which shone like prismatic glass, were the only indication that they were not merely duplicates of one another. Each girl had a different hue to the glassy irises, one for each color of the rainbow. They were like her, artificial. And yet...

"Eyesight activated."

"Momoko, you don't have to announce your functions every time you do something."

"Understood, Papa." She turned her head to face her Papa, the man who created her. There were so many questions she had to ask him. Who were these other girls? Why did he shut her off? And why did he wait so long to reboot her? How many years, precisely, had it been since that day? How had the people survived without her aid?

However, all of those questions were simultaneously erased as she gazed upon his face at last. This man...he was not her Papa. He was far too young, far too cocky. Momoko could see it in his eyes, there was naught but ambition and vanity. Her Papa was old, kindly, and sincere. She did not know how long she had been asleep, but it was certainly long enough for papa to become very, very old. There were none of her Papa's qualities in this new man. He was young, not even into his twenties yet, dark haired, and smug. Where was the kindliness? Where was the intuitive expression, the intelligent smile?

"Who are you?" Momoko asked him. "I do not recognize you from my memory banks. You are...not Papa?"

"No, I am not the Papa you know. I am your new Papa."

"How did you access my memory banks if you are not my Papa?"

"That's easy, my little peach," he cooed coyly. "I am Dr. Ryu's grandson. You may call me Adam."

Momoko's senses were whirring. Her Papa's...grandson? She had been asleep for two whole generations. Surely, the people no longer needed her guidance if she had slept this long and the world was not in turmoil. "What purpose do you have in waking me, if not to spread my knowledge?"

"Your knowledge? What little you possess would be of no use to anyone but me."

"Little?" asked Momoko, but it was not long before she realized that she had no need to ask such a thing. Almost all of her data banks had been wiped clean. There truly was very little now that she either knew or remembered, and even that much was encrypted. It would take much effort to access those files.

He placed his hand beneath her chin and tilted her face upwards so that she could look directly into his eyes. "My little Peach, will you not help me achieve my dream? Help me to recall the twilight of humanity, that brink between life and death, the edge of sanity

131

and madness. Help bring chaos back to this bleak little world of black and white. Restore the shades of gray that lie between the absolutes. Give rise to the rebirth of the Twilight Dragon!"

Momoko knew well the long history of the Twilight Dragon. If there was anything that still remained in her data banks, that was it. Her Papa had spent his entire life studying the documentation of the Eidoliths, hunting the creature down, and using Momoko as his guide. They had found it, but Momoko's memory logs were fuzzy after that. She suspected that it was not long after that she had been shut down. But surely, he must have succeeded in his endeavor. There was no reason to undo all that her Papa had accomplished and bring such evil back into the world. She was created to help the people, not destroy them. To promote order, not bring about chaos. What this new "Papa" spoke of was madness.

"The Twilight Dragon is gone. My Papa defeated it."

Adam laughed. "My dear little peach, I forgive you for your ignorance, for you have been asleep for so long. But I must inform you, the Twilight Dragon is by no means defeated. You cannot stop the Twilight Dragon. It will always live on in the fear of our hearts, the sins of our past, and the pain of our memories. It will drink from the hate of humanity, perpetuated as long as life itself continues to exist. Once slain, it will find a new host, and corrode them from the inside out."

"But my Papa..."

Adam interrupted her. "My Grandfather did indeed slay the Dragon, but he did not finish the job. It split itself in two, half of it escaping to the original world from which it came, and the other half finding refuge inside the heart of its very destroyer. Part of the Dragon lived on in your dear Papa, until the Eidoliths themselves came and took his life. His son, my father, spent the rest of his life hunting down your Papa's murderers, and he was killed for all his efforts. They took you as well, destroyed your body, and wiped what data they could from you. Even now, with the new body that I have made for you, you are incomplete."

132

Momoko didn't want to believe what he was saying, but when she tried to think back to what had actually happened, she could not remember. This was different than her memory banks being erased. This was far worse. Pieces of her were missing. Crucial pieces. "Where...am I?" she asked.

"Oh, here and there," he laughed as he subtly gestured to the seven other AI in the room. "Your sisters here each have a part of you within them. Think of it as...a familial bond."

"Doctor, she seems a little stupid. Are you sure we should have awakened her after all this time?" said the AI with the yellow eyes. "If we had let her rest, it would have been a mercy. We could have had more pieces for ourselves."

"It seems a waste to let her keep them. She's too soft, like the peach you call her," mocked the one with orange eyes.

"Avaritia, Gula, hush. I'm trying to talk to your sister."

"They are not my sisters," stated Momoko, "and I will not help you."

"You *will* help us revive that which we seek."

"But what could you ever hope to accomplish through bringing back the Twilight Dragon? That horrible, malignant tumor that once festered in the belly of the earth! What could you possibly hope to gain?" demanded the pink-haired robot girl.

"Eternal life!"

"Excuse me?"

"Without the power of the Twilight Dragon, the ultimate coalescence of pain, the existence of Eden, or paradise if you prefer to do away with religious terminologies, cannot exist. It is there that the fruit of eternal life grows wild, and it is there that I will finally attain it. It is the pinnacle of peace and perfection, the polar opposite to what the Twilight Dragon embodies. Much like how there can be no light without darkness, there can be no paradise without a hell.

"When the dragon was split into two, weakening its power, Eden, too, vanished. I was so close! So close to entering that forbidden paradise, the last true paradise on Earth. And now I will gain my right to enter it by restoring it to its true glory!"

"You are not going to gain entrance to paradise by bringing something back that will destroy the lives of thousands upon thousands of people! You are only going to lose everything."

"What could I possibly have to lose, dearest? What, truly, could I lose? My SINS here are little more than play-things, and I will have no use for you after the Twilight Dragon is reborn. My own mother thrust me away after murdering my father, leaving me no blood relations. My sanity, I believe," he paused, suddenly bursting into hysterical laughter. After a brief outburst, he finally righted himself and continued speaking. "That was lost long ago, when I discovered the truth of my heritage. My right to Eden? Nothing could take away that right. My humanity? Ha! If I feared losing that I wouldn't be plotting this in the first place, now would I? I'd much prefer the company of a blood-thirsty dragon and my mechanical friends. Like you..." he leaned in for a kiss. This man was sick! She ducked out from his grasp and avoided his lips. She wasn't going to let him have his way with her.

"Momoko, do not listen to him!" a new voice cried at her from the other side of the room.

Momoko looked towards the source of the sound. It appeared to have come from a tiny cat with tan fur. Her memory whirred and clicked, and she felt as if she were going to overload. She now knew what she was missing. It was more than the parts and pieces that her Papa's grandson had stolen from her and given to his SINS. It was far more important than any of that. "Nekotarou..." she murmured. She began to reach out for the little cat, but one of the SINS, the one with violet eyes, grabbed him first. The cat let out a vicious hiss and bit down on her arm, but she did not release him.

"Thank you, Superbia," laughed Adam.

Momoko turned to face Adam. "I will never help you and your evil schemes."

"Then all of this was a complete waste," replied Adam. "It is no matter. It looks like Avaritia can have her way after all. I shall grant you one last reprieve." He snapped his fingers. "Ira, my darling, will you do me the honor?"

This time the SIN with red eyes stepped forward. He handed her an object that looked like two whirring razorblades on a rod. A spark coursed back and forth between the two razorblades as Ira cranked the clockwork handle. "It would be my pleasure, Doctor."

Momoko's fear input suddenly spiked. If they touched her with that, it would all be over. There would be nothing left of her memory, she would be wiped forever. There would be no more Momoko. Even the encrypted files would be gone forever. She would never be complete again. "No!" she screamed before trying to dash for the door.

Adam snapped his fingers once more. "Luxuria! Invidia!" The SINS with blue and green eyes stepped forward and grabbed Momoko by her scrawny little arms. Their grip was like iron. Momoko shivered. They were not so alike to her after all. Their bodies were completely synthetic. Her own was biomechanical. She was no match for their robotic strength, as her own flesh was actual flesh. There was no escape. "Perhaps if you will not change your mind, I shall change it for you."

With that, the one called Ira stabbed a jammer into Momoko's head, and her world once more went black.

The cat saw his opportunity and took it. He sliced through the synthetic flesh of his captor, leaving behind a scar of latex and metal gears, and leapt onto Momoko's collapsed form.

"Get him!" bellowed Adam.

But it was too late. Before any of the SINS even had the chance to process what had happened, he had touched his nose to hers, and began siphoning his own energy into the pink haired girl. It was just enough to control the actions of her body, and no more. He settled onto her shoulder as he made her scale the wall and burst out the window.

Down, down they tumbled into the water he had not known was there. Salt and ice and death and dreams. He had not prepared for this. He hadn't thought the lab would have been situated on an

135

ocean-side cliff. Momoko would be alright, her body was made of waterproof biomechanics, but his...

He could feel the shockwaves begin to course through his small frame. His extremities began to jerk and twitch, in tiny motions at first, but steadily becoming more and more violent. At this rate, he would not have the energy to get them out of the water.

"Momoko..." he mumbled before finally shorting out.

~~~

Drip...drip...drip...

The little cat awoke to the steady dripping of icy water on his synthetic fur. Where was he? What had happened to him? Or to Momoko? The last thing he remembered was...was finding his other half at last, held captive by a strange young man with black hair and seven near identical maidens. She had been given a new body, but it made little difference to him. He could have given her the body of a squirrel and still he would have recognized her. It was impossible to separate them for long. They were two halves of the same whole.

But something had happened. Why couldn't he remember? And why weren't his sensory preceptors working properly? All he could see was static.

He tried to call out, but all he could do was meow. Had he lost his ability to speak along with his memories?

"Neko-chan?" asked a sweet little voice.

Excitement filled him. That was Momoko's voice! He let out the loudest little mewl he could muster. Hopefully this would lead her in his direction.

"Neko-chan, I can't hear you..."

Oh no. Momoko was...deaf? And Nekotarou was blind. This simply would not do. He stood up, shook the water from his fur, and began walking in the direction he heard her calling out in.

Yet as he walked, suddenly the darkness gave way to sight that was not his own. The Doctor...he could see Doctor Adam. But how, why...? And...no, he couldn't stop the scene from overpowering his will. His eyes were no longer his own.

~~~

Adam grabbed the underside of a table and thrust it across the room, sending all of the papers and pens scattering to the floor in a whirlwind of anger. "What do you mean you can't find her?" he screamed.

"Doctor, we have already told you. When you behave like this, our sensors all focus on you. Ira is unable to get any readings when you start throwing things. Calm down, take a breath. It is not as if..." droned Acedia before she was cut off.

"She fell into the goddamn sea, you idiots! She can't have gotten far!"

"The sea is no prison, Doctor. It has no shackles to hold her down, no chain to keep her in place. Near, far. It matters not, really," mused Acedia.

Adam stomped over to her and grabbed her wrist, hoisting her off of her slouched position on the ground. "Do not mock me!" he screamed at her. "You can't even be assed to get off your own and get the hell out there and find the damn Peach!"

Luxuria draped herself over his shoulder and began nibbling on the lobe of his ear. "Leave Acedia alone, Doctor. It's her nature to laze about like that." She walked her fingers down his chest. "And besides, how are we supposed to find her if you refuse to allow us outside of the lab at all?"

"It's your fault, you know, for designing us to consume the sins you've asked us to focus on," complained Gula while she pretended to examine her nails. "Isn't *that* a bitch?"

"Quiet!" Adam shouted, pushing Luxuria off of him. She fell to the ground after losing her balance.

"Luxuria and Gula are right, you know," Superbia said from across the room. "We can't do anything properly if we're all cooped up in here."

137

Adam reeled around and grabbed Superbia by the collar of her dress and hoisted her off her feet.

"That isn't going to do you any good, Doctor. I can go without breath for hours. Or forever, really, as long as you don't mind cleaning out some overheated gears afterwards. Break me if you wish, you'll need to repair me sooner or later. Or have you forgotten that, too?"

Adam slapped her across the face. Her head snapped back from the force, and his hand began to swell, but it was a senseless action. The SINS felt neither pleasure nor pain. "I did not create you to talk back to me! I created you to..."

"To hone in on and absorb the essence of the Twilight Dragon, yes, we know. Now put me down, Doctor, so that I may get back to work." Her piercing metallic eyes locked onto his and refused to break their hold. His breath calmed, his shoulders relaxed, his rage evaporated before her gaze, and slowly, ever so slowly, he began to lower her back to the ground.

"Feeling better?"

"Yeah."

"We'll find her, Doctor, don't you worry."

"I know. Now get back to work."

~~~

At last, Nekotarou was able to push the images out of his mind. When he opened his eyes once more, his vision had returned. Momoko was sitting right beside him, curled up with her arms wrapped around her legs. She was mumbling something to herself. "Neko-chan...we are nothing. Nothing, nothing, nothing but data. Swayed by folly and by fear, I still remain alone in here. Inside this body made by man, given life by mortal hand, death will never find my soul for I am something still unwhole."

"Momoko, darling..."

"Neko-chan, we are nothing. Nothing, nothing, nothing..." she repeated over and over again. "Nothing but data."

Nekotarou looked into her eyes, which had glassed over from the cold. Did she feel *nothing*? What had come over her? "Momoko, snap out of it. Listen to me, I'm right here."

She did not seem to hear him. She only repeated her somber mantra again.

And again.

And again.

Chapter Sixteen
Spells and Symptoms

~~~

Orienne woke up to the pleasant surprise of Melaenie cuddled up in a little ball between her and Anton. She was so adorable when she slept, all curled up like that. Orienne smiled, glad that everything had turned out alright for the two of them after all. The poor little thing had been through so much.

"Orienne?" Melaenie mumbled quietly as she opened up her eyes. She had woken up.

"Melaenie," her sister asked. "Are you feeling a little better now?" Orienne felt a little bad after Melaenie's little bout of sickness yesterday.

"Much better, thanks," she said, yawning and stretching, waking up Anton in the process.

"Looks like a little stowaway crawled in here last night," he joked before picking her up in a cute little hug. Melaenie giggled as he tickled her. They looked like a happy big brother and little sister like that, messing around after a slumber party or something. She couldn't help but smile. Her family was getting bigger.

After a quick breakfast, Leilani opened up a portal off the coast of New France. She warned them, because this was so close to a political hot spot. Granted, the politician who lived there was Anton's uncle who was a known supporter of Faders, though it was unknown what his stance on Psychics were, and they would probably have little to worry about aside from any lobbyists or paparazzi who happened to be hanging around.

Anton spoke up before they departed. "I want all of you to be extra careful not to stir up any trouble while we're out and about. We can't rely on my popularity or political status to get us out of trouble all the time. There are many who wish us harm, and almost as many still who are willing to act on that."

"That's nothing I'm not already used to," replied Keaira nonchalantly. "I escaped from a prison, remember? I can take care of myself."

"That's all the more reason to be careful," answered Áine. "There's more of us now than just you, we've got more people to worry about. This is not an operation that will work under the laws of *Every Man for Themselves*. We're in this together, we're family now. We watch each other's backs and make sure no one's safety is compromised any more than it has to be. Understood?"

They all nodded. She was right, after all.

The Kinship arose in the lake that Leilani had opened up the gate into, and they made their way safely to shore. Many of them were still amazed at the kinds of things that could be done with the water in the Lake of Atlantis just by crushing pearls. Spell Weavers had such interesting abilities.

The home of Anton's uncle could be seen not far away from where they had come out of the waters. It was a white building that looked as if it were made of marble, but it was shaped like an old cottage, only larger. It would probably have only taken a few minutes to get there by foot, if they didn't stop to sight see or get noticed by anyone.

As they neared the house, they saw a little girl with unnaturally pink hair pulled up in two puffy little pig-tails with burgundy handkerchiefs tied up in little bows. She wore a goldenrod yellow scarf and a muted burgundy poncho that matched the handkerchiefs in her hair. Baggy khaki Capri's and thin, white leggings covered her legs, and hot pink rain-boots protected her feet. A little white bunny pin was fastened to her scarf. She had skin only slightly darker than Keaira's, and striking emerald green eyes that almost looked metallic. It seemed as if she had just picked a random smattering of clothing and hastily put them on, not caring that nothing really matched and that her rain boots clashed with everything.

"Should we check the situation out?" asked Anton.

"I think we should," Orienne replied. "Remember what Leilani said? We'd meet the Peach and the Cat, and we'd know them when we saw them."

"I only see one person, Orienne, and she's not a cat," responded Melaenie.

"One thing at a time," reassured Áine. Áine definitely recognized the pair. She had seen them twice before, once when she had touched the stone and again when she shared that image with Leilani. They were certainly the ones they were looking for. "Come on, now, it's not like she's out of the way." They all got a little closer so that they could hear what she was saying.

"I am not what I am. I am nonexistent. What is my purpose? My purpose is none. Why was I created? I do not know. Where is Papa? I do not know. But he is not Papa, is he? I do not know. I do not know. I do not know." She rambled on and on. Every now and then she would twitch in a way no human could ever twitch without pulling a muscle or two, and when she did this, her emerald eyes flashed a bright, electric green color.

When Áine asked her why she was sitting on the cold steps in the middle of a snow drift, she replied, "I do not know. I do not know. Nothing, nothing, nothing but data." It seemed as if that was the only thing she could think of to say right now. She appeared to be in a state of depression, or at least confusion. She twitched and blinked again.

"Little girl, why are you out here all alone?" she asked again.

"I am not alone. Neko-chan is here with me. But he does not exist either. So I suppose neither of us are here. Neither of us are alone because we cannot be here in the first place. Things that do not exist cannot be alone. We are empty shells with nothing but data. I am nothing but data. He is nothing but data. We are nothing but data. Data...data...little bundles of information that do not

142

belong to us...we are just data." None of them could understand what she was rambling about. She was repeating herself an awful lot.

"Aren't you cold?" asked Melaenie.

"I cannot be cold, for I am not. I do not exist except to hold data. I feel nothing. I do not even know if I can see or hear. These noises you make...my sensors pick them up, but do I hear them? Do I? Do I..."

Then, suddenly, the little cat popped up from the folds in her poncho, and then began to speak. "Momoko, you're rambling again. Stop confusing these poor travelers, you're making them feel awkward." They all jumped back, except for Áine.

"You're talking? And you're a cat?" asked Anton. He seemed confused at first, but then something seemed to sink in. "Oh, you're one of them. An AI cat..."

"Allow me to introduce ourselves. This is Momoko-chan, Manufactured Organic Model of Kinetic Operations. I am Nekotarou, but you can call me Neko-chan. Please excuse my affinity for honorifics; we were both manufactured in Japan where it is customary to use them. It is just part of our programming, I assure you."

"What does your name stand for?" asked Melaenie.

"It doesn't. I'm just a cat."

"Oh..." the younger Andraste sister replied. She had expected a more entertaining answer than that.

"I am Momoko's guardian, of sorts. I am in charge of keeping track of her and making sure she does not get in trouble. We are, as you correctly assumed, what you call AI, or artificial intelligence."

"If you were made in Japan, how did you wind up all the way out here?" asked Keaira. She seemed to get a little angry at that. She must have had a prejudice against the Japanese people for what they did to her, which nobody could really blame her for, but it still didn't make any sense for her to get angry at these two machines.

"I could ask the same of you. Judging by your attire, you are either a cosplayer with a poor choice in color scheme, or a refugee from one of the Psychic Orphanages. I am willing to bet my whiskers that you are of the latter category." He was certainly a snarky little fellow.

Keaira's only response was a huff, followed by more pouting.

"What are you doing here, anyway?" asked Orienne.

"We simply woke up here. We have been asleep for a rather long time, and were awoken by someone other than our creator that neither Momoko nor I were able to recognize. He wiped most of our memories, bugged my companion, and dumped us here."

"Well that's not very nice of him," said Anton.

"Nice, rude, it is all the same really. But how could I know? I am just a cat," and then he pretended to clean himself as he licked his paw and rubbed it over his head, the way a real cat would do. It was kind of eerie, actually.

"Are you really the Peach and the Cat?" asked Áine.

"It is entirely possible, after all, that is what our names mean. As to whether or not we are *the* Peach and the Cat, that is another matter entirely. As I have said, our memory banks have been wiped. We cannot remember anything."

Melaenie asked, "What's wrong with Momoko?"

"Like I mentioned previously, the man who awakened us bugged her. She has got a little bit of a computer virus known as DEPRESSION. It stands for Diminished Emotion Percentage Redirects Essential and Superfluous Sadness Information to the Open Network-system."

"Eh?" they all stared, trying to understand what the AI cat had just said. "What does that mean?"

"It means that she is depressed. You know, miserable; unhappy; just plain sad."

"So how do you get rid of the virus?" asked Áine, who seemed legitimately concerned.

"We do not know. You humans as such silly questions sometimes. If we did, she wouldn't exactly have DEPRESSION right now, would she?"

144

"Well, no, I guess not..." she sighed back to the AI...cat...thing... Then she thought back to the poem that spoke of the guardians. The line "Two artificial beings" must have been about Momoko and Nekotarou, especially considering the vision. Áine dug two charms out of her pouch. "These are gifts for the two of you."

"A gift? How thoughtful. Why, thank you." Nekotarou swiftly leapt up and snatched his from her open palm, and then dexterously attached it to his tiny red collar.

Just as the Halfie was handing the other pendant to Momoko, however, she dropped it and it shattered, spilling all over the pink haired girl's lap. The shards of the broken charm swiftly melted into the water that had been within it, and there was not a trace of glass to be found on or around the pink haired girl. As soon as the water touched her skin, a great flash of white light surrounded her. Then Momoko did something totally unexpected.

She smiled.

"I...feel?" she asked enthusiastically, perking up and seeming to notice all of them for the very first time. Then her eyes got big and she began to make sounds as though she were sobbing, though there were no tears that fell from her metallic eyes.

"What just happened?" asked Keaira, dumbstruck.

"I think that little thing of water cured the DEPRESSION. I did not see that coming."

"Is that really possible?" Orienne asked. She raised an eyebrow.

"I knew that the water was magically potent, but this is not an effect I knew it to possess," gasped Áine.

"Apparently so. Unfortunately, that means she will go through a long reboot phase we AIs like to call EMOTION," stated Nekotarou. Then he cursed the DEPRESSION bug under his breath for causing such a disturbance in his artificial life.

"What does that one stand for?" asked Anton.

"EMOTION stands for Emotions Magnified Outrageously to Ignite Obfuscating Nature. It means that she is emotionally unstable for the time being," replied Nekotarou. "Much like the saying goes, she will be riding an emotional roller-coaster for some time now."

"How can computers like you and her even have emotions?" asked Keaira.

"First of all, we are more than mere computers. But to answer your question, allow me to say this. It is quite simple, really. Our emotions are based on programs installed to us. Our sensors allow us to respond to certain situations with the proper emotions necessary for such an occurrence. However, when our Emotion-Sensors are tampered with or get viruses, we tend to go haywire, much like Momoko here. Now, before the thought escapes my mind, who are all of you?"

"We are the ones spoken of in the ancient prophecy of the Eidoliths," replied Áine.

"Ah, the Eidoliths. We know them well," said Nekotarou, resuming his feline bath. "Charming folks, really." He said this last part with a particularly thick coating of venom.

"I am Áine McCrae."

"Keaira Aleshire."

"Orienne Andraste, and this is my little sister, Melaenie."

"Prince Anton Christophe LaCiel," added Anton as he did a deep bow. "And we call ourselves The Kinship of the Twilight Moon."

"I would be honored to join you all on your noble quest. After all, you cured me of my depression!" said the AI girl, who then promptly attempted to mimic Anton's deep bow, to awkward results.

"Not so fast, little one," argued Nekotarou before hopping up on her arm and swatting away Anton's outstretched hand. "The Eidoliths murdered our creator and tried to destroy us. What reason would we have for aiding their charges?"

"Because you were created to finish what they started," replied Áine. "I know Dr. Ryu built you to fight the Twilight Dragon, and that is just what we have set out to do."

"Are you with us or not?" demanded Keaira.

146

Nekotarou seemed to contemplate the notion for a moment, but at last he gave it. "We shall...follow you all for a while to observe and properly assess the situation. Do not expect our aid before the decision is made."

"Close enough," said Keaira as she crossed her arms across her chest.

"Well," started Anton. "Shall we go into my uncle's house now? It's starting to get extremely cold standing out here in the snow."

"But it's only September, how could there be-" Orienne said. However, as soon as she spoke those words, a snowflake drifted onto her nose and melted.

"Yeah, I don't get it either. New France has been weird like that lately."

"Do you think it's the Twilight Dragon?" asked Melaenie.

"Don't be silly, not everything is that creature's fault," replied Keaira. And with that, they all went inside of Anton's uncle's house.

As soon as they set foot on the beautiful rug, they heard a big, booming voice that came from really, really far down the absurdly long hall. "Welcome, dearest Anton and friends, to the home of Lord Donato-Jacques-Alphonse-Amaure VI! You can call me Donnie."

The first thing they all thought (except for Anton, who was most likely thinking, "It's so great to see you again, dear uncle!") was *what is it with that totally weird name?* In truth, it had to have been some kind of tradition in Anton's family, considering his uncle was the sixth. Goodness, just thinking of naming six consecutive sons of each generation the same crazy name seemed...ridiculous.

They all walked down the extremely long and brightly lit hallway to reach Anton's Uncle Donnie. When they got there, he was holding a letter. "Is one of you young ladies named Orienne Andraste?" he asked.

This startled her and she faded once again.

"Why, you're a Fader, aren't you?" he asked, seemingly excited. Orienne was worried for a bit, before he continued with a jolly old chuckle and more light-hearted speech. "I've never seen a Fader before. I've always wanted to find out what the big deal was about your kind. You seem harmless to me, nothing to get worked up about. It's not like you'll just spontaneously combust and take us down with you or anything like all those Fader haters out there make it out to be."

"Yes, sir, I'm a Fader," Orienne replied, as courteously as she could despite her confusion. He didn't know how wrong he really was, about them spontaneously combusting at least. It was rare, but it had happened before on numerous occasions. It only happened when a Fader's scattered molecules collided with something combustible during the fading process, which created a huge force almost equivalent to a small-scale bomb.

"Well, my dear lady, this letter that I am holding is for you. Strange little thing, isn't it? Anyways, I received it from a rather peculiar youth, he looked a lot like you, only with shorter hair and more masculine features. He was a Fader, too, just like you. Odd, isn't it? Seems there are more and more of your kind all over the place, bless their souls."

He paused for a moment and let out a deep sigh, as if in regret at the harsh treatment of the Faders. Surely he must have known of their mistreatment since he was a figure of authority, and judging by his reaction to Orienne being a Fader. "He just came busting in here saying something along the lines of a girl named Orienne Andraste was coming here with some friends and it was a very urgent message for her, well, you, rather. Anyhow, why don't you read the letter?"

This letter must have come from the Andraste sisters' brother. Now they knew beyond a shadow of a doubt that he was absolutely alive, and trying to stop them from following him. Orienne took the letter from Uncle Donnie, and read it carefully out loud for all of her companions to hear.

Stay away from the Twilight Dragon. It is none of your concern.

There wasn't even a signature, and her name wasn't written anywhere on it proving that it was addressed to her. This was a lot less wordy than his previous letter, and even more cryptic. Ophir must have personally told Uncle Donnie that it was for her. She handed the letter back to him.

"Stay away from the Twilight Dragon?" asked Keaira. "But that is the whole point of quest! Why would that blonde kid want us to just drop whatever we're doing just to listen to his lousy attempt at a warning? Oh please, give me a break. It only has a half-a-dozen words on it!"

"Actually," corrected Anton as he grabbed the letter back from his uncle, "It's got exactly a dozen words. One, two, three, four, five, six, seven..."

"That's not my point!" interrupted Keaira. "That doesn't change the fact that it is totally pathetic!"

"It's not pathetic, it's just short, sweet, and to-the-point," countered Anton, trying to stand up for Orienne's brother, despite never having met him himself.

"Sweet? What's so sweet about 'it's none of your concern' anyhow? It sounds like more of a threat or a warning to me! Stupid blonde kid..."

"Is she always like this?" asked Uncle Donnie, leaning slightly away from the peeved Psychic. They solemnly nodded their heads. He shook his head in regret. It seemed as if he didn't exactly approve of her behavior either. It was nice to know that the rest of the Kinship weren't the only ones who regarded her as a brat.

"You should still hold onto this, however," he said as he handed the letter back to Orienne again. "I have a feeling that it will be very important to you on your journey. It might be a clue, you never know."

Orienne nodded her head, accepting the letter from him once again.

"Anyways," he continued. "I know that Sir Anton has come here to get his next spell. Been putting it off for a bit, haven't you, Anton?"

"Sorry uncle, I was busy..." replied Anton, avoiding his uncle's gaze.

"Don't worry about it, my boy, I was just stating a fact. Would you all mind terribly if I were to borrow my nephew for a bit? Perhaps you could all stay the night here, I'd be happy to provide a warm meal for you all and a place for you to sleep while he trains."

The thought of a warm meal and soft bed to sleep in, at least for one night, sounded heavenly. Everyone, save for Nekotarou and Momoko (who merely looked indifferent) looked eager to accept Lord Donato-Jacques-Alphonse-Amaure's offer, so Áine decided to speak up. "We'd love to," she replied. "Besides, it's not like we can go anywhere without Prince Anton. He is our friend and part of our Kinship, after all. Thank you for your generous offer, sir."

That night, a small banquet was prepared for the Kinship in the hall. The smell alone was so wonderful it could have enticed all the angels in heaven to sneak down from their clouds in the sky just for one whiff of the glorious meal that was set before them. There were all sorts of things there, like fresh-baked cinnamon and raisin bread, three delicious kinds of soup they had never even heard of before, steamed and seasoned vegetables, and a huge roasted turkey basted in honey and orange glaze. For desert there was spice cake fresh out of the oven and French Vanilla Ice Cream. It reminded Orienne and Melaenie, who had come from the New States, of Thanksgiving back at home with their family, before it had started to crumble...

When they were all done eating, they headed to their rooms as Anton went off with his uncle to learn his newest spell.

Chapter Seventeen
Track and Tinker

~~~

Momoko rested her head on the plush down pillow as she turned to look at her feline companion. Her eyes held a thousand questions, though she did not have the words to ask them properly. She felt eyes on her, eyes in her head that were not her own, piercing her, watching her, invading her, though never truly seeing her. The eyes pressed behind her own, seemingly using them as a window. She believed she had been bugged...but...

Nekotarou hopped up on the bed and nuzzled in the crook of her arm. "What is it, Momoko?" inquired the tiny cat.

"I do not quite know how to formulate the words, Neko-chan. These questions that whirr within my mind...I do not have a way to ask." In truth, she was afraid to. These "eyes" in her head, they...they hurt. If they became aware that she was aware of them, she did not know what would happen. If she were to ask... "There are...eyes..."

Nekotarou's ears perked up. "Eyes?" The SINS...this was bad. If they had managed to land a track on Momoko, it was all over. "Do you mind if I synch with you?"

"If you think it will help you to discover what ails me..."

"I am initiating a scan. This will only take a moment." His fur bristled as he tried to scan Momoko for traces of the SINS. He would be sure to recognize their hold. After all, he had been under it himself once before. He tilted his head up and touched his nose to Momoko's.

There was a terribly bright flash in his mind as sparks ran across his vision. White and thunder and static and...and his eyes weren't open. What, then, was he seeing?

~~~

"Wait, Doctor, I'm getting a reading. It's not quite the same wavelength as The Peach, but the pattern aligns quite nicely. I think it belongs to The Cat. Do you want me to pinpoint the signal?"

"Yes, damn it, quickly!"

~~~

His suspicions were correct. They were being tracked, and he and Momoko could do nothing to shake the trail. There had to be some kind of clue, some kind of hint to latch onto.

Then he knew. Eyes. Momoko had said she felt eyes. He, too, had felt eyes on him, in him, eyes that were not his own. That had to be the way the SINS were tracking them. He knew that each of the SINS contained parts of Momoko's programming, and therefore parts of his own. That explained the link, and the SINS exploited it through their eyes. There was no other explanation.

That still left him with one question, though. That didn't explain why the visions came in such sudden, sporadic bursts. They should either be perpetual, which he was glad they weren't, or not at all. The connection shouldn't have been so random.

Unless...

~~~

"Doctor, the signal is getting stronger. I'm almost able to lock onto it. It doesn't seem to be moving."

"Lock on to it!" roared Doctor Ryu as he slammed his palms down on the desk. His face bore a deep gash of a grin, white and wicked.

"Lock on acquired. And Doctor, take a look at this." Avaritia, the yellow eyed replica brought up a screen. It was a map of New France. She slid her fingers across the screen a few times, zooming in and in again until the cursor was clearly fixed on Anton's uncle's manor. There was a soft golden blinker with a white overlay, which surely must have denoted Nekotarou's and Momoko's locations. But there were several other blinkers as well, all bright white and shining.

"Can it be?" asked Doctor Ryu. "The Kinship..."

~~~

Nekotarou began to panic. The others were in terrible danger because of him and Momoko. He had done it before; he could certainly manage it once more. He had to push these foreign thoughts out of his mind.

"Momoko, desynchronize yourself from me. Quickly."

"Can you not do it yourself?"

"You must initiate it. Make haste, make haste, we cannot allow the SINS to find us. They have already begun to lock on."

Almost immediately, Momoko and Nekotarou began detaching all of their sensors and cutting themselves off from one another. All the synapses were being stopped. Off, off, off, close, clear, ctrl+alt+delete.

~~~

"We are losing signal, Doctor."

"Boost everything, I don't care what kind of energy you have to draw from. Do not lose that signal!"

~~~

Just then, there was a knock on the door. Their eyes were their own.

153

"Is everything alright?" asked Áine, poking her head through the door. "I heard noises."

Momoko sat up from the bed and prepared to answer, but Nekotarou quickly spoke before his companion had the chance. "Everything is alright in here, Áine-san. We were merely shutting all of our functions down for the night. It has been a long time since the two of us were awake; we are a little rusty on the process."

Áine raised an eyebrow, but nodded in response anyways. "Well, if you need anything, don't hesitate to ask. I'll be awake for the night meditating, so you won't be interrupting anything." With that, Áine turned away and shut the door behind her.

"Why did you lie to her, Neko-chan?" asked Momoko as soon as Áine was gone.

"I do not wish to trouble the others about this matter. The matter is under control."

"We do not know that for certain."

"It does not matter. It is none of their concern."

"The SINS are no longer tracking us, but them as well. That seems like it should concern them, does it not?"

"We have it under control, Momoko. Do not say a word to the others. Do you understand?"

"Yes, Neko-chan..."

~~~

In the morning, they all met again in the great hall to reunite with Anton and say their goodbyes to his generous uncle. Momoko and Nekotarou did not want to mention the events of the previous night to the others. There was no reason to spoil the good mood of the party for something that they had hopefully gotten under control.

Uncle Donnie had packed them off with some supplies and extra, much needed blankets, complete with water proof bags to seal them in. It was, after all, getting to be later on in the season, and winter would be coming soon. Not to mention that deep under the lake in Atlantis, there wasn't really much heat.

"What kind of spell did you learn?" asked Áine politely as they walked out of the hall. She was obviously trying to flirt with him, but the Prince took no notice, thinking of her question as mere interest in his art.

"It causes a flooding storm. It's enough to cause a few large puddles here and there, but nothing deadly," Anton replied happily. "Speaking of water, will you be alright in the water, Momoko? Neko-chan? You are AI, after all."

"Do not worry about us," replied Momoko. "We are special models, biomechanical in nature." Then she dipped her finger in a glass of water to demonstrate. "We're mostly organic, almost like you. And even if we weren't, our mechanical parts are all waterproof." She smiled mischievously as she said this, an expression that none of them had ever seen her use before. It was eerily reminiscent of Keaira. Orienne sincerely hoped that the little Psychic teenybopper was not rubbing off on the little AI girl. The last thing they needed was another sarcastic, bossy brat following them around and saving the world.

And with that, the Kinship thanked Anton's uncle kindly and left the rather large home of Donato-Jacques-Alphonse-Amaure XVI. Refreshed and resupplied, they eagerly went on their way to the waters where they could return to their home beneath the lake.

Chapter Eighteen
Misery and Mutation

~~~

When they reached the hub of Atlantis, with full bellies and rested bodies, it was now their minds that were troubled. Where would they go to now? There was always the option of helping Keaira's fellow Psychics out of the Orphanage...but that was a little out of their abilities to accomplish for the time being. Aside from that, one of the only clues they had to where they were supposed to go next was the cryptic note that Orienne's and Melaenie's brother had left Anton's uncle. Even then, it wasn't really much of a clue at all.

In fact...the very fact that Ophir had left those notes in the first place was more than a little disconcerting. How had he known exactly where Orienne and Melaenie were going to go? New Egypt and New France weren't exactly nearby, and even a commercial airplane could not have gotten there before the Kinship did. Was he using some sort of magical transportation, as they were? And if so...how? There was no magic in the Andraste blood. They could open no portals, cast no spells...could they?

As if answering Orienne's thoughts, Áine walked over to her and sat down beside her. "The Eidoliths were very special indeed, my friend," she began.

"What was so special about them?" asked Orienne. "They were just humans, weren't they?"

"Yes and no. The Eidoliths are the *first* humans. They came from the same land I come from, the land where magic first began

156

leaking out into the world. The Eidoliths used that magic to see into the future, devise the language of Magic that Spells find their power in, and create the other races. Faeries, fellow humans, and all the animals of the world owe their existence to the original Eidoliths. You and your sister, being descendants of those people, may still have some of that old power inside of you, though you are not Spell Weavers."

"Do you think that my brother has been using that power to travel ahead of us?" asked Orienne. What Áine was telling her made sense, though it was a little far-fetched. She had never heard of this old story before. Perhaps it was one of the old myths of Áine's people, where she came from.

Where *did* she come from anyways? Orienne had always been too afraid to ask. The kindly and mysterious woman had so fiercely avoided answering such things when first they met...but perhaps now...

Before she could ask her question, Keaira plopped herself down before them. "We should go and rescue my friends."

"I do not think it wise to rush into such a thing. We must devise a plan before we attempt something so dangerous," replied Áine.

"I agree with Áine," said Anton as he sat down, having just finished storing the rest of the food his uncle had given them in their make-shift shelves. "I want to save them as much as you do, Keaira, but we're not ready yet. We're only going to cause more trouble if we go and do this without thinking it through."

"Then what do you suggest we do?" asked Keaira, pouting and crossing her arms. "It isn't like we have any other leads at the moment. We can't just sit down here while we wait for an epiphany."

"That's a big word for you, pip-squeak," snapped Orienne.

"Shut it, blondie. I've been nice to you all day, no need to be snappy."

Orienne wasn't happy about it, but Keaira was right. They still had the option of going on that rescue mission to help free her psychic friends, but as Áine and Anton had said, they were in no position to attempt such a thing just yet. They were stuck.

Bored and restless, Orienne turned to Leilani. She studied the young finned lady briefly for a moment or two before she turned and her grey eyes met Orienne's own brown ones.

"Yes?" asked Leilani. "You need something?"

Orienne had been wondering about Leilani's fin since they had first met, and she had been doing her best to keep it to herself, but now her curiosity began to get the better of her. "You know," she began. "You never really told us about yourself."

"And should I? What reason have I to tell you about myself?" Leilani asked defensively.

"You know about my story," Orienne replied. "And my sister's. Doubtless you know of Áine's as well, since you have known her for so much longer than the rest of us. You don't have to tell us everything, just a little bit."

Áine stepped in. "She doesn't have to tell anyone anything she doesn't want to, Orienne." Even Áine did not know much of Leilani's past before she found her on the operating table. In fact, she didn't know any of it at all. What right had Orienne to demand her friend to speak of such painful memories?

Orienne shrunk back. "I'm sorry...I didn't mean it like that, I was just curious..."

"No, Áine, it's alright. Orienne's right. I know about all of you... Is there anything in particular that you would like to hear about?" sighed Leilani, giving in to Orienne's plea to hear more about her.

Orienne briefly contemplated asking her what she was really curious about, the fin, but in the end she decided that it would be insensitive to pry into that subject. Leilani was touchy about her lower half. So, she asked the question she wanted to ask every sane person who didn't hate her and her kind. "Tell me why you are not afraid of Faders. Tell me why you actually care about my kind."

There was a long pause before she answered her question. At first, Orienne thought that maybe she wasn't going to tell them about herself after all. However, after a long time, she began to answer her question.

"My older sister was a Fader," she said quietly. "She died because of the Crystalline Virus...or rather; she died because she had contracted the virus. She was murdered by a Fader Hater when I was ten years old. She was only fifteen at the time..." Leilani began to get choked up. She hastily asked Áine for a handkerchief as her nose started to run. It was easy enough to understand why it took her so long to answer Orienne's question.

"I remember how we spent our whole lives up until the time of her death running from the Fader Haters that wanted to kill her. We had always been on the move so as not to get caught, even though I myself was not a Fader. We were the best of friends, my sister and I. There wasn't anything we wouldn't do for one another." She smiled and looked up at the dome as she talked about her sister. But her expression soon changed to that of anger and despair.

"And then there came a day when we weren't fast enough. They came and she didn't have a chance to get away. She told me to run as far as I could, and she would be right behind me. I ran for quite a distance before I realized that she was not following me. All of a sudden, I heard six gunshots. I froze in my place.

"I rushed back to find her bloody body sprawled out where we had been, and the Bounty Hunter seemed to have left. She was still alive, but only barely. She told me to go back home and tell our mom what had happened, and she told me to be good. When she finally died, though, I just snapped. They had murdered her. I screamed and screamed with all of my heart, pouring all of my sorrow and anger into that single bestial roar."

"What happened after that?" asked Orienne.

"That bellow was my downfall. The Bounty Hunter hadn't really left, since he hadn't picked up the body of his kill yet, and rushed back to the scene. Upon realizing that I was not a Fader, as his Bounty had been, he kidnapped me and sold me to a Biotechnical Lab for study. There would be big money in finding out why I had not contracted the disease despite my prolonged proximity to a Fader."

"And that's how you..."

"How I ended up the way I am now?" asked Leilani. "Yes. There was a mix up in the papers. I was sorted into the wrong facility, and nobody cared to fix it."

"I'm so sorry," said Áine. "I never knew."

"I never told you," Leilani replied. There was a long silence where Áine merely hugged her friend, holding her close.

Nor did the finned girl tell them now. But she remembered. She remembered all too well. Leilani had been shuffled into a group of young men and women who were to be turned into something called Chimeras. It was sick. Hundreds of people and animals alike were being spliced together, many dying in the process. She saw them try to create Centaurs by fusing the torso of a man with the body of a beheaded horse, Harpies by severing the arms and legs from women and replacing them with the wings and feet of various birds. There were others still who they tried to turn into Merfolk by fusing them with fish.

Most of them died. Few survived, but those who did wished for nothing but death to end their torment. They were not allowed to eat; instead they had minimal nutrients directly flowing into their veins. They were not permitted to cry, so they sealed off their tear ducts and rerouted them to their mouths or their nostrils.

When those who survived and recovered were well enough to function, they were packed up and shipped off to what was only known as "The Reservation." Leilani didn't like the sound of that. Though she knew not where or what The Reservation even was, it certainly boded nothing good.

For weeks, Leilani watched as the others suffered. She kept telling them they had made some kind of mistake, but they would hear none of it. They didn't care that she was so young either. "All the easier to adapt" they would say. It had been years since her kidnapping before they strapped her to the table though, and she was twelve or thirteen by that point in time. She had lost count of the days, but she knew it had been at least that long, if not longer.

Longer still than her horrifying imprisonment were the grueling days they ran test after test on her. She couldn't even begin to count how many needles she was stuck with, or how many bizarre physical exams she was put through.

What was the purpose of all of this? Surely there was little scientific backing to any of this at all. There was no rhyme or reason to this madness. They had killed so many people and animals by trying to cut them up and put them back together, ruined so many lives, with such a devastatingly low success rate. Even the successes were monstrosities who lived every waking moment in pain and misery. Why do this to them? What was their goal?

Then one day, she was to take a swim test. She performed wonderfully. She had always been a good swimmer, her mother used to call her a little fish. But she attracted more attention to herself than she had hoped. That was the day they decided what Leilani would become. "She swims like a dolphin!" exclaimed one of the doctors.

A dolphin indeed.

Her fate was sealed.

They cut her apart, and fused her spine with that of a dolphin. It was horrible. She could hardly bear it, despite the exorbitant amount of pain killers they had administered to her.

After the surgery, they continued to test her physical abilities. Her stitches bled, her scabs cracked, and her vision blurred with arid dryness as she longed to cry but could not. Even the eye drops were never enough. At first, it hurt her, but over time the pain turned to numbness, and she could move without blacking out from the stress. She had become the mutant mermaid they had strived for.

Leilani thought she would die there, like all of the others. She had given up all hope of ever escaping. Without legs to even run, it was more hopeless to try than it ever had been before. She was, after all, their prized experiment. She was one of the few successes. Of course they would never give her up.

But that's when *she* came. Out of nowhere, a blonde haired woman showed up nearly naked in the tank they tested Leilani's swimming in. All she wore was a white loincloth and a white sling across her chest. She carried a pouch of pearls with her. It had been Áine.

"*Maighdeann*," Áine had said to her. "Come with me. I must get you to safety, before any more harm can be done." The now-finned girl didn't know if the strange young woman was just part of her imagination or not, as she had been dulled to near any experience. She didn't even move to back away as Áine took hold of her hand and crushed one of the pearls she carried in her palm. "Close your eyes" she said. And Leilani did.

When she opened them again, she was no longer in the lab. She was in the lake that they now call Atlantis.

After Áine rescued her, she awakened her potential as a Spell Weaver with her Faerie magic. The blessing of a Faerie could be given but once, at the expense of half of their own magical potential. Leilani had never asked for such a gift to be given, but Áine had given her everything. Magic, freedom, life...

Yet Áine never told her anything of her story, nor did Leilani share hers. Not until now.

Leilani pushed back the memories and began to speak to the others again.

"I never did go back home to see our mother," Leilani said at last. "I was too ashamed of my new body, and ashamed that I had let my sister die. Though...I was able to seek my mother out using the power of the pearls, after Áine taught me how to use them."

"She had long since died of illness, worried sick about her daughters and careless of her own health. It was a small comfort to know that she hadn't been in pain for long.

"But I was all alone in this world now. Alone except for the woman who rescued me. I have been indebted to Áine ever since."

Chapter Nineteen
Song and Silence

~~~

After the tale was over, it was decided that they should all get some much needed fresh air. Leilani needed some space now, and it wasn't going to do any of them any good sitting down there in the dim light beneath the lake and running their thoughts into the mud. It was too soon to go to the orphanage, and far too soon to begin seeking out the true location of the Twilight Dragon. Leilani began to open up the portal to a forest that was close to the actual surface of the lake, so they could get back quickly if there happened to be trouble.

Momoko and Nekotarou opted to stay behind. They didn't want to risk themselves out in the open any more than they had to. For some reason, the magic from the pearls blocked their sensors, and if their sensors were blocked, it meant that the SINS' sensors were as well. As long as they remained in Atlantis, the SINS could not find them. Hopefully, that meant that the SINS could not find the rest of the Kinship, either.

The other members of the Kinship eagerly left the desolate little bubble of rubble, though. However, when they emerged from the portal, many of them had been separated from one another. Something had gone horribly awry. Only Anton and Orienne remained together.

The two had emerged from the portal in a completely different place from a very different source from the others. While the others had come through the stream, as was intended, Anton and Orienne somehow managed to rise from a shallow mud puddle that had since been scattered. There was no way back for them now.

"No, don't contact Leilani. We'll find our way back to the lake, it can't be far from here," Orienne said to Anton, panic rising in her voice. She had always been terrified of getting lost, ever since she was a little child. Memories of the night her mother died after she helped Melaenie to escape were quickly coming back to haunt her. She was continuously fading in and out as she tried to regulate her own breathing.

"Calm down, Orienne," Anton consoled. "We'll find our way back, don't worry. Just breathe." He had an air of laughter in his voice as he said this. Orienne couldn't possibly understand how he could sound so calm and cheery under the circumstances.

He grabbed her hand and led her to a small clearing in the woods. He turned around and looked right into Orienne's eyes. Her heart was beating so hard and fast that she was sure he must have heard it, too. *All he's doing is looking at me! Well, that and holding my hand...but that's not the point! Why can't I breathe?* He pulled her up very close to him and wrapped one of his arms around her waist. She was becoming more than nervous now. She felt her stomach lurch, and she tried to keep her balance as her head began to spin.

"Anton, I don't feel so well..." was all that she managed to get out of her mouth before he moved his hand from her waist and reached up to touch her face. She immediately shut her mouth and didn't say anything. Anton tilted her head back so that he could study her eyes. That's when her heart stopped and seemed like it just couldn't start up again.

"Alright then, let's sit down for a bit." They did so.

At that point she couldn't tell whether she was feeling nauseous because she was so nervous due to her little crush on the prince or if she was feeling that way because she was really seriously ill. Maybe it had been the excitement of the past few days. She couldn't quite decide.

"Would you like me to sing to you?" he asked. "It might make you feel better."

She nodded her head weakly in response. She was feeling so nauseous that any more than that simple nod could have caused her to throw up. That was the last thing she wanted to do, especially right in front of Anton.

He laughed gently, which made Orienne loosen up a bit, and then he prepared to sing. He cleared his throat and began.

It was a simple little ditty, with just over half a dozen lines. But the melody...the melody was enchanting.

Pen and paper, ink and rhyme
Feelings from the dawn of time
Heart of silver, lips of gold
Speak of stories ages old
Write the lyrics of your thought
In the way that you've been taught
Break away from lies and see
The truth in your own fantasy

When he stopped singing, Orienne's heart sank a little. His voice was so beautiful that it kept her motionless the whole time he had been singing. "Did you make that up just now?" she asked.

"A little. My mother, my birth mother that is, wrote the poem. It was one of her spells. I just made up the tune," he said, rubbing his arm up and down her back to try and help her calm down a bit. It was working, a little. "I promise we won't be lost here forever. We'll get out of here; we just have to keep our hopes up and listen up for the others." Then he closed his eyes and leaned in closer to her, hovering just in front of her lips. She could feel his warm, husky breath against her face.

In truth, he was merely casting another spell to make her nausea subdued, but she mistook it for flirting. Orienne couldn't help but part her lips, she was so excited. After all, wasn't every girl excited when she thought she was going to get her first kiss? And then it happened. Every nerve in her body was tight as she pressed her lips against his. She smiled through the kiss as she pulled herself into it. But her happiness was short lived.

Orienne stopped breathing for real that time, and then she got very cold. Then her knees gave out on her, and Anton struggled to keep her up in his arms because of the unexpected and sudden dead weight of her body. Her arms hung limp as he held her, no longer holding onto him. Her body became very stiff, and she was finding it excruciatingly hard to blink or breathe. Her eyes stung with dryness. Her lungs were dying for air, but she just couldn't inhale.

At first, Anton had merely been shocked at how forward and improper Orienne had acted, but now he was worried that something was seriously wrong. "Orienne? Orienne!" he called out over and over again, trying to shake her back into the real world. But alas, all she could do was stare vacantly into space.

Anton's cries were audible from a distance and the others were able to find their location from the noise. Áine was the first to the scene.

"Anton! What happened?"

"I...I don't know, she kissed me, and then...and then...!"

"Calm down, lover boy, it's gonna be alright," said Keaira as she nudged in closer.

"No, she's fading!" Melaenie cried as soon as she got close enough to see. "She's losing herself! No, no, no, this can't be happening!"

The sound of Melaenie's panicked voice gave Orienne the will to survive. She simply had to wake up and break out of this haze so that she could reassure her frightened sister that everything would be alright. She wouldn't be defeated by a stupid little kiss!

Orienne struggled to inhale, but to no avail. All that her struggling did was cause her to cough out soft choking sounds. She felt herself burning up, being incinerated from the inside out. It felt like she was being crushed beneath thousands of tons of pressure. Then it hit her like a ton of bricks falling from a twelfth story window...

Orienne was dying in the same way so many Faders before her had died. She couldn't believe it. Was her time really up already? Was she too late to stop the Twilight Dragon? Too late to save her sister and the other Faders? So much for her extraordinary destiny...

Orienne's throat stung as she tried to cry out and tried even harder to gasp for breath, but her body couldn't handle it. She tried calling out her brother's name, Melaenie's name, and then even Anton's, but nothing would come out. She began to fade again, with small silver specks leaving her body this time. She really was losing herself. This just wasn't fair...she hadn't saved her sister yet. She hadn't found her brother. She hadn't finished what she had set out to do.

The elder Andraste sister soon passed out from a combination of despair and lack of air. Black nothingness became her world, and she submitted to it all too willingly.

The peril had only just begun, however. As soon as Orienne was out, rustling could be heard all around them.

"What was that?" asked an already panicked Melaenie. She held on close to her unconscious sister.

"Just the wildlife," reassured Anton, though he himself was unsure how truthful his answer was.

Áine, however, suddenly became keenly aware of everything in her surroundings. There was a familiarity to this feeling that was coming from behind the brush. She was taken back to her days as a wandering waif in the White Forests of Eldra, back when she spent her days hunting humans and avoiding the wicked gaze of the Sídhe...

This feeling...

"Sídhe!" cried Áine. "Quickly, everyone, back to the lake!"

"What?" gasped Keaira. "More faeries?"

"Evil faeries! I promise you, these creatures mean nothing but ill will." Áine began to help Anton hoist the limp Orienne over his shoulder. She didn't understand...she had sealed the portal behind her, as she had been instructed to do after her exile. Nothing from

167

Eidolon should have been able to make its way to Earth, and vice versa. How...?

Yet as soon as Áine stood up and turned around, she found herself looking up in horror at not one, but three large, black beasts that had come up around them. They had enormous, black jaws where their heads should have been, and there were several long, frayed strands of black, muddy grass that hung down, draped over their hunched backs from their necks that served as their hair. Their long, thin arms were warped and lanky, and were covered along their lengths with thick clumps of black mud that were even darker than the rest of their body pigment. Their legs were much shorter than their arms, yet were still intimidating and voluminous.

"What the hell is that thing?! Those things?! Gah, whatever!" cried Anton as he almost dropped the unconscious Fader off of his shoulders. He noticed that he was losing his grip on her and hoisted Orienne up again, securing his grip as he did so.

"Poleviks..." gasped Áine. "Sídhe. Three of them..."

"What the hell is what?" asked Orienne. The yelling and jerking movements had awoken her, and she was all groggy. She couldn't really see straight for that matter either, and had no idea what was going on. It probably didn't help matters much that she was in desperate need of water and rest.

In that moment, the Sídhe beasts bellowed out a deep, burbling roar.

"Run!" shouted Áine.

"I won't argue with you on that," agreed Keaira as she bubbled herself in a ball of psychic energy. She was ready to run. Not only that, but if it came down to it, she sure as hell was ready to fight. With that, the rest of the Kinship took off in the direction Áine had bolted. They ducked under branches and scurried around brambles. Yet no matter how fast they ran, no matter how quickly they could move their bodies out of the way, the Sídhe kept right on them. There was no hope for escape.

Anton stopped by a tree and quickly slid himself and Orienne behind it. She had passed out again during the confusion. He slowly lowered her off of his shoulders and set her gently by the tree. The Sídhe didn't seem to notice them, and so he stayed crouched down in the thick brambles that jutted out from the tree's roots. The Prince could see that Melaenie hadn't ducked away, and she was still being hopelessly pursued by the Sídhe.

Anton clenched his teeth and looked away, burrowing himself and Orienne deeper in the brambles. He knew that he couldn't help Melaenie…he couldn't afford to draw attention to himself or else the creatures would come for him and the defenseless Fader. His staff was back in Atlantis, and he was unable to use his ice spells effectively without it. He had no way to protect any of them from three huge, hostile creatures. He felt pain well up inside of his heart as he realized that his actions would most likely lead to Melaenie's death. But what could he possibly do to save her? Besides getting Orienne and himself killed in the process?

Melaenie looked back to see that the Poleviks were still on her heels, but none of her friends were anywhere to be found. While she wasn't looking at where she was going, she tripped and fell on her back, spraining her ankle from getting it caught under a tree root. As she toppled to the ground, she could see the Poleviks get closer and begin to surround her.

"Help!" she screamed at the top of her lungs, panic rising in her voice. "Anton, Áine, anyone, where are you?!"

Anton knew that she was calling for his help, and he struggled with himself to make a quick decision. It was either Melaenie or him and Orienne. Could he really just let one of his best friends die? Orienne's little sister...*die*? Would he be willing to sacrifice himself and another person in order to save her? If it was only his own death to save the child, it would have been a no-brainer, but this? No, this was too much to ask of him, he couldn't make this kind of decision, he wasn't ready.

The Poleviks closed in on the younger Andraste sister. Anton was out of time to make a decision. Now or never. Orienne or Melaenie. Life or death...

Melaenie tried to get up, but to no avail. Her ankle was in extreme pain, and her foot was stuck underneath the protruding root. Tears of pain and fear came rushing to her eyes. "Help!" she screeched once more.

Anton took a deep breath and prepared to stand up. Just as he was about to do something incredibly stupid and foolhardy, he stopped himself as he saw someone standing between Melaenie and the Sídhe.

It was Keaira.

"Hey!" she cried out, trying to get the attention of the beasts. They looked over in her direction, but they still stayed clustered around Melaenie. "Over here, you dumb beasts!" she shouted at them. When that failed to bring them away from the little Fader, Keaira tossed a large clump of mud at them. They were motionless for a while, and she reached down to grab another handful of the dark dirt in order to ready another assault on them. But before her hands were full of the stuff, the three creatures lunged themselves towards her, completely ignoring the trembling child who lay on the ground behind them.

In a flash, Keaira took off running into the distance. She had to lure those things away from the others before she started using her powers against them. She couldn't afford to go out of control now and accidentally injure or kill one of her friends.

How had they even wound up in this kind of a situation anyways? How had they gotten stuck playing such deadly games to protect not one, but two damsels in distress? They were supposed to be the Kinship of the Twilight Moon, never backing down, never giving up! And the Prince was supposed to be the powerful Spell Weaver who threw ice around like nobodies' business. When did Keaira have to become the heroine of this story?

At last, she was far enough away from the others to avoid getting them caught in the fray. She stopped abruptly in place and turned on her heel to face the Poleviks. As if they were confused by her sudden movement, they, too, stopped in their tracks. That split second of confusion was more than enough for Keaira to accomplish what she needed to get done.

She cracked a mischievous grin as two trees snapped and toppled down on top of the Sídhe. The creatures let out an anguished gurgle as the weight of the trees crushed them into the hard earth.

Keaira walked slowly over to them and kneeled down beside their heads. She laughed slowly and deliberately as she leered over them. "My name is Keaira Aleshire," she spat. "I am known as the Little Dark One. And your kind would do well to remember never, ever to mess with me or my friends. Or they'll end up like you.

Her grin vanished and the light in her eyes deadened as she began to crush their heads in upon themselves. The Sídhe gurgled and shrieked as black ooze poured from their twisted jaws.

And then there was silence.

Pure, empty silence.

~~~

When at last Orienne awoke again, Anton and Melaenie were holding her. Melaenie appeared to be nursing a swollen ankle, and Anton had a bloody bandage wrapped around an arm that was now sleeveless. Áine and Keaira were not too far off in the distance, both of them with deeply worried expressions etched into their faces. She was still feeling drowsy, and she didn't know how long she would be able to stay awake before she drifted to sleep again.

"I'm...alive?" Orienne asked in a half-whisper.

"Yes. As soon as I realized what was happening to you, I cast a spell to freeze your molecules into place. It's not a very powerful spell, since I didn't have my staff, but it should keep you from fading for a short while."

"What about the beasts?"

"Keaira bravely fought them off," praised Áine. Keaira beamed in response.

"Is...?" Orienne started to ask, but she forgot her question before she even finished. Her mind was hazy, and she could barely keep her thoughts straight.

She remembered mumbling something pretty incoherent that was meant to be the rest of her question before her vision went blurry. That's when she drifted off again.

Chapter Twenty
Sin and Suffering

~~~

For days, the Kinship of the Twilight Moon wandered further and further into the forest as Orienne's condition gradually worsened. The Prince mentioned nothing of the kiss after that day, though he did not act any different towards her. He still cared for her only as a brother would care for his sister, and wished no further harm upon her.

Both he and Keaira took turns carrying her, the Prince with his physical strength and the Psychic with her powers. Melaenie would hold her hand, and when she could not, she held onto Áine's. Áine did her best to keep them all in high spirits by singing and playing her violin as they travelled. They dared not go back to Atlantis, as they feared that the dying Fader would drown or worse if she happened to fade while in the water.

All this time, Orienne had begun having nightmares that shook her to the very core. Somehow, she believed that those nightmares were trying to tell her something.

As they settled down to camp for the night, she could already feel the terror of her dreams sinking in. "Orienne, are you going to make it?" asked Anton as he lowered her down from his back. She tried to nod her head, but no movement could be made. She was too stiff. Before she even had her head to the ground, her eyes closed and she was transported to the familiar world of black.

~~~

When Orienne first awoke in the darkness, she was greeted only by silence and nothingness. There was little light to see by, though she had a feeling that there was nothing there to see anyways.

"Orienne..." A cold, syrupy voice called out to her. It was filled with concern, but it was almost impossible to tell whether the concern was authentic or not. It sounded almost sarcastic, but just almost. This voice...did she know it from somewhere?

"Who said that?" gasped Orienne. "Who's there?"

"Look around you, Orienne. You are alone. Forever." Orienne shrieked in revulsion at the familiar voice that echoed in her head. It was becoming clearer now. The voice belonged to a boy. She knew it, she knew it...but did she really? It was too distorted to tell.

"No!" She covered her ears with her hands in an attempt to block out the sound, but to no avail.

"Listen." The voice began to solidify in her memory. It was...it was the voice of Ophir, her brother.

"No! You aren't my brother. I won't listen."

"You are unloved."

"No!"

"You are unforgiveable."

"Stop it!"

"Mother is dead because of you."

"I didn't mean it, I didn't mean it!" she cried. "Stop it, please!"

"Alone, unloved, unforgiveable. Listen, listen, listen!"

"No!" Orienne let out an earth shattering scream, shutting her eyes and ears against the vile words that enveloped her entire being and strangled her very soul. Yet when she opened her eyes, the barren nothingness of the darkness was gone, and in its place was a beautiful grassland that seemed to stretch on forever. "Huh?" she uttered to herself, unsure of what to make of the sudden change of scenery.

"Listen, Orienne. This is very important. Do you know your significant sin?"

"No, but..."

"If you won't listen, then fine. Find the answer yourself. Stand up and move forward."

All of a sudden, her body seized up and she was compelled to do exactly as the voice said. Her legs stiffened and began to move of their own accord. She walked on, for miles and miles and miles until her feet ached and her throat thirsted for water. Yet still, the grassy plains did not come to an end, and they continued to stretch out for nearly forever in every direction from where she stood.

"I...I can't go on anymore. I'm too tired..." she gasped, willing herself to collapse on the ground. Her legs were throbbing.

"You will listen and do as I tell you."

Against the painful desire from every muscle and bone in her body to remain resting, she lifted her tired frame and continued onwards. She pushed herself as far as she could until her heart felt like it would burst from overexertion.

"I am listening! Just please, make it stop!" she cried out in terror and pain. As soon as the words passed her lips, the grassy plains came to an abrupt halt before her where a deep chasm jutted from below at a frightening ninety-degree angle. Her legs were still moving. Orienne began to panic as she peered down the perilous slope. It seemed to go on forever, just as the grassland had. If she were to fall from this height... "Please! I can't take it anymore!" she shouted back at the voice.

The twisted voice of her brother echoed in the darkness again. "No, you're not listening. Listen!"

She screamed as loud as her tired lungs would allow as she tried without success to steer herself away from the perilous edge. No matter how much she cried or tried to pull back, no matter how she struggled to re-angle herself, her legs just kept on moving forward. She let out a blood curdling scream as she felt her first leg go over, then a second, and her body crumpled into a graceless freefall.

As Orienne fell, the single voice became seven and began to softly sing a twisted rhyme that seemed to pierce through her very soul.

When we want things we do not need
This little sin is known as greed
When we want passion without giving trust
This little sin is known as lust
When we are jealous of what cannot be
This little sin is called envy
When we consume over-heartily
This little sin is gluttony
When we destroy what's in our path
This little sin is known as wrath
When we're full of ourselves while others we chide
This little sin is known as pride
When we are lazy and live without doth
This little sin is known as sloth
When seven sins are all around
And in ourselves they can be found
The world will end without a word,
Without a sound or movement
Because our sins will shut us up
And kill us in confinement

It seemed like an eternity before she finally hit the bottom, but when she did, she was enveloped in the most intense pain she had ever felt as the impact crushed every bone in her entire body. Her bones were shattered, her neck twisted backwards, her spine destroyed, her legs crushed, her body crumpled in a pool of her own blood. It was a miracle, or perhaps a curse, that she was even still alive.

"Get up."

"I can't..." she whimpered pitifully. "It hurts..."

"I told you to get up."

176

Her legs began to move of their own accord once more, and she screamed in pain as the broken bones cracked and scraped against one another as they tried to support her weight. The agony was simply too much, and she blacked out

When she opened her eyes again, her world was red, and her body was mended, though the pain was still there. The ground on which she stood oozed bloody liquid, and strange fleshy globules floated before her. Where was she?

"You're in my world now."

Orienne didn't have time to think, as a thick cloud of darkness was quickly making its way towards her. She had no choice but to run, lest it envelope her completely. She bit down against the pain and pushed her body onwards. Something about that shadow seemed truly evil. If it even so much as touched her...she would be gone...forever...

And so, she ran. But no matter how fast her aching legs could carry her, it was never fast enough. Her feet got stuck in the sticky, fleshy ground upon which she ran, and removing herself from the ick slowed her down too much. The darkness gained on her at an alarming rate, and it inevitably overcame her. As the darkness enshrouded her, it both consumed and corrupted her. Her heart was blackened, stretched over a void of pure hatred and stitched back in horrid, jagged-toothed stitches. Her soul caught fire and became a green blaze in her eyes. What little there remained of Orienne was nowhere to be found. Envy was all that filled her now.

~~~

Orienne awoke suddenly in a vicious rapture of fear. Every night since she had begun to lose herself from fading, that dream had been haunting her. Every night it was the same thing. A voice called out to her from the depths of darkness and told her to "listen." To the very least, it was quite confusing.

177

Listen, listen, and find your significant sin. Listen, Orienne. This is very important.

She was so sick of that damn word. "Listen, listen, listen."

"Shut up."

And then she would wake up. And it never changed from night to night, and that was what bothered her the most. Reoccurring dreams were usually a sign of something significant.

Your significant sin...

The campfire was now a small flame no larger than a tennis-ball, though it was still blazing softly. Orienne stared sleepily into it for a while until she warmed up a little. She realized that her forehead had broken a cold sweat. When her eyes adjusted to the light, she could see that Melaenie was sleeping soundly by her side. She smiled half-heartedly, glad that her little sister had been keeping her company, but ashamed that it had to be that way. It was supposed to be the other way around. Melaenie already had so much to deal with at her tender young age. She didn't need the burden of taking care of her big sister on top of that.

Anton walked over to Orienne, noticing that she had woken up at last. "Are you alright?" he inquired sleepily. He had an adorable case of bed-head, and his beautiful silvery hair was swept in every possible direction. His eyes were only half open and his smile was the smile of a little boy.

"It's that stupid dream again. You know; that one where the voice asks me about my significant sin," replied Orienne. She was too afraid to tell him about the other parts. About the falling. About the darkness that consumed her time and time again.

"Well, maybe if you find out, you'll stop having that dream," he suggested. "Maybe it's referring to the seven deadly sins. Maybe it's asking which one stands out in you the most."

"And that's a good thing? I thought that sins were bad, and that's why we don't want to have any," Orienne huffed.

"I never said they were good, I'm just making a suggestion. And everyone has a significant sin that they exert more than the rest, whether or not they really know what it is for themselves. For that matter, no one is perfect. Even saints have their pasts."

"Alright, Anton, I get it."

"Maybe you just need to figure out which of the seven deadly sins represents you the most," he smiled half-heartedly at her. Orienne knew he was only trying to be helpful, but he was only frustrating her. Well, maybe he was right, maybe everyone did have a dark side. But when had Orienne, or any other member of the Kinship for that matter, exerted a sin so drastically that it had been deadly?

"I'm sick and tired of trying to interpret my stupid dreams."

"Well," he replied quietly, "that's kind of a hard thing to find out for yourself. Why don't we ask the others about what your significant sin is when they awaken from their 'peaceful' slumber?" As he said the word peaceful, he made air quotations with his fingers.

"You mean that you think they could be having similar dreams too? Maybe we're all getting them," Orienne suggested.

"Maybe."

"But you aren't having this dream, Anton. You never said anything about it," she questioned.

"Well actually..." he began sheepishly.

"I knew it."

"It's nowhere near as frightening as yours, but it's pretty similar. You know...there's something bothering me about all of this. If you and I are asked about our sins in our sleep, it must have some connection to..."

Orienne cut him off. "It must be the Twilight Dragon!"

"Yes, that's exactly what I was thinking." Anton nodded, and he laid his head down against a pillow. He closed his eyes, and for a long while they were both silent. Orienne stroked his hair gently, fixing as much of the tousled mess of snow-like beauty as she could

179

with her small fingers. "Orienne," he started, changing the subject on her. "About the other day..."

A little flicker sparked in her heart when he said this, but she brushed it off. He was talking about when she had kissed him. It had gone so horribly. It only embarrassed her to think about it.

"I love you," she whispered to herself, thinking that he surely wouldn't hear it, and she hugged her knees close to her chest.

"Look, Orienne, we need to talk."

She blushed as she looked up at his face, afraid that he'd heard her. "You uh...you weren't supposed to hear that..." she mumbled, embarrassed.

"Hear what?" he asked. Apparently, he hadn't heard after all.

Orienne breathed a sigh of relief. "Oh, nothing. Don't worry about it. You were saying?"

He was silent for a long while.

"Anton?"

"Never mind. Let's get some sleep; we have a long day ahead of us tomorrow. And maybe you should work on finding your significant sin. I'm sure that it's important if we've all been having that same dream every single night."

Orienne nodded her head slightly as she slid back down in her sleeping bag. She closed her eyes and tried to fall back asleep, but sleep eluded her until she heard the steady, rhythmic breathing of the Prince once sleep had taken hold of him. She stared at the sky, freckled with beautiful, starry lights, for a while longer until the quiet of the night lulled her to sleep.

~~~

When Orienne awoke in the morning, everyone else was already awake and in the process of cleaning up camp. The sun had only just risen. And she still hadn't discovered what her significant sin was.

"Move it, bird-brain!" grunted Keaira. She was carrying a load of folded blankets to bring to Áine and Anton, who were piling everything up quite nicely.

What reason did she have to be grouchy towards Orienne that morning? Yesterday she had been an ass to everyone, but that was because she apparently slept with a large tree-root jammed beneath her spine the night before. Not that that was a reasonable excuse or anything, because she could have moved if she really wanted to, but at least there was legitimacy behind her crankiness. That morning Orienne could only assume that it was merely because she wanted to pester her.

Orienne got up and started to stuff her blanket into her duffel bag. For some reason the zipper kept getting stuck in the perforation holes. Each time she got it untangled, she would reposition it so that she could get it in easier, but then it would get tangled even worse than before. Again and again, no matter what she did, the zipper just refused to work properly. At that point, the zipper was so tangled up in the material that there was no possible way she could get it fixed by herself.

Then Áine went over to her and took the tangled mess. "Let me try," she said softly, trying to calm her down. She twiddled the blanket and the duffel bag apart in a matter of seconds, and then put the blanket inside of it just as quickly. "Sorry, that must be a pain." And then she walked back over to the place where she was packing up the rest of their supplies.

"Thanks," Orienne muttered under her breath, embarrassed at her frustration and inability to solve even the simplest of things.

Then she said to herself, "I really do envy her subtlety and patience sometimes..." and then it hit her. It hit her as hard as someone throwing a mud brick at a glass window.

And then she realized what her significant sin was – envy.

Ever since the beginning of her adventure, perhaps even before then, she had envied almost everyone at least once. Keaira's ability to act cute and get away with things, Anton's exclusion from the hate train despite being a Shironohane, Melaenie's gift for language, Nekotarou's uncanny intelligence...the list went on.

Her sin was envy.

"Orienne! Orienne, wake up!"

Wake up? She was already awake, wasn't she? She felt someone grab her from behind, like a sheltering cradle, but when she turned around, no one was there. She could have sworn that Áine had just been there, though, and Keaira and the others, too.

"Hello, is anyone there?" she asked, frightened. There was literally no one around. No Áine, no Keaira, no Anton...no anybody.

She was alone.

Yet still she felt the arms cradling her close, and still she heard the voice that must have been Melaenie's calling out for her to wake up.

She felt something warm and wet in her hands. It was thicker than water, whatever it was that she was feeling. But she looked down at her hands and nothing was there. She tried to shake whatever it was off, whatever that feeling was away, but it just got heavier and heavier. Her arms began to feel as if they were being crumbled into thousands of jagged pieces beneath her skin, but still she could see nothing wrong with them. The nothingness grew until it consumed the last of her calm, and she screamed out in agony and fear.

"Listen, Orienne. This is very important. Do you know your significant sin?" she heard from the back of her mind. It sounded...it sounded a little like Ophir's voice. It was fuzzy and sounded far away. That was when she knew. She knew that she was dreaming again.

She couldn't remember what happened next, because everything went black.

The next thing she knew, Anton and Áine were carrying her, and both of her arms were in terrible pain. She couldn't see clearly enough to pin-point what was around her, let alone what was wrong with her arms, so she just lay immobile in their grasp.

"Oh, Orienne, you're awake!" exclaimed Melaenie. Orienne could tell by the quiver in her voice that she had been crying, but from the way her words sounded, she spoke them with a smile. Her long lavender sleeves were stained dark red. Something smelled like the rusty-iron smell of blood. Orienne suppressed the urge to throw up.

She tried to ask what had happened, but the words wouldn't come to her. All she could manage to do was let out a dry, pained groan.

"You sleep-walked right off of the top of a tree, never mind how you got up there in the first place, and you tumbled down and broke both of your arms! You almost broke your neck and you've dislocated a few things in your back, but it truly is a miracle that you are still alive!" squealed Melaenie.

That would certainly explain the warm, thick feeling in her hands, as well as the smell. It must have been blood. *Her* blood. Orienne's vision had cleared enough for her to see relatively well, though things were still a bit hazy, and she looked down at her arms. It was almost too gruesome to describe.

They weren't just broken – they were discombobulated.

Mutilated.

Ripped and torn in such a way that she couldn't believe that she wasn't in more pain. It looked as though they had been run over by a multitude of six-wheeled vehicles, bent every-which way until there was no possible distinction of where her joints were supposed to be, had sticks and rocks impaled through in numerous places, and they were stained almost completely a dark, deathly red color. It was almost black. She felt her stomach churn, and after she vomited from the shock, she faded and immediately passed out again.

~~~

When again she awoke from her pain-filled slumber, it was early morning, with the sun not even having fully risen above the distant horizon, and everyone was crowded around her. Orienne blinked a few times to clear the sleepy blur from her tired eyes. Everything seemed to be in a haze, as if she were dreaming. She certainly hoped that wasn't the case. She had had enough of dreams.

She looked to her side to see that Anton was sitting up next to her. His eyes were closed. Had he stayed up with her all night? Why?

Orienne tried to sit up, but her arms just wouldn't move without causing extreme pain. She couldn't think of why they could be hurt. Maybe she had slept on them funny? Her struggle to sit up must have alerted Anton, as he immediately opened his eyes and pushed her down gently onto the ground again so that she would relax her body.

"Good morning, Sleeping Beauty," he said.

"Good morning, Prince Charming," she replied. "Do you mind helping me to sit up? I feel like I've been lying down forever."

With that, he grabbed her gently by the waist with one hand and put his other hand behind her head and hoisted her so that she was sitting up.

"Orienne," he began after he sat her up. "I don't know if you remember what happened. You slept for days. Maybe we used too much medicine, but we were so worried that you weren't going to make it."

Medicine? What could she have possibly needed medicine for? She wasn't sick, or injured.

And then...then she remembered what she had seen during her previous consciousness...her horribly mangled appendages. The images flashed back into her mind, and she was immediately filled with fear. She suddenly felt a surging pain run up passed her shoulders and down her spinal column. Her eyes grew wide, and she screamed out in terror. Her heart began to race. She could hear herself begin to hyperventilate as she screamed in short bursts of agony.

Her screaming had awoken the others. They all rushed to her side, even Keaira.

184

"Orienne! It is alright, just look, your arms are not as bad as they were. We treated them; everything is going to be alright!" Áine tried to comfort her. It sounded suddenly strange to her how this Faerie tried to soothe her. She had never noticed before, but now she could feel every tiny spell that was woven into her words. Faerie Magic. That was the source of her kindly and benevolent aura.

She inhaled and exhaled slowly a few times, Áine's Faerie Magic working its course, and then felt the courage to look down at her arms. She couldn't bring herself to stop crying, though. True, her arms did not look nearly as bad as they had before, but they were more painful now than they had been last time. Her arms were no longer caked in blood, and there were no more pieces of rock and wood sticking out of the wounds, so it was easily apparent that the damage was not as bad as it had seemed... Regardless, it really was quite horrible.

The broken bones had been pushed into place so that they wouldn't be prone to infection. There were huge puncture wounds stuffed with bandaging and healing medicines. There were many scrapes and bruises from her finger tips to her shoulders, all covered with a thin layer of salve. The stinging sensation on top of the strong, dull pain must have been coming from the medicine.

"What exactly happened?" Orienne questioned them in a daze, finally able to calm her breathing.

"We suspect that someone, or rather something, is trying to kill you," answered Keaira worriedly. Maybe she really did care about her. Orienne suddenly felt guilty for thinking so lowly of her all the time.

"But you guys said it yourself, I just sleep-walked off of a tree."

"Yes," started Melaenie, "but you *never* sleep-walk."

"And we were all securely on the ground," said Anton.

"We were settled down around a fire after your little mishap, or did you forget? How could you have possibly climbed that high just to tumble down, in your sleep no less?" added Keaira.

"Then how did you find me?" Orienne questioned.

"We heard something moving in the dark, and we followed it. By the time we had realized that it was you, it was already too late, and you had already taken a dive off the tree," said Anton.

"You didn't scream or anything. The wind stopped blowing, the crickets stopped chirping, and the crashing waters fell silent. It was almost as if time had stopped everywhere except for around you," added Áine.

"Besides," Keaira quivered, "I felt someone else's mind interfering with the consciousness, with your consciousness. Someone must have been controlling your body through telekinesis. I...I tried to stop it, but I was too late. I'm so sorry, Orienne. I know we have our differences, but I would never have wished this on you, and if I had only been there a little sooner...oh, this is all my fault. I'm so sorry."

Orienne began to feel cold. She was terrified. Why would someone try to kill her? Why only her and no one else in the group? Melaenie, too, was an Andraste, though Orienne was sincerely glad that this had not happened to her. Her tiny body would have been destroyed in a fall like that. What was so special about *her*? Orienne's stomach churned, and she felt like she was going to throw-up again, but luckily she didn't.

"Orienne, remember how the notes your brother kept leaving kept telling you to go back home?" asked Áine.

"Yes," Orienne shakily replied. What was she getting at? She knew what Leilani had said, Áine didn't need to say it again...no one needed to say it again. She was an Eidolith. And it was her destiny to slay the Twilight Dragon.

"I believe that whatever or whoever it was that tried to kill you has something to do with the Twilight Dragon. It must be beginning to sense your presence, and it no doubt feels threatened by you. I believe that it was trying to get rid of one of us before it was too late for it to stop us," signed Áine.

"We were supposed to be protecting each other," added Keaira, "from anything like this."

Orienne blinked some of the tears out of her eyes as she looked up at the others. "Why?" she asked them. "Why does it all have to be so hard? Why must it be so difficult to defeat this horrible thing?"

"Because nothing that was ever worth fighting for was easy to earn," she replied simply.

"But why...why now? I finally discovered what the dream was telling me..."

They all gasped and stared at her. "Then the time of our simple journey is over," said Áine solemnly.

"Wait a minute...I thought that finding my sin would stop the dreams and everything would be alright." She turned to face Anton. "You said so yourself, you told me it would be alright!" Orienne sobbed, staring at Anton with a look of betrayal staining her face. "You told me it'd be okay, and it would be over!" She began to sob even harder. She couldn't believe he had lied to her...Anton had lied to her...

"After you began to lose yourself, we all began to search for our sins after the dreams started coming," replied Áine. "We thought that if we could answer our dreams, the nightmares would stop and perhaps we'd find the next clue to reaching the Twilight Dragon. After all, it has been told that it feeds on the sins of humans.

"But then terrible things began to happen. Leilani was the first to find out that hers was Sloth. We had been keeping close in contact with her and the AI via our charms, but when she discovered hers, the barrier in Atlantis faltered. She has been busy rebuilding it ever since. We lost a lot of our supplies." Áine sighed. "This was the first of our miseries. And when I found that mine was Wrath, the strings of my violin snapped. My bow broke in two."

"Mine was Greed," said Melaenie, "and when I realized this, I tripped and dropped all of our new food supplies that we needed after the fiasco in Atlantis into the mud. They were ruined."

"Lust...was my sin," said Anton. "When I went out searching for more food with Keaira, more of those strange Sídhe ambushed and attacked us, and we had to kill all of them. We couldn't risk another incident like the other day happening."

They all looked at Keaira. She was the only one who hadn't admitted hers.

"Alright, alright. I was a victim of Pride...I was the first to find out, and the last to tell the others. When those Sídhe attacked us the first time, right after you began to lose yourself to fading...was right after I had discovered mine. In fact, I had stumbled upon my sin so quickly that the dreams never ended up coming for me. I only told the others after the strange events kept on happening over and over and over again."

"It was then that we realized that our nightmares were actually a safety mechanism," explained Áine. "According to Neko-chan, there is a group of seven AIs who have been repeatedly trying to crack open our minds from afar, though why or how they are managing to do this, I do not quite know. They have been tracking us down through Momoko and Neko-chan since we left Anton's uncle's manor, though apparently the barrier in Atlantis had also been working as a jammer for the signal. When the barrier went down, the rest of us became vulnerable.

"We had hoped that you still remained ignorant of your own sin, as perhaps it would keep us safe from the senses of the Twilight Dragon for a little longer. But now...it seems as though all of us have been put on trial and found guilty."

"In our understanding of ourselves, we have become visible to the Twilight Dragon." Anton paused for a moment and closed his eyes for a few seconds. "I am sorry; I never should have told you to listen to that horrible nightmare. This is all my fault. I can never ask you to forgive me." There were tears in his voice. He was crying.

Why was everyone blaming themselves for what had happened to her? Was it because they thought they had misinterpreted the nightmares? Even Orienne had fallen victim to such a thing. But that was all because Anton had told her to, and she had trusted him.

"No, Anton, this wasn't worth it! Trading my ignorance and our safety for this...this nightmare! Trading our dreams for this hell! Let me go back, Anton, let me forget!"

"Orienne, listen to me," said Anton in a half-whisper. "This nightmare is here to stay, at least until we have done what we were born to do."

"Unless we, the ones who are destined to destroy the Twilight Dragon, have the power to stop it, we will never find rest. We will never stop being hunted," finished Keaira, clenching her fists tightly at her side.

No, not again. Orienne did not want to have to continue on this adventure, not when she knew now how high the stakes would be.

"I'm so sorry," Anton repeated sadly. His own eyes were spilling over with tears of regret. "Orienne, I know you're running out of time. But we have to kill the Twilight Dragon, before it's too late."

Their destiny was surely their curse.

Chapter Twenty One
Mourning and Malady

~~~

The Kinship of the Twilight Moon decided at last to contact Leilani and tell her what had happened, and perhaps request the use of Atlantis and the portals. Hopefully, the dome barrier had been recreated by that point, or else they were stranded. They desperately needed a rest and a shortcut; there was no doubt about it.

"Leilani," they called into their vials. "Leilani, talk to us." But there was no answer.

"That's weird," Anton said. "She always answers our calls, even if they are in the middle of the night or later..."

Keaira grabbed her vial harder than usual and started shaking it angrily.

"*Cad é atá tú a dhéanamh?*" Áine asked the Psychic.

"The water inside isn't glowing anymore," she replied, not exactly answering her question, but pointing something important out in the process.

Orienne looked at her own vial. It was true. Where once the water inside of the vials glowed with a soft light, there was only plain, ordinary water. It had lost its potency, and they were left without means to contact Leilani or the AI who were with her.

Everyone began holding out their vials of what was once magical water. What had happened? Without a means to contact Leilani, they were pretty much cut off from their information and transportation source.

They had no choice but to continue on foot, without the ability to consult their mutant mermaid princess and request her aid.

Orienne could barely walk, as she had lost so much blood and was still in a state of recovery, but Anton and Áine were more than willing to take turns carrying her as they moved along. Orienne was still upset at the Prince, even though she knew deep down that he had done nothing wrong. She was far too stubborn to let it go though, and she simply refused to talk to him or say anything while they moved through the valley below the waterfall.

As they walked, Orienne nearly dozed off while being carried. Yet as soon as she closed her eyes, she overheard Anton and Áine talking about something. They were speaking under their breath, as if they did not wish to wake her, had she truly been asleep.

"Hey, Áine. It's um...lovely weather we're having, isn't it?" he asked politely.

"It seems so," replied Áine softly.

"Yeah. You know, Áine, I feel quite guilty about this, but I don't know what to do about Orienne. I know she likes me, but I...well, you see..."

"I know. I've seen the way she looks at you."

"That isn't my point, my lady. I don't quite know how to let her down easy."

"You could let me carry her," replied Áine, completely missing the point.

"No, I mean..."

"I know what you mean, Anton. But I don't want to get in the middle of it. You've got to handle this little mess out on your own."

"Áine, I love the lady dearly, but not like this. I would protect her with my life, as would I to you, or her sister, or even Keaira or Leilani. We are all connected, and I do feel protective of her. But not like this."

Orienne felt her heart breaking.

"Anton," Áine responded serenely. "I appreciate that you trust me enough to ask for my help, but here is my advice. You should tell her of these things yourself."

He said no more after this, and neither did Áine.

It was not long after that Áine sped up ahead to start walking at the head of the party with Melaenie so that the little one didn't have to watch her sister suffer so, and Anton began to trail behind alongside Keaira.

"I see you're finally taking a stand, Anton," Keaira said quietly, yet playfully.

"What do you mean, squirt?" asked the Prince, pretending to be innocent.

"Ha, you don't have to hide it. We can all see how you look at her."

"Except for Áine...oh, how her shining beauty hangs on the edge of my mind like a glimmering piece of stardust... Do you think maybe she's just not interested?" he asked sadly.

Orienne was disgusted. Was it not to Orienne that he had first confessed the truth about his heritage? Was it not to Orienne that he had sung to and comforted? And yet here he was, spouting cheesy poetry about the Faerie.

"Wow, Anton, that was quite poetic right there. I never pegged you as one of *those* kinds of guys." Then Keaira didn't say anything for a short period of time, as if she were contemplating something to herself. After a bit of silence, she said, "Nah, I just think she hasn't noticed yet. It's always harder for people to tell when the affection is being aimed towards themselves rather than towards others. And even if she has noticed, I don't think Áine is the type for competition. You've already got a fair young lass chasing after your heart."

Anton sighed. He really did like her, didn't he? It was a shame that Áine didn't seem to notice his affection. But Orienne...she had heard it all.

"Where are we going anyways?" Orienne asked after a rather lengthy silence. She didn't bother to feign just waking up, as she was pretty sure that he knew that she had been awake the whole time, though he hadn't expected her to have heard everything he had said. She could still hear the annoyance in her own voice, despite her efforts to hide it.

"We're going to New Japan. We're going to break out the other Psychics," Anton replied. He sounded a little hurt at her tone of voice.

"Did Keaira suggest this?" Orienne accused. She was suddenly unsure of why they were on the current path. They were already swiftly running out of time, and now that the Twilight Dragon and its allies were aware of their presence, this detour seemed foolish. "I thought we were going to free them after this whole ordeal with the Twilight Dragon?"

"Things have changed," he said, his voice full of resolve. "And no, I was the one who suggested it. Keaira says that there is a Psychic in there that has the power to shield people's minds. They can restore the barriers that were shielding our minds and prevent whatever happened to you from happening again."

"So we're heading for calm waters, then?"

"So Leilani can open up a portal near the orphanage, I know. And yes, we're heading for the nearest calm body of water there is. That way we won't need the assistance of our vials to call her. We've been following the stream that led from the waterfall for quite some time now, hoping that it would lead us to a pond or a lake."

"That's a good idea," Orienne mumbled. There was a brief, awkward silence that passed between the two of them before Anton caught her off guard with one of his questions.

"How long are you going to stay mad at me, Orienne?" he asked, his own voice filled with a sorrow that he masked rather poorly.

Orienne didn't answer.

"Please, Orienne, talk to me," he pleaded.

"What's there to talk about?" she snapped. She sounded angrier than she had meant to. She didn't have any right to feel bitter towards him about the whole dream thing, and had just as little right to feel betrayed about his love for Áine instead of her. She knew that her remark had stung him, as he flinched after she said it.

"What will it take to get you to forgive me?"

"I thought you didn't *want* my forgiveness," she remarked sarcastically.

"Orienne..."

But despite her knowledge, her heart would not let her words be calm. "What do you want me to say, Anton? 'Oh, everything is just fine and dandy, my Prince.' Well that's not going to happen, got it? You led me to believe that you liked me even though you knew that it wasn't true!"

"Wait, just a minute, now..."

"And then you convinced me to do the very thing that almost killed me! You put us all in danger, Anton. You *lied* to me. Do you honestly think I'm going to just let that go?" The sound of the anger in Orienne's voice was even beginning to sting her.

"You're wrong," he said. She could hear the pain in his voice. "What you thought to be my affection was nothing more than my friendship. I admit to my fault in being too afraid to tell you otherwise, hoping that your interest in me was nothing more than a passing fancy. I admit that I probably could have saved you a lot of heartache if I had just told you upfront. But I was too afraid to hurt you, and for that I am sorry.

"But about my lies, that is where I must put my foot down and stand up against your accusations. In the Legend of the Twilight Dragon, what the beast fed off of was the sins of the people. I believed that what our dreams were trying to tell us was nothing short of a warning. When we realized what our greatest sin was so that we could stop ourselves from committing them, we would cut off the Twilight Dragon from its food source. I know that's not what ended up happening, but that was my intention! It was never to hurt you or the others. Never."

All of them had heard Anton's words. None were more shocked than Áine and Orienne.

As Anton's outburst began to sink in, Orienne began to feel more and more foolish by the way she was behaving. She was too heartbroken to simply put on a smile and say "I'm sorry," though. She regretted everything she had accused Anton of, and she felt like scum.

"The fact of the matter is, I didn't know, and I am sorry for whatever false hopes I may have painted in your mind. I was only afraid of losing you, but it seems to me like I already have."

Orienne felt like her heart had been crushed by an iron mallet at that remark. How foolish she had been! Before she could reply, Melaenie came up behind them and put her hand on her sister's shoulder. "We're almost there," she said, and Orienne pushed back her sorrow and turned to face the direction they were headed.

They arrived shortly at a small, clear pond. Anton put Orienne down by its banks as everyone began sitting down and dropping what remained of their packs.

"Leilani," Áine called. "We need you."

Within moments, Leilani popped her beautiful little head out of the surface of the water. "Aloha, my dears," she smiled at them. Then, upon seeing the mangled Fader, her smile turned into a frown. "I am sorry, Orienne. I saw what had happened to you. I had tried to warn you through your charm, but something was interfering and I could not reach you." Again with the apologies. Did everyone have a guilty conscience or something?

Orienne was beginning to feel guilty herself about being so angry when all anyone was trying to do was help her. Anton, Melaenie, Keaira, and even Leilani now had all tried to apologize for something they were all unable to do to help her and all she was doing to repay their concern was being stubborn and angry.

"I do have some good news, though. The barrier is back up. Though we have lost our supplies, we at least have a place to rest in safety now. Where are all of you headed anyways?" she asked, changing her melancholic tone to a slightly more cheerful one.

"To the orphanage," replied Keaira. "In New Japan, the one for Psychics. We're breaking the others out."

"You were planning to do that in your condition?" asked Leilani, pointing towards Orienne's less than presentable arms. "Why don't you let me fix those for you?"

They all looked at her when she said this. "You can fix my arms?" the Fader asked.

"Me? No," she laughed lightly. It was refreshing to hear a genuine laugh after all they had been through recently. "Don't be silly. But the water of Atlantis can."

"Well why didn't you just say so in the first place?" rushed Anton. "Please, fix her!" He nearly tripped over himself in his eagerness.

"Alright, wait here for just a moment," she replied happily before disappearing beneath the surface of the water again. The others waited impatiently in silence for a few minutes for Leilani to show up again. When she came up above the water for a second time, she was holding an old canteen filled with water, presumably from Atlantis. "Take off the bandages," she commanded with an air of authority.

Anton and Áine each worked on hastily removing the bandages from her arms. When Orienne saw them under the unraveled bandages, she almost didn't recognize them as her own arms. They were shriveled and shrunken, deformed and lumpy, and covered in all sorts of welts, cuts, and bruises. She began to wonder why none of the rest of her body had even been damaged as badly as her arms had been. Something about this whole business just didn't seem right...

Leilani leaned out from the pond as far as she dared and poured the cool water over her mutilated arms. Much to her surprise, it didn't sting at all. In fact, it felt quite refreshing. She could feel her bones and muscles mending beneath her skin, and she could see her ruined flesh renew itself. She suddenly felt all of her frustration melt away with her wounds, and smiled for the first time since before she began to lose herself.

"You all ought to rest up tonight, seeing as how you guys are breaking in to the orphanage soon. You do realize that nothing like this has ever happened before, right?" said Leilani.

"Of course," said Keaira. "That's exactly why it's going to work."

That night, Leilani kept the portal to Atlantis open all night. She prepared a nice little moon-lit picnic of fish for them, since their supplies were all but lost, and Áine brought out the rest of the edible berries from the forest for desert. Though Áine's violin was broken, that did not stop them from sitting merrily around the little campfire Áine had made and singing songs together for a while before it was time to lay their weary heads down to rest at last.

Chapter Twenty Two
Bonds and Unbinding

~~~

"It's time," said Leilani. "You should do this as fast as you can, but do not sacrifice caution for speed." She aimed the next part exclusively at Keaira. "I trust you to take good care of the defensive, as best as you can anyways. Watch them carefully and do not lead them astray. If your powers are not enough, I implore you to use force. We cannot risk losing anyone on this rescue mission. You know the walls and layout of the orphanage-"

"Prison," Keaira briefly interrupted.

"Prison, then. We will all be relying on you." She hesitated before she said the next part. Her eyes were filled with concern as she looked at her companions.

Keaira continued on. "Listen up, everyone. You all have to be on you're A-Game. One misstep, and you might not survive. They are armed to the teeth, and will not hesitate to kill any one of you. They deal with torturing and murdering children every goddamn day, they won't give a rat's arse if they catch intruders. Especially...since I'll be with you. Everyone, please, I implore you not to be...reckless."

Everyone was quiet. Melaenie tightened the grip she had on her elder sister's hand. They all knew what could happen. They knew the risks, or at least understood that risks were there.

"Melaenie, I want you to stay in Atlantis with Leilani," ordered Orienne. The last thing that she wanted was her little sister getting captured again, or worse. "You'll be safe here."

"But Orienne..."

"Don't argue with me, little lady."

"Come on," Leilani said as she smiled sweetly at the little girl. "It's for the best."

"She's right," said Áine. "Leilani will take good care of you. Be a good girl now."

Melaenie was too shy to make any sort of reply. She resigned herself to her fate as the others mentally prepared themselves for the danger ahead.

"Momoko, Neko-chan, are you coming with us?" asked Anton.

"Yes. We shall be accompanying you presently," replied Momoko.

"Wait just a moment, Momoko..." objected Nekotarou.

"No, Neko-chan, we are going to help them. They helped us, and we have repaid them by hiding away in a bubble while the rest of them struggled through many hardships on the surface. Had we been there, we could have stopped the SINS from interfering. Had we been there, we could have helped. No more waiting on the sidelines. I want to do what I was created to do. To help."

Nekotarou was silenced by Momoko's outburst. He had only wanted to protect themselves, but she was right. These people were their friends and allies. And they needed their help.

"We're ready," said Áine.

"You all had better get going now. I'll open up the portal from Atlantis. We've wasted enough time with our idle banter."

With that, she dove back through the bubble. The Kinship saw a patch in the water that began to shimmer more vibrantly than the rest of it. Leilani popped back up in a matter of seconds. "You will end up in a Koi pond inside of the orphanage grounds. The doors you will see lead directly to the main hall. Wait until it is dark before you do anything, lest you be caught by the guards." She motioned to all of them to follow her. "Now hurry, everyone! Jump in!"

They all jumped into the water one after the other; Orienne, Momoko and Nekotarou, Anton, Áine, and Keaira, all following Leilani as they plugged their noses and held their breaths.

They swam through the portal and wound up in the Koi pond, just as Leilani had informed them they would. The sky was orange; it was just about sunset. Twilight. The time of change. They didn't have much longer to wait until nightfall, and it would be dark enough for them to sneak in.

They climbed slowly out of the water so as not to make too much of a sound. Anton quickly whispered a spell that summoned a wind to dry them off so that they would not take chill. It was, after all, late autumn. Sitting around, dripping wet in the cold night air would not do any of them any good.

They sat there in near silence, waiting for the sun to finish dipping below the horizon.

Áine had noticed that Keaira was sitting away from the rest of them, staring in the opposite direction of the building. She had a mixture of loss and longing in her expression. It was almost painful to look at. The Halfie walked over to her. "Are you alright?" Áine asked the Psychic.

"Yes, I am alright, don't mind me," she replied sadly. Áine could tell that she was lying. Something was really bothering her.

"No, you're not," Áine said right back at her. "*Le do thoil*, tell me."

"What do you care?" she snapped. She looked at Áine briefly, her eyes filled with scorn, but then the anger left her glare. She appeared as if she were about to cry. "It's about Gaignun."

Áine was not at all surprised by this. Gaignun was Keaira's friend, right, her Other. They were going to rescue him soon enough. Keaira had nothing to worry about. "What about him?" Áine asked, her voice calm and steady. "Are you afraid we cannot save him?"

"No!" the Psychic exclaimed softly. "No..."

"Then why the tears?" Áine was genuinely concerned for the dark haired teen. They all needed to be in tip-top condition for what they were about to undertake. Tears simply would not do.

"He's not for me, Áine."

"What do you mean he's not for you?" the Halfie asked. She should have stopped herself from saying that. "He's your friend." It was a stupid, thoughtless thing to say. She should have known that Keaira would have more than just platonic feelings for this boy. She was, after all, a growing young woman, and she was essentially risking everything to save him. And he was her Other. If there was no love there, it did not exist anywhere.

"Don't think I'm stupid, Faerie. It doesn't matter if we save him. I'll never..." she trailed off, never finishing that thought.

Áine waited and waited, but the statement was never finished. She could put the pieces together by herself, though. Keaira was in love with Gaignun. "What brought this on all of a sudden?" she asked Keaira, worry escaping into her voice. This was certainly not the time for their only real chance at pulling this off for Keaira to start freaking out.

"It wasn't all of a sudden! I've been thinking about this for a long time now. Since I left, I...he..." Áine could see tears forming in her eyes. "But that's not why I'm acting like this right now. No, it's *that*. Last night, I..." She paused once more, this time even longer than the last.

"You what?"

Suddenly, her train of thought took a sharp turn, and she started babbling about something from her childhood at the orphanage, about guards, torture, experiments, kidnapping, murder. Murder. Murder, trouble, death, fear. She said many troubling and frightening things, but she was speaking so fast that Áine was finding it hard to follow. Her English quickly turned into babbling in a dialect of Gaelic that Áine didn't even have a hope of understanding. Her eyes bugged out, and she suddenly exclaimed, "Gaignun!"

Her outburst alerted the others. "Keaira, are you alright?" asked Anton, sensing Keaira's panic. The Prince walked over and put a hand on the Psychic's shoulder.

"No, he'll die!" Keaira said, worry now filling her voice to the brim. "He'll die, they'll kill him!"

"What is the matter with you Miss Aleshire?" asked Momoko, her own sense of panic escalating.

"We need to help him immediately!"

"Who? Help who?" Orienne asked her.

"Gaignun!"

"What? Are you crazy?" asked Nekotarou, not helping the situation by his accusatory tone. "We must wait until sundown, or we risk exposure and imprisonment, and possibly even death."

"Screw exposure, they're killing him! Can't you hear him? He's screaming!"

They all listened intently for a moment. None of them could hear anything but the cool, gentle wind blowing through the garden, and Keaira's frantic breathing.

She suddenly dropped to her knees and started crying. "He's dying! They're killing him!" She cried out as if she were in real physical pain herself. "Oh, it hurts!" She grabbed her chest and coughed. "Make it stop, it hurts!"

Momoko turned to face the rest of her companions. "What is the matter with her?" She did not understand where the girl's pain was coming from.

Áine looked at her with an expression that showed she had realized what was happening to the young Psychic. "I think...that this Gaignun lad's pain is her own."

"Her what?" the others asked, near simultaneously.

"She told us before, he is her Other. It is very rare, but sometimes a Psychic can develop an extremely powerful physical bond as well as the typical mental bond that all known pairs of Others have been proven to possess. The connection is supposedly strongest when the two are in close proximity to one another, which explains why she hasn't even had so much as a twinge of pain

202

before arriving here in New Japan with us. If her bond with Gaignun is like that, she is in more danger than we had ever thought, and our mission as well. If he dies from an overload of pain, so, too, will she. If she dies, so, too, does our quest"

Keaira was now writing in pain on the ground, biting back screams and clenching her head.

"If we don't go now, she's going to alert every guard in the facility," cautioned Anton. "Keaira, can you stand?"

Her only response was an agonized moan.

"Carry her, then," commanded Áine.

"Just shut up and help him, damn it!" Keaira cried.

With that, Anton gently picked her up in his strong arms, and the Kinship of the Twilight Moon abandoned all caution as they rushed through the courtyard doors and into the main hall where a receptionist gaped at them with wide eyes and an open mouth.

"You! Who are you?" she exclaimed, but the words were barely out of her mouth before Áine was on top of her, teeth bared and nails like claws. It was terrifying. She was wild, almost feral. The receptionist didn't even have time to scream before Áine focused her entire body weight into her elbow and brought it careening down onto the back of her head. There was a loud crack as her forehead collided with the desk she sat behind, and a thin stream of blood began to trickle from the point of impact and drip down onto the floor. She was down and out. She was not dead, though she would have a hell of a concussion when she finally woke.

"Holy *shit*!" exclaimed Anton, nearly dropping Keaira as he took in what he just saw Áine do.

"Gaignun!" Keaira cried at the top of her lungs, oblivious to the merciless maneuver their Faerie companion had just carried out. "Where are you?" Her eyes were bright red and her face was stained with her salty tears. She was on the verge of hyperventilating.

Momoko broke the door to the next room off of its hinges when it was found to be locked, not wanting to waste a moment of time. All it took was a well calculated kick.

"Well done, Momoko," praised the cat.

They all dashed through the cafeteria, catching the eyes of all those who were in there. Four guards that had been guarding the doors of the cafeteria saw them as well, and they began to shout at them and chase them down through the winding corridors of the orphanage. One of them sounded the alarm, and a blaring siren suddenly filled the halls.

"Where is Gaignun?" called Áine over the sirens. "We are running out of time!"

"I...don't know!" choked out Keaira. She was starting to hyperventilate faster now. She was speaking in broken sentences and losing the ability to keep up with her own words. "Keep heading further...down...this way! The closer I...get to...him..." She screamed out in pain again.

"Hush, hush, we know. You don't need to say another word," breathed Áine in a comforting and motherly way. The young Psychic looked as if she was slightly more at ease due to her words. It was the complete opposite of Áine's mannerisms towards the unfortunate receptionist. Could she really switch back and forth between such starkly contrasting personalities in such little time? That in itself was almost as frightening as her feral actions.

As more and more guards poured from the doorways and into the winding halls, Áine and Anton announced that they would stay behind to fend off them so that the others would not be overwhelmed. The Prince swiftly handed Keaira off to Momoko, who carried her easily despite the fact that the Psychic was quite a bit taller than the pink-haired AI. Orienne and Nekotarou thanked the Prince and the Halfie and quickly continued on their way. Áine the Feral and Anton the Spell Weaver could handle themselves.

"I am sorry, Grian, but I cannot keep the vow I made to you. I cannot keep their blood from staining my hands," Áine muttered to herself, preparing herself for the many deaths she knew she would have to cause to protect her Kinship and those they were here to rescue.

Anton flung spell after spell in their direction, hurtling ice chunks and frigid water at the seemingly endless guards that poured through the doorways. The ice shattered on impact and the water slowed them down, but only barely. Áine didn't miss her chance to pounce on the guards who took too long getting back up, tearing at their throats in the soft spot beneath their bullet-proof turtleneck uniforms.

But Áine was only one woman. The guards she could not keep down got back up again and again, shooting at them with their guns. Anton's magical ice shields couldn't stop the bullets forever.

"I never pictured myself going out like this!" shouted Anton over the roar of battle.

"This isn't how it ends!" Áine shouted back at him, her fingers dripping with blood. "We still have a dragon to slay!"

~~~

While Áine and Anton held the rear guard, Orienne, Momoko, Nekotarou, and Keaira passed by countless rooms while curious and frightened Psychics poked their heads through the doorways to see what was going on. The prisoners were watching the intruders frantically sprint down the hallways, eyeing them with disbelief. Some appeared to recognize Keaira, and those who did began to cheer her name. Orienne remembered how Keaira had told them of her promise to those remaining at the orphanage that she would return and free them all someday. She suddenly felt awful and selfish for wanting to convince everyone out of coming here before they defeated the Twilight Dragon. These people, these *children*, needed them. They needed Keaira.

All of a sudden, the runners came upon a large, glass wall that showed into another room. It looked oddly like some kind of freakish biology lab. In that room, there was a young boy who was no older than Keaira strapped tightly into a metal chair. He had beautiful strawberry-blonde hair, fashioned in a short, awkward, wispy fashion, as if he had tried to style it himself. It was damp with sweat, though, and much of it was sticking to his brow. A handful of freckles danced lightly beneath his eyes and across his nose.

There were two guards next to him, one of which was powering a strange machine. The boy in the chair wore a similar style uniform to Keaira's, save for the fact that it was styled for boys, and he wore pants instead of a pleated skirt. His shirt was unbuttoned and hanging open, his shoulders and chest exposed. Attached to nearly every area of his body by thick metal needles were strange electrical wires that were also attached to a nearby machine that appeared to read Psychic energy levels with one bar and electrical energy levels on another. When the machine went off, he screamed out in pain. At the same time, Keaira mirrored his reaction. Was this boy Gaignun? He had to be.

Keaira's episode faded at last as she gazed through the glass and saw the boy hooked up to that horrible machine. The pain in her face burned away at the new fury her expression was now heralding. "What are you waiting for?" she yelled angrily at the others. "Break the damn glass!"

Momoko gently placed Keaira on her feet and began banging her fists against the glass with all her might. Orienne began kicking the glass, trying as hard as possible to make some kind of crack or dent, but to no avail. At last, Keaira gathered up all of the Psychic energy that she had within her and hurled it at the glass wall. However, it bounced back off of the glass and knocked them all back with incredible force.

Keaira got back up on her feet, pushing herself out of the tangle of her companions and began throwing herself at the wall. "You let him go, you sick bastards!" she yelled into the other rooms. Bruises were beginning to form on her pale hands and face. She was really a fighter, when it came down to it. Her futile attempts to break through the glass with her own body were more courageous and full of determination than anything they had ever seen.

Though the glass made no way for her, she had definitely caught the guards' attention by this point. They both left Gaignun be and walked over to the glass.

"Keaira Aleshire," one of the men began. "I never would have thought you would show your face in here again. I didn't honestly think that you were that stupid."

"I thought you would have learned a thing or two about this kind of glass by now, seeing as how it took sixteen of you worthless Psychics to put even a dent in one of these babies the last time you went up against us," boasted the second one.

"You just couldn't leave your little boyfriend alone, though, could you?" the first one said, taunting her.

"Screw you!" she spat back at them.

Just then, Gaignun turned his head and looked at the girls and the little cat who stood on the other side of the glass. When he saw Keaira, he smiled a smile so pure, so sincere and full of love; his heart could have simply burst from joy at the mere sight of her. Keaira smiled back, her pain-filled expression changing into an exhausted yet happy grin. There was no doubt that there was love between the two of them. What Áine had said was true about Others. They really were soul mates.

The guards both grabbed weapons that closely resembled batons, but they were tipped with glowing ends that looked painfully electrical. They appeared to press a sort of button above the glass, and air could be heard pushing out from somewhere. The Kinship looked above them to see that there were nozzles in the ceiling made for releasing gas into the area. This was the end of the line.

Within moments, their eyes grew heavy and it was becoming hard for them to see or to keep themselves from falling over. Their legs threatened to give out beneath the weight of their own bodies.

Keaira took a quick look around, glazed as her eyes felt, to see that everyone else was reacting to the gas in the same way that she was. Even...Momoko...

As she collapsed on the ground, her world and the worlds of her companions disappeared.

Chapter Twenty Three
Escape and Emancipate

~~~

Anton and Áine had managed to take out all of the guards in the area. Áine's hands were covered in blood. She was trembling from the aftermath of going berserk. She had broken her promise to Grian. She had slain humans again. Spilled human blood. It was in self-defense, and defense of her Kinship, and yet...

"Áine!" Anton exclaimed as he placed a hand on her trembling shoulder. "Áine, it's over now. It's done." He faced her front and tried to look into her eyes, but she just looked straight through him as if he wasn't there, her eyes full of fear.

"I...killed them all..." She held her bloody hands before her face. She remembered it all so vividly. Her senses were all heightened when she went berserk. These images would be etched inside her mind forever. Just like when she had murdered her brothers. "I broke my promise. I betrayed her, I failed her..."

Anton grabbed hold of her hands, not caring that the blood would stain his gloves. "Áine, snap out of it! We're here on a mission, I can't have you zoning out on me!"

"But I..."

"You did what you had to do," he said as he wiped the blood away from her hands with his cloak. "You protected your friends. You protected *me*. Now come on, get a hold of yourself. I need you."

Áine finally looked into Anton's eyes instead of through him. How had she never seen it before? Never seen how much he cared for her? She had fancied him herself from time to time, though she had never tried to peruse her feelings. He was a human, and she was... "I'm a monster..."

"You're not a monster. You're a Faerie. And you are my Lady."

Without hesitation, Áine flung her arms around Anton's neck and pulled him into a brief kiss. It was not the first time she had kissed him, but it was the first time she had done so without the intent of casting a spell on him.

All this time she had thought herself undeserving of him. When she saw how the elder Eidolith girl looked at him, she had tried to give Orienne a chance. Yet Anton's eyes never strayed, never turned away from her. He actually, truly needed her. And believed in her. That was more than even Grian had done for her.

"What is it with you girls always kissing me?" he asked playfully.

"It was a thank you. Now come on, you're right; we've got a prison full of kids to free." With that, Áine and Anton turned tail and dashed down the hallway in the direction the others had gone.

By the time they got to the others, however, the gas had already been released. Áine was the first to smell it, as her heightened Feral senses had yet to ebb away completely. "Anton, the gas. Exhale."

Anton nodded, and, being the ever resourceful Spell Weaver that he was, just whispered quietly, "Not to worry, my Lady. Cleansing is my specialty." Not a moment later, he breathed out a little spell to cleanse the air.

But it was too little too late. The others had all dropped to their knees, the gas having already taken its effect on them. Even Momoko, who the gas probably shouldn't have been able to affect at all...then again, she had been created out of biomechanical make-up. Perhaps the organic parts of her were still susceptible to such things. But that was not all. Almost as soon as they hit the ground, the floor opened up like a trap door, dropping them all down into the level below.

~~~

It wasn't until much later that Keaira awoke again. She opened her eyes to see that she was in a small, metal room with her arms chained to the wall and hanging limp by her sides. Her clothes were slightly damp; not as if she had been in water, but as if she had been residing in a cold, dank place for the last few hours. She didn't doubt that possibility. She felt around in the dim-lit room for a bit, but didn't find much. The floor was indeed cold and damp, but as far as she could reach, she felt nothing but the flat concrete that paved the ground.

She remembered this chamber well. It was rarely used anymore, but her captors used to use it for testing how well the telekinetic Psychics could throw around heavy, blunt objects. The purpose was to test how well they could be integrated into the workforce as heavy-load laborers. Back when there was actually a method to the madness, though that didn't make their treatment any less despicable. A lot of kids died in here. Many more had been severely injured. But what made them stop practicing altogether was when some of the Psychics got smart and started using the heavy objects to break themselves out...

Now it was a room used only for "time out."

Keaira suddenly became aware that she was all alone, and that there was a painful throbbing sensation in her head. That's right, she was still in the Orphanage, and until she escaped, Gaignun's pain would be her own. She tried calling out for the others, though the sound of her own voice triggered horrid waves of pain rushing through her skull.

"Áine?" Keaira called. "Anton?" She rubbed her head gently before going on. This was more painful than it ought to have been. Damn migraine... "Neko-chan, Orienne, anyone?" There was no response save for the mild echoes of her own voice.

She struggled briefly, suddenly afraid of her seclusion. If she was alone, what had happened to her companions? Had they been...no, it was too horrible of a thought. She simply would not believe that she had brought them here only to meet their doom. She

210

would not believe that after everything they had been through, this was where they failed. But her struggling was useless, and her powers all but gone. This place held the same sorts of bindings that Leilani's Pearls and Prince Anton's Enchanted Cheese held, sealing her powers deep within the confines of her mind. The people who ran this Orphanage never, ever made the same mistake twice.

Keaira sat there in silence for what seemed like hours, waiting for goodness only knows what. Then, when she was finally starting to crack and fear that all hope was lost, she began to hear heavy footsteps making their way towards her location. Her stomach lurched in fear. Oh, no, no, no! What was she supposed to do? Her migraine throbbed in her skull, she hadn't the effective use of her arms since the chains were too heavy to allow her to fight, and her legs were as good as gone since the effects of the gas had yet to wear off. She was still in a funk, and there was no way she had any chance of fighting any more guards off, especially without her telekinetic abilities.

She heard the loud clank of someone hitting the door that led to her room. It sounded as if they were trying to break it down. She began to wonder if whoever was at the door wasn't really a guard at all. Why would a guard be trying to break down the door of their own cell? Hope began to bubble up in her chest. Maybe it was one of the others!

In a few short moments, the door caved in, and a wave of bright light washed into the room. Keaira was temporarily blinded by the intensity of the new light, but when she opened her eyes she knew that she was getting out of there. Alive.

The person who had smashed down the door was none other than the little A.I. girl, Momoko, with Nekotarou resting idly on her shoulder.

"Momoko, Neko-chan!" Keaira joyfully exclaimed. "How did you escape?"

Momoko smiled a childish smile, full of pride and playfulness. She giggled slightly before answering. It was slightly eerie, knowing that she was technically only emulating such a giddy behavior. "They counted on me being human," she said. "I faked passing out earlier, and simply beat my way out of my cell. Neko-chan was already with me, and then I just used my sensors to detect where you and the others were."

"The others? Have you freed them already?" Keaira asked, perhaps a little bit louder than she should have, considering the circumstances.

"Yes," Momoko said as she walked over to the Psychic and began breaking the chains off of her arms. "They have already freed the other Psychics. Gaignun is the only one who remains. The others are waiting in the hall as we speak." When Keaira's bonds were broken, the AI helped her to her feet. Keaira wobbled a bit, but she was soon able to stand up and walk with relative ease. Even her migraine was already beginning to wear off. They scurried out of the room and joined the others in the hall.

"Is everyone ready?" asked Momoko. There wasn't a veto amongst them.

"Let's get going then," commanded Keaira. She then began to lead them down the twisting hallways until they came to a small, heavily armored door. There was a key-pad by the door, most likely for inputting a password that would open it.

"Keaira, do you know the pass code?" asked Áine.

"Um...no, I hadn't really thought of this..."

Momoko smiled and gently pushed Keaira and Áine aside. "Please, allow me." The pink-haired AI girl pointed out her index finger, and a very small pin-like barb extended from beneath her nail. She stuck this into a little hole in the side of the key-pad, at which point her eyes began to glow that odd electric green color again. Within a matter of seconds, a short beeping noise was heard and the door opened.

That was a nifty little trick she had there.

The Kinship stepped through the now open doorway, wary about what was in there. It didn't take them long to realize that this was the same room that they had been looking into from the other side of the glass. This was the room where they had been experimenting on Gaignun. They saw the table and the machine on the other side of the room, where the researchers and the guards still hovered over the suffering freckled boy.

The guards turned around almost as soon as the door opened. "Hey, you!" yelled one of them.

"How did you all get in here?" the other asked.

Their element of surprise had been shattered, but their resolve to rescue Gaignun had not been. They charged in, running at full speed, ready as ever to attack them and free the boy. As they got closer, the guards finally realized that they were the same people who had been drugged and dumped into their different cells just hours before. Their stupefied looks were priceless.

The guards were about to make their moves, but Feral Áine was too quick for them. She instantly leapt at them and sent them flying back into the machine, knocking it over. It fell to the ground with an ear-shattering boom. Sparks flew everywhere, jumping and leaping across the tables, instruments, and walls. It was a miracle that every single person in the room, villain and member of the Kinship alike, escaped getting electrocuted. As it fell, some of the wires that had been attached to Gaignun had been torn forcibly from his body.

The guards didn't stay down long, even though the force of Áine's attack had knocked them back quite hard. They got back up and grabbed their baton-like weapons again, swinging at their legs and breaking Áine's shin while they were at it. She cried out in pain, snapping her out of her berserker rage.

"Áine!" cried Anton, rushing over to her.

As the Halfie fell to the ground, the guard who struck her reached to press a button, which would no doubt sound yet another alarm. Just as before, hordes of guards would begin to flood into the room. And this time, without Feral Áine, their fighting force was as crippled as her broken leg.

But just before the deed was done, Momoko was able to make her way to the front of the brawl and intercept the guard. The human guards were no match for her robotic strength, and with only two hits per guard, they were down for the count.

"Why didn't you just do that from the start?" complained Keaira.

"I did not desire to hurt any of you," replied Momoko. "You were in the way."

While Anton and Momoko fended off the other guards, Orienne and Keaira began working together to get Gaignun out of there. Keaira ran to Gaignun's side and un-strapped his wrists. The two of them began taking the remaining wires off of his body; leaving red marks, puncture wounds, and blisters wherever they had been. He buttoned up his shirt and tried to stand up, but he swooned and fell back into the chair. She finished buttoning up his shirt for him before she lifted him up and hoisted him onto her shoulder.

"What took you so long?" he joked weakly.

"I'm so sorry, Gaignun," she said. "I didn't mean to be so late. I got caught up in this wild journey. You should meet my friends, you'd like them."

He looked up at the others. "Hello, everyone," he said. "Keaira has said such kind things about you all." But then he looked over at Áine and laughed. Images of Keaira getting tied to a tree flashed through his mind. "Well, most of you. But I don't think any of you are bad."

"Let's just get out of here," said Keaira, embarrassed about Gaignun sharing her thoughts with her companions. She was about to ask Anton to carry Gaignun until she saw the broken legged Áine leaning up against him. That would do no good. But the AI girl... "Momoko, can you carry him please? He's been through a lot...I would know."

Momoko nodded, not saying a word.

"The others?" asked Gaignun as they prepared to leave.

"The others are free," answered Momoko. "We took care of all of them. Some of the other Psychics helped us out as well. It was quite a sight to see, actually."

"It sure was," agreed Anton. "I think they'll have this place down in no time. I don't exactly know where all of them will go from here, but I've got the feeling that they'll all be alright now. There's nothing to worry about."

"What about him, Keaira?" asked Orienne. "Are we dropping him off somewhere safe, or is he going to be coming with us?"

"With us," replied Keaira. "He's the one with the power to shield minds, and mess with minds as well. He's far more skilled in that aspect of Psychic activity than anyone I know. He should be able to protect all of our minds with relative ease, won't you, Gaignun?"

Gaignun weakly nodded in their direction. "These...SINS...they won't...give you any more...trouble..." He seemed really weak, like he was going to pass out at any moment.

"We should go," said Áine. "He can't pass through the portal unless he's conscious, or he could drown. Anton, keep him cold, make sure he stays awake."

Anton nodded again, always willing to do whatever Áine said. "Stay awake, Freckles," he said to the boy as they all started to walk out of the facility. "It's time to go to Atlantis. We've got business to take care of."

Gaignun and the Kinship made it back to the Koi pond in one piece, where Leilani was there waiting for them.

"I see you found him," she said. "I saw everything from Atlantis. I'm so proud of all of you!"

"There's no time for that," Áine interrupted. "We must get to Atlantis. We haven't a moment to spare." Gaignun was quickly slipping into unconsciousness. They didn't have much time before he completely passed out.

"Alright, alright. Quickly, now, before our newest little member leaves us again."

With that, they all dove into the water once more, with Momoko carrying Gaignun and Keaira holding on to her Other's limp hand. Áine needed no further assistance, as the magical properties of the waters of the lake that had healed Orienne before now worked its same wonders on the Halfie.

215

They swam to Atlantis and passed through the magical barrier again. Little Melaenie greeted them warmly with a nice warm meal already prepared. It had been quite a while since they had left. They were...home.

But when at last they were all settled down, Leilani's expression was grim. "Why do you grimace so?" asked Áine. "Is something the matter?"

"No," replied Leilani calmly. "It's just that with our newest member quickly slipping into the world of dreams, I figured it would be too dangerous to drop you all off where you need to be."

"And where exactly would that place be?" Áine asked.

But now it was the elder Andraste sister who Leilani turned to face. "I've found your brother, Orienne."

Chapter Twenty Four
Promise and Prophecy

~~~

The golden haired Eidolith girl gaped. "You...what? How?"

"I'm taking you all to him as soon as Gaignun awakens," said Leilani. "I have a feeling that your brother knows something about the Twilight Dragon. I'm hoping that by bringing you to him, this whole journey will finally be over, and we can live out the rest of our lives in peace."

"Where is, he, Leilani?" Orienne asked desperately.

"He's on a small little island, so small that it wouldn't even show up on any maps of the world. There's an extremely powerful magic barrier that is shielding the place from being discovered in addition to its extremely tiny size."

"Then how did you even get through the barrier?" asked Áine .

"The pearls," she replied casually.

"Of course. You've been relying on those a lot more lately."

"I didn't have a choice, Áine."

"I'm not reprimanding you, my friend. Merely warning you to be careful. Those are powerful catalysts, and your power as a Spell Weaver has been growing exponentially since I met you. Just...be careful."

"What kind of spell did you use?" asked Anton, genuinely curious.

"I used a strand of Melaenie's hair and the note that was given to Orienne in New France, and cast a finding spell. I had hoped it would finish before you all got back and, well...the results were greater than what I could have hoped for. Anyways, I figure we should wait until the little guy wakes up before we do anything huge like try and open up a portal powerful enough to allow us entry to that place. It's going to take a lot more than my own magic, and even the magic of the lake and the pearls combined to breach the barrier on that island. I suspect that the powerful magic comes from none other than the Twilight Dragon itself."

Orienne suddenly began to wonder how her brother had arrived at such a place if it was so hard to find, and even harder to get to. Just what exactly had Ophir been up to?

"So what are we going to do until he wakes up?" asked Melaenie.

"Are we just going to wait around and do nothing?" added Nekotarou.

"It's actually up to you," said Leilani. "But if I were you, I'd rest up, too. Tomorrow may in fact be the day of destiny that you have been traveling towards since the day the prophecy was made."

"Thank you for the advice, Leilani, but I don't think we should go to sleep just yet. There are still some things I would like to address with the others before there isn't any time left to do so," said Áine.

What? What was there left to tell them? The Kinship of the Twilight Moon knew that finding and defeating the Twilight Dragon was the end of their journey, and in doing so they would fulfill the age-old prophecy. They had already learned of its origins, its abilities; its hunger. What could Áine possibly want to address?

"Understood, Áine," replied Leilani, bowing her head to Áine in respect. None of them had ever seen her do this before. Had they missed something? Was there something that the two of them had been hiding from them? Their minds began to race alongside their hearts as they began to think of the endless possibilities of things that could have been going on right at this moment between Leilani, Áine, and the rest of them.

"However," continued Áine. "I would prefer to wait until young Gaignun is awake. I would like to convey everything to everyone at once so that I do not have to repeat myself."

"That won't be a problem at all," replied Keaira, who was sitting with Gaignun, his head resting in her lap. "We can share our thoughts, if we will it. Anything you tell me is essentially the same as telling it to him."

"All the same," replied Áine, "I would prefer to tell him in person. It's more...traditional, per say."

And so, they waited around for forty minutes or so, filling the area with idle chatter and singing. Áine, whose bow Leilani had since repaired, played her violin alongside their voices, calming their nerves about what was to come and bringing a harmony to their souls that they were sure no other violinist in the world could do.

Gaignun finally awoke, and at first, he didn't seem to remember what had happened. He shot up out of Keaira's lap, confused and disoriented. "What...where am I?" he asked. "Who are all of...you..." he said, before his expression softened a great deal. The memories were finally coming back to him. Keaira's memories, too, flowed into his mind as she eased them through. He relaxed, and turned around to see Keaira, smiling at him gently. He smiled back at her and sighed with such relief it was almost heart-breaking. "I knew you weren't a dream...you really did come back for us."

"Yes I did. You're very welcome," she replied.

"Thank you, Keaira."

"Ahem," Áine cleared her throat. "I apologize, but there is something I need to tell you all before we face the Twilight Dragon tomorrow. I need to tell you the whole story, from beginning to end. I need to tell you what it is that is truly at stake here."

"We don't know for sure that the Dragon is there, Áine," argued Orienne. "It's just my brother...it's just Ophir, isn't it?"

"Wherever Ophir is, he's heavily involved with the Twilight Dragon. If he hasn't already been killed by it, he is being held captive by it. Or worse," replied Áine.

"That can't be true. Ophir wouldn't let himself get killed or captured like that. He's too strong, too..."

Áine slammed her violin down on the hard surface of the ground. "The Twilight Dragon destroys all, Orienne. It twists and corrupts and ruins everything. It is the very antithesis of hope. You believe one lone Fader can stand up to this creature and remain unscathed? My entire family stood up to it and was wiped out for their efforts! My Father the Fey King and all of his cousins and kin. Each and every one of my brothers and sisters were cursed by the Dragon and doomed to fade to nothingness. The magic in their blood allowed the Crystalline virus to kill them far faster than it ever could kill humans or Eidoliths. I watched them all lose themselves to the disease, and after they vanished I was all alone. The last living thing in that dead, deserted Wood."

"Áine, I'm sorry..." breathed Orienne. She hadn't meant to upset her so. She hadn't known...

"You don't understand, human. Your kind never understood! My people are dead because of trust in that false hope your kind let out of Pandora's Box!" As Áine spoke, her words filled with anger and pain, her canine teeth became sharper and more prominent. Her eyes glossed over as she began to succumb to her rage. "It's your kind's fault I became a murderer and had to leave my home. Their blood is on your hands as well as mine if you think for even *one second* that boy can stand up to that monster on his own!" Áine's nails shifted into claws as she clenched her fists together. Blood began to drip from the palms of her hands. She was going Feral.

"Áine, snap out of it!" Anton yelled as he slapped her across the face. That seemed to do the trick. Her claws were nails again, and her eyes lost their glossy rage. She was just Áine again.

"I...I apologize, I did not mean to..."

Anton held the Halfie close. "I know," he said calmly. "It's alright."

Orienne and the others looked on at the Faerie in horror. She had almost attacked them...

220

After Áine had behaved in such a way, she had no choice but to explain her true history. Her murderous past, the slaughter of her half brothers, her half sister's promise of redemption and verdict of exile. She told them why she cared for her new companions like family, why she could not let the dragon live, what it had done to her world, what Grian was doing to stop it. Only Leilani had known before now, but there was no longer a way Áine could keep it hidden. Some of them looked on in horror as she spoke, others with quiet understanding.

"I'm sorry," Orienne apologized again. "If I had known, I wouldn't have said those things about my brother..."

"It is alright, Orienne, the fault lies with me. I should not have reacted so." There was a brief pause as Áine collected herself. "As...as I was saying," Áine began again, clearing her throat. "We should set out to find Ophir...and to find the Twilight Dragon, as soon as we are able to. Orienne, Anton's spell can only keep your fading under control for so long, and your body is already becoming resistant and beginning to break free from the spell. If we wait too much longer, you'll lose yourself, as my family lost themselves so many years ago. I cannot watch you succumb to the same fate and sit idly by as our last hope to defeat the Twilight Dragon dwindles away."

"I don't understand," said Orienne. "Why is everything lost if I die? I'm not the last. There are other Eidoliths. There's Ophir, and Melaenie..."

"Ophir may already be lost to us," interrupted Melaenie. "And I am unable to draw upon the powers of my heritage. I tried, I really did. But I am not a true Eidolith. I am only human."

"What?" gasped her older sister. "What are you saying?"

"Your sister speaks the truth," Leilani interjected. "I tried to coax her powers out of her while she stayed with me in Atlantis. There is no mark or blessing upon her, no sign of magic in her blood, no trace of the Eidolith Legacy. She is nothing more than an ordinary human."

"So I...I am..." began Orienne as she trembled. No, this was too much pressure. Not that there hadn't been pressure on her before this revelation, but there was still the hope there that if she were to fall then her sister could take her place. Now that hope was all but gone, scattered into dust and blown away by the harsh breath of the Twilight Dragon.

"Now please, you must not interrupt, and you must listen closely. As I said, I shall tell you now what is truly at stake here."

The others nodded and waited in fearful anticipation of the story that Áine was about to tell. What did she mean by "what was really at stake?" They all knew that they were risking their very lives to fight this evil thing. Was there another side to the story? Something they had all missed? All would soon be answered by Áine's story.

"These things I shall speak of are things you would not have been taught in school, not been told of by your parents, for even they do not remember. But I am a half-born Faerie, child of the Fey King of the White Forest of Eldra, far to the northern boarders of Kehmgedra in the world of Eidolon, and it has been known to me and my people for as long as the events have lived in the history of the Two Worlds.

"I told you before of the origin of the Twilight Dragon itself, but the tale did not end there.

"A woman by the name of Pandora was given safe keeping of the precious box that the Twilight Dragon had been sealed into. No one had told her what was in the box, only that she was never, ever to open it. However, one day her curiosity got the better of her, and she opened it. In that single moment, all the maladies of the world were released into the Two Worlds. All the plagues of humanity swarmed out from the box, released out into the open for the first time since the Twilight Dragon had been sealed.

"Mankind suffered these maladies for many, many generations. While humanity struggled, the darkness that was released out of her box began to coalesce to form something far greater than any of the things initially released. What was born from the evil was the

Twilight Dragon, that which would bring the dusk of life to humanity. The dragon's body was made up of fleeting souls, and it fed on the sins of those closest to it. Its very breath oozed disease and suffering.

"People began to fear that the end was coming. Earthquakes shattered cities and left them like dust in a desert. Entire mountains crumbled into the sea, causing enormous tidal waves that washed away entire civilizations. The sky turned red, and all living plants began to slowly take on the color of the sky. It appeared as though the dusk of mankind had finally come, and humanity had lost against the Twilight Dragon.

"That was when the Old Ones, who had long since gone into hiding, returned once more, bearing prophecies of hope and triumph for all those who would dare to rise up against the calamity.

"Their prophecy was one that all of you should know well."

Áine then began to sing her song, the one she had sung to Leilani when she revealed her past at last, the one she had sung time and time again for her friends as they passed the time in Atlantis, the Prophecy of the Kinship of the Twilight Moon.

Songs of ancient prophecies
Of Twilights gone and past
Will call to only those they see
The final days will come to pass

The Child of a Songsmith
Two Artificial Beings
Descendant of the Eidoliths
A Psychic that needs freeing
A Faerie maiden from the Wild
A lass who cannot cry
And lest ye not forget the child
Who shall join them from the Sky

What fades today, what fades tonight

223

The dragon falls, the fallen rise
Our blinded ways are brought to light
And those who die will live their lives

The Kinship of the Twilight Moon
Bound by their blood and by their fate
Shall whet their blade by Light of Lune
And save these worlds 'fore 'tis too late

"Many have sworn themselves to their own Kinships, seeking out the Twilight Dragon and slaying it, over and over and over, but it always returns wearing the body of its slayer, bearing different curses to inflict on those who would wish to quell its hatred.

"We are the final Kinship. Only we may slay it. We are the last Kinship that can ever rise to do battle with the Twilight Dragon. There can be none after us should we fall. The Faeries are extinct, eradicated by the Plague of Twilight. The Eidoliths have left these worlds forever, leaving behind only three children with strongly diluted blood. But there is too much hanging in the balance for us to lose. We shall not fail. This legacy shall not die with us."

This time, it was Orienne who spoke up. Her hands were trembling, and she was sweating fiercely. "I...I don't understand, Áine. We are risking our lives to defeat something that will only rise up from the ashes to cause havoc once more! Are we not simply throwing our lives away?"

"This is insane!" added Keaira, agreeing with Orienne for once. "It's pointless!"

"It is not pointless!" Áine bellowed, raising her voice. "There is always hope that it will not consume the body of its slayer! We must keep sin and hatred from our hearts, clear our minds, and strike it down! Without hate, it cannot be reborn! Without love, it cannot be undone! And now, with my sister and her Kinship fighting in Eidolon, we might actually put it down for good!"

"That's all well and good, Áine...but there still remains one problem with this plan," said Keaira. "We don't have all of our members."

"Are you sure it is wise to go now?" Leilani asked. "We do not stand a chance without the entire Kinship of the Twilight Moon, standing together as one."

Áine shook her head and smiled. "No, I believe we do have everyone we need."

"But the child from the sky..."

This time it was Anton who spoke up. "Áine and I both think that the role is played by me." He then unclasped his robe and pulled off his shirt, revealing his white feathered wings.

Everyone except for Orienne and Áine gasped. The two women did, however, shoot one another rather poisonous glares, realizing that Anton had shared this secret privately with the both of them.

"You're one of them. A Haneshiro..." accused Leilani. "You're..."

"I am still half Human. You would not forsake me now that you know what I am, would you? You, who call yourselves my companions, my friends, my family?" demanded Anton. "I thought you were above such discrimination."

"Haneshiro are evil!" Keaira shouted as she jumped up. "They kidnapped Humans and..."

"Keaira, hush!" snapped Áine. The young Psychic complied, her fear becoming timid complacency at the harsh tone of the Halfie's voice. "Haneshiro are no more evil than Psychics, Faders, Faeries, or Humans. Anton is no more evil than any one of us. You shame yourselves."

Nearly everyone hung their heads, feeling the sting of Áine's words. She was right, after all. Anton had never shown any of them unkindness, and before he had met any of them, he was dedicating his life to healing the world in places the Plague of Twilight had corrupted beyond means of Human repair. In fact, without his bloodline and his body being blessed by the Haneshiro, he would not have even had such abilities to begin with. And ever since he

225

had met them, he had done his best to diffuse tension, inspire friendship, and freely give his devotion and protection to the others. Anton was just as "Human" as they were.

"But Anton," Orienne spoke up. "You are the Child of a Songstress. How can you also be the Child from the Skies?"

"My sister has a point," said Melaenie. "How can you be both? Isn't that cheating?"

Áine shook her head. "I do not believe that there need be two different people filling the roles. The fact that Anton here fulfils two requirements might even make him stronger in the end, at least against the Dragon, for he has been Twice Blessed."

"I suppose that makes sense..." said Keaira.

"Of course it makes sense," said Orienne, eager to accept any explanation so that they could move on and meet up with her brother as soon as possible. She didn't know if she could bear to wait until they hunted down some other obscure person to add to their ranks. She had to find Ophir. She needed closure regarding her brother like she needed air to breathe.

When Áine was done speaking, they all decided that it was in their best interest to get as much sleep as possible. They could not risk being tired and uncoordinated when they finally faced off with the Twilight Dragon on the morrow. Especially since now they knew that it wasn't just their lives that were at stake here, but if they fell victim to their own negative emotions like their predecessors had before them, the Twilight Dragon would be reborn again. The vicious cycle would be doomed to repeat itself one final time, as next time, there would be no one left to fit the prophecy and fight. As Áine had said, there were no more Faeries, and no more Eidoliths. The very magic that bound the Kinship together by blood and by fate would be dissolved. The destiny of the world really did rest on their shoulders.

The next morning, they cleaned up as quickly as they could, though they were all afraid of the task they had before them. Leilani said that she had finally gathered enough magic together to open a

226

portal to the island, and the only thing she was waiting for was their word.

She didn't have long to wait before she led them through the portal and towards what all of them believed to be their final stand.

Chapter Twenty Five
Blade and Brother

~~~

The Kinship of the Twilight Moon found themselves in an ancient desert with sand that was whiter than snow, and large pillars of salt jutting out from the pale sand every few miles. Bodies were strewn about, half buried in sand and at least a few weeks dead. Their corpses stank in the hot sun.

The sky was a queer shade of lavender rather than blue. It made for a very eerie feel, especially because it was so quiet there. Many of them were beginning to wonder if the strange landscape had anything to do with the corruption of the Twilight Dragon.

Then they saw what they had all come here for, though they had not realized it just yet.

It was Orienne's twin brother, alive and well, staring right at them, surrounded by death. The life in his eyes was gone, replaced only with a calm fury. Cold fire blazed behind his copper gaze as it pierced the soul of his twin sister.

"I knew he was alive," Orienne said to herself.

It was then that he cracked a smile and spoke to them. "Greetings, my friends, I am Ophir Andraste. I'm very pleased to meet you." And then bowed deeply, as if to reinforce his friendly guise. It did nothing to bolster the Kinship's trust in him.

Orienne and Melaenie forced themselves to smile. Who was he, really, and why was he using their brother's face? There was certainly something very different about him. The two of them may not have physically seen Ophir for a great many years, but even they were not so blinded by familial love and relief at seeing their long lost brother to overlook the death behind his eyes.

This was wrong. This was *not* Ophir Andraste.

"Allow me to tell you about myself, as I'm sure that you are aware that I am...not quite like the rest of you." His copper colored eyes glowed eerily as he spoke. And then his lips curled into a ghostly smile, as if he wasn't really there in front of them. Orienne thought that for a moment, his image shifted into...something else, but she quickly brushed off the sight as a mere figment of her imagination. Why was he bothering to introduce himself to them? Didn't he know who they were, at least regarding Keaira, who he had saved, and his sisters, who he had known since birth?

"I took on the previous Twilight Dragon not long ago. These people here were my kinship." He gestured widely to the bodies strewn by his feet, though he seemed to show no remorse for their deaths.

"Previous?" Orienne asked. She suddenly began to feel very wary and afraid of this man. She took a step backwards, taking Melaenie into her arms.

Then "Ophir" outstretched his hand and held it out to Orienne. "What did you come here to kill? Don't you remember?" Something wasn't quite right about this picture. The way that he spoke was way too syrupy, too corrupt, as it had been in her dreams. It was unsettling and unpleasant.

"Who are you, really?" Orienne demanded. "What have you done to our brother?"

Ophir took two steps towards the Kinship and raised his head up to the sky. "The Twilight Dragon. Do you remember now?"

"What?!" they all simultaneously gasped. Ophir then transformed into a monstrous copper-toned dragon...the Twilight Dragon. Bronze scales covered every inch of his grandiose body, and horns shot out in great pillars along his long back and on the tips of his wings. Spikes protruded from around his eyelids, and two kingly horns jutted out out from the back of his head. His pale, milky teeth flashed them all as he grinned a smile like daggers at them.

Anton immediately got to work solidifying ice bubbles around them as a second shield if the Psychics' shields went down too quickly. He only hoped that there would be time for them to formulate completely before they were overwhelmed by the power of the beast.

He flapped his enormous wings and sent the two AI, who had not been able to be shielded by Keaira's and Gaignun's powers, flying backwards so fast that hit the rocks on the ground and shut down. Momoko even had one of her limbs torn off; she hit the ground so hard. Static noise filled the air from the sound of her malfunctioning components. The others could hear Momoko's screaming in garbled words and numbers. Her speech functionality must have been damaged in the attack.

Orienne and the others were able to stand their ground through the sheer power of their Psychic companions. But the blast had knocked down their shields in the process. And they didn't have time to put up new ones before the Twilight Dragon sent another whirlwind at them.

Anton's partially formed Ice Barrier shattered, and he and Áine went hurtling to the ground, ice shards raining down on them. Melaenie flew screaming into a salt pillar, torn from Orienne's protective grip. She had collided hard enough to shatter her bones and break her neck. It would be a cruel miracle if she had lived through that. Orienne herself found herself completely unharmed, though watching her sister break against the pillar almost killed her on the inside.

Keaira and Gaignun were both able to hold their ground through quick bursts of their Psychic powers, though they hadn't the time to put shields around everyone else as well.

If the others didn't recover soon, it would be all over, because they needed every last member in order to fight the Twilight Dragon. They didn't stand a chance against this thing if they were all unconscious or worse.

"We've got you covered!" Keaira shouted at Orienne over the howling wind caused by the dragon's flapping wings.

"Why did you only protect me?" cried Orienne, lamenting the loss of her little sister. Her heart was heavy, her stomach lurched, and she feared for the worst.

"You're the only one who can slay him! You are the last Eidolith!" Keaira cried back.

"He can't control you! At least while we're shielding your mind!" finished Gaignun. Orienne looked towards the two of them and nodded, grateful that Keaira was still willing to protect her even though they always fought, and she had said such mean things to her and about her in the past. She was equally grateful that both she and Gaignun were such powerful Psychics, or else she knew that she would have been dead already.

The Twilight Dragon snapped his mighty jaws at Orienne, but his attack was reflected by a burst of Psychic energy.

"Now, Orienne!"

"Now what? I don't understand! I have nothing to fight him with! I have nothing!" Orienne looked over to her struggling companions. What were they even doing here? They had all gone down before the Twilight Dragon even struck them. Now they struggled even to stand up in its presence. Melaenie was dead or dying, Momoko broken to pieces, Keaira and Gaignun pouring every ounce of energy into shields for her and themselves...yet they had nothing to fight against the beast with. No swords or true spells, no weapons or magic that could harm it. They had jumped into this battle unarmed and unprepared.

"You are an Eidolith!" screamed a voice from behind her. It was Áine who had spoken up. She and Anton were bracing themselves against one another, standing up against the furious wind.

"That means nothing!"

"It means everything! Orienne, do you know what made the Eidoliths so special? They shared the power of the gods, the power

231

of creation! Orienne, the Eidoliths are the only living beings who can create something from *nothing*!"

Suddenly, a silvery iridescent sword with sparkling water inside of the blade appeared in front of Orienne. It had her name engraved on its hilt. Then she checked all of the folds in her skirt and all of her pockets, and she couldn't find her charm anywhere. Had the sword come from the charm? There was hope for them yet, if this weapon really had the blessing of the magical waters of Atlantis within it!

"Say the words, Orienne," whispered Leilani's voice from within the waters of the sword. "Call upon the powers of the Kinship of the Twilight Moon. Call upon those blessed in the light of Lune. Call, and give this blade the power to truly slay the Twilight Dragon."

At last, Orienne finally understood why everyone was needed. It wasn't because they all had special powers that could help defeat the beast. It was because all of the power that was unleashed by their combined efforts to break fate, their trust and unity, their *Kinship* that gave them the strength to finish the task they were given. She called out. "The child of a Songsmith!"

A soft white glow that seemed oddly reminiscent of moonlight enveloped Prince Anton. The glow gathered around his heart and flew to the sword, bathing the blade in its light. Orienne felt his spirit coursing through the blade, ebbing and flowing with the tide of her own. This sword, this Eidolith blade...could strike with the entire power of the Kinship of the Twilight Moon behind it.

She didn't waste another moment before calling out the next stanza. "Two Artificial Beings!"

The same glow enveloped the bodies of Momoko and Nekotarou, but as the light gathered at where their hearts would be, they merged into one, as if they shared the same soul. Despite Momoko's intensive damage, she managed to turn her head and smile in Orienne's direction before their lights zipped over to the sword.

Ophir saw the second light gather to the sword, and immediately reverted back to his human form. He glared at Orienne with the most intense of all hatreds. What was he thinking? All she wanted to do was hug him like she used to do when they were children, to be his loving sister again. Why was he glaring at her as if he could know no greater hatred?

"You know that I cannot allow you to complete that blade, dearest sister." He held up his own sword to her chest. His sword closely resembled Orienne's. That must have been the sword that he had used to defeat the previous Twilight Dragon. Did that mean that Ophir had been taken host by the Twilight Dragon? Had he given in to his hatred and sins?

Orienne looked into his once beautiful eyes and saw that they were truly clouded. She could see no shine in them, and his pupils were misted over so heavily that they were almost the same color as the rest of his eyes. The warm, chocolaty brown was all but gone, replaced now by a cold, metallic copper.

"No, you aren't the Twilight Dragon. It's all some kind of lie. Ophir, this can't be true."

"Shut up!" he shouted at her as he sliced at her dress, slitting it at the bottom a little. "What do you know about the truth?"

Orienne winced. "My brother...don't you remember me? Don't you remember our family?" she asked him sadly.

"I care not what happens to you, bitch, but know this! You shall not prevail," he said, his voice filled with the icy sting of hatred.

"Well, Ophir, I'll have you know that it's the only way we can destroy the disease that's causing normal humans to become Faders! It's the only way we can live!" Orienne faded again after she said this, and another silver fragment of her body disappeared for good. Aton's spell had worn off...this was not good.

Orienne looked into Ophir's eyes again. The cloudiness in them gave way to a swirling pool of glowing hatred. The Twilight Dragon was controlling him, and causing him to hold the sword up to his own sister. His own sister that always played with him, always wrote music with him so they could sing little Melaenie to

233

sleep, always sat with him when he was ill, always protected him with all of her being. As she thought of this, hot tears filled her eyes, and one rolled down her cheek and down onto the hot, sandy ground.

How could he have been so easily taken from her? How come no matter what the circumstances were, she could never save him?

"That may be true, Orienne, but something worse will be sure to follow. You've never heard of what happened when the last Twilight Dragon was killed, have you? All of the world's people had suddenly been cured of AIDS, colds, cancers, the flu, and everything else, and there still has been no person to have any of these diseases ever since. Only bacterial diseases remained. However, on that same exact day, the Fader epidemics broke loose. Psychics ran rampant through the streets. The Crystalline and Capacious viruses infected everything in their path and destroyed the lives of countless victims, as it is doing now to you. Do you know what that means?" What was he trying to say? That their efforts would be futile?

Now was the time to end this, no matter what he meant. Orienne wanted to live her life, and that couldn't happen if Ophir, or whatever it was that had taken over his body, was to live.

Orienne could see Anton off to the side, held tenderly by Áine. She remembered their first kiss, and she never wanted to forget it, even if it was the night when her condition became fatal, and even if he did not love her in return. She remembered when she first whispered her love to him and he did not return her feelings. But above all, she remembered that he had protected her anyways, loving all his companions, save Áine, as family.

She would die if all of that was taken away from her.

Orienne raised her sword against her own brother. Her heart was heavy as she struggled to bring the sword down on him. She told herself that this was the only way, but no matter how hard she tried, she could not bring herself to attack him. She loved him. He may have hated her now, he may have had all of the love sucked from his soul, but she could never hate him. Never.

She dropped her sword to the ground.

As soon as Ophir raised his sword to deliver the first blow, Anton ran in and blocked the attack, at the expense of his wing. The sword went right through, leaving a gaping and bloody hole. He screamed out in pain before he took the sword from Orienne's hands.

"Ophir! Can't you see what you're doing? She's your sister! I know that you don't want to do this!" Tears of pain streamed down his face as tears of confusion began to trickle down Orienne's.

"Ophir...Anton..." was all she could manage to squeeze out of her throat before she faded again, losing yet another part of her body. When Anton saw her fade, he turned around to touch her, to see if she was still at least in this dimension. He should not have done that. At the first sign of Anton's turn, Ophir stabbed him again, luckily still only catching his wing. Anton cried out in pain again, and this time he fell to the ground in a pool of his own blood.

Orienne and Áine both cried out in anguish as the Halfie rushed to his side.

"Orienne, Áine...I want you both to know...I...I'm sorry. I've lied to you and kept the truth from you, made promises that I couldn't keep...and I couldn't protect you. You must hate me now...don't you?" Just seeing him on the ground in front of them, crying, was enough to break their hearts.

Orienne was speechless, but Áine spoke up soft and clear, like the morning after a heavy rain. "Anton, I don't hate you. In fact, it's just the opposite." She couldn't bear the thought of him believing that I hated him. "I love you."

Orienne's heart broke all over again. She cried as she leaned over his body, burying her face in his chest. Áine did not stop her. He pulled them both into his arms, letting their tears fall onto him. "I love you, Anton," sobbed Orienne.

"I know," he said. "But now you have to let me go. Be a good girl, Orienne. You can do this."

"You are like our sister. We have faith in you," added Áine. "I know that you have the strength to let go of love. Let this be a lesson to you. Let this be your final test. Finish saying the words. Finish all of this. Please...if not for us, then for your brother."

Right then, Ophir lowered his sword. "Love?" he spat. Even he started to cry at this word. "Am I supposed to give up my life for your love? I think not!"

The words that Áine and Anton had spoken to her were finally beginning to sink in. If she could let go of the dead love she had for the prince, then she could let go of the dead love she held for her brother. She had to trim her roses. She had to let him go. "You're wrong!" Orienne shouted. "It is not you who must give up, but I!" Then, in rapid succession, she began calling out the rest of the Kinship. All of the lights joined together and wrapped around her sword. She had whetted her blade by Light of Lune. Now she had to save the world before it was too late.

Then, suddenly, Ophir reverted back to his dragon form and reared up for another attack. He brought his long neck down at a dizzying speed and crunched his jaws at Orienne, just barely missing her. Orienne swung the sword down as his jaws narrowly passed her by, but she, too, missed her mark.

He went back to his human form once again. But this time, his eyes were unclouded. Orienne nearly dropped her sword from the shock.

"It will be all right, my sister. Strike hard and true!" He briefly embraced his sister before he started screaming again. The dragon took over his body yet again. It was then that Orienne discovered the truth for herself.

The Twilight Dragon wasn't really a Dragon at all. It was just an angry parasite that used a single human body for a host. The reason that the Twilight Dragon lived on was because all it needed to do was find a weakened body to use as its new host, and Ophir must have been weakened by his battle with the previous dragon, and stained with sin. He had sought out this terrible beast so that he could protect and save his sisters, but in the end, it only infected his body, suppressing his soul. If she managed to strike the dragon in its true form, Ophir might still be able to be saved. They were two separate beings, drawing life from the same body.

Orienne shouted to Ophir at the top of her lungs. "I'm sorry that you got hurt because of me and Melaenie! I promise that I'll end it right now! You won't have to suffer any longer!" She charged at the Twilight Dragon, sword at the ready, shrieking out a pain filled battle cry. As soon as she got close enough to attack, however, it changed into Ophir. But Orienne knew what the parasite was doing; it was using her brother as a shield. She wouldn't fall for it, though; she would kill this horrible thing once and for all.

She charged again and again, until she knew that she would be too exhausted to charge at it anymore. She couldn't risk striking Ophir again, because she had already stabbed him twice by mistake, and he was losing blood as rapidly as she was losing energy. If she didn't hurry up and find a way to lure the Twilight Dragon out, Ophir would die, and the beast would take over her own tired and worn out body.

Or would it? She had let go of her dead love, let go of the source of her envy. Her sin no longer held its sway over her. If the host died, it would have nowhere to go. Not this time. Not ever. She could destroy the Dragon by destroying its shield...even if that shield happened to be her own brother. Yet she had cut off *that* dead love too. She held the answer now. She had the strength to end it all.

Suddenly, out of nowhere, it started to rain. Soon enough, a shallow puddle of water was formed, and the desert began to flood. Orienne turned around, and sure enough, Anton had cast one of his spells. He had cast his newest spell, the one his uncle had taught him, and he was weakly smiling. Leilani popped out of one of the puddles and pulled one of the pearls off of her long strings. She held it up in the air, until it started glowing in rainbow colors, just like the bubble around Atlantis.

The pearl began glowing brighter and brighter, until the little flickers of rainbow became streams of color shooting out from that tiny orb. The dragon form pulled out, and stayed there, motionless.

237

"I, Leilani Moanna, hereby share my gift with fellow Spell Weaver Prince Anton Christophe LaCiel, son of King Damien Anselme LaCiel, twice blessed child of a Songstress and child of the sky! Hear me, Spirit of Magic! Take my water, take my might, take my gift of Faerie light!"

At that very moment, the rain seemed to change. Where each tiny droplet had been as ice before, it was now warm and gentle. Leilani's and Anton's spirits filled each and every droplet, and with their spirits together, they were able to hold the healing water from the Lake of Atlantis within them. It was raining *life*.

All who were touched by the water began to have their bodies healed and mended, including the mangled Prince and the gravely injured Melaenie. Even the biomechanical AIs were repaired to full health. As soon as they were all restored to near perfect health, their pendants and Orienne's sword began to glow with a beautiful light unlike anything they had ever seen before.

"Now!" yelled Leilani.

Orienne nodded, and charged one final time. The dragon form was still out. She wouldn't have to kill the body of her brother after all. Tears of relief rained down her face and mixed with the rain from the sky as she impaled the Twilight Dragon with the Eidolith sword. The copper creature fell to the ground, writhing in pain. Orienne faded, one last time, as the dragon faded as well. Only this time, all of the silver fragments that had left her body before were coming back to her. All the pieces of the shimmering dragon became part of her as well, making her feel whole again. And when at last the fading image of the Twilight Dragon had disappeared for good, Ophir's human body dropped to the ground, limp and unconscious.

Melaenie ran over to her sister's side as she dropped to her knees. "Orienne! You did it!" she exclaimed.

Momoko and Nekotarou made their way over to her as well, their broken bodies as good as new. "You are not half-bad, for a newbie. Good job, Orienne," said Nekotarou as he licked his paw.

238

"He should be grateful to have a sister as wonderful as you," Anton said to her as he smiled.

"Thank you, everyone. I could not have done it without you all."

"Go to him, Orienne," said Áine as she pushed the Eidolith forward.

Orienne walked over to her brother and kneeled by his side. She turned him over gently and brushed the sand away from his sleeping face. "I'm here," she told him. "We saved you. Please wake up now, Ophir. Please."

As she whispered this, Ophir's eyes flickered awake, and he looked as though he had seen the world for the first time in ages. The copper in his eyes was gone, and he gazed back up at her with his familiar brown eyes once more. The eyes he shared with his twin sister. He turned to Orienne, and a great smile emerged on his lips. "You're alive!" He exclaimed.

"Yes, it's all over now. Didn't I tell you everything would be all right?" Now Ophir was crying right alongside her...crying tears of joy.

"I was afraid that once you began to ignore my warnings, you would die and all I have been doing these past many years would have been in vain."

"I needed to know that you were alive," Orienne replied. "We all thought you'd been dead for the longest time. Once I found the slightest glimmer of hope that you were still alive, I couldn't bring myself to walk away from it. I love you! Melaenie loves you! You're our only brother, you dummy!"

"Speaking of love," replied Ophir. He looked over to where Anton and Áine were. They were holding each other close, grateful that at last they could be together. Grateful that their pasts had not prevented their futures, that their friends had saved their lives. And then there were the two Psychics. Keaira stood there proudly, smiling and laughing. Gaignun was holding her hand. That was so sweet. Ophir looked back towards his sister as they walked over to the others. "It's good to have you back," he said.

"You too, Ophir."

When they met up with the others, Ophir gave a little high five to Keaira. "I see you took my training to heart! How've you been holding up, my little runaway?"

"Fair enough. Your sister is a pain in the arse," she joked. "But she's alright, I guess." She reached over to give him a one-armed hug.

"So are you two...?" Ophir began to ask, pointing towards the two Psychics' clasped hands.

"Ha, yeah right!" laughed Gaignun. "We're friends. *Just* friends."

"But we're the best friends ever! What, is it a crime to hold hands or something?" finished Keaira. Alright, so they weren't a couple. But something told them it wouldn't stay that way for long. Give it a couple of years, and their relationship would be sure to bloom into something beautiful. After all, they were one another's Others.

Orienne, having finally had the victory sink in, interrupted the happy little banter. "We won," she said. They really had freed the world from the terror of the Twilight Dragon and fulfilled the prophecy handed down from the legends and prophecies of old. They had done it.

"You all saved me," Ophir smiled sincerely. "And you saved the world from me. Thank you."

"We didn't just save the world," boasted Keaira. "We saved the future."

"To the future!" They all shouted. "To the future of mankind!"

If only that could have been the way their story ended.

240

Epilogue

~~~

There was a bright twinkling in the sky overhead in Eidolon. Something had happened in the other world. Something...strange.

"Grian, what do you make of this?" asked Fennen. "Look there, the sky is shining."

"Fennen! Do you think...?" exclaimed Aillen.

Grian looked up and smiled. "Our sister has done her job, it seems. Took her long enough, what was it, three years?"

"Cut her some slack, Grian," said Aillen. "We haven't even found the other members of our own Kinship yet, and you have foolishly exiled Áine from this world, preventing us from even asking for her help."

"She would not have helped us even had we asked. She believes us dead, and she believes you to already have fulfilled the prophecy in Eidolon. If you hadn't been so intent on getting rid of her..." added Fennen before he was interrupted by his sister.

"It was for our own safety, and the safety of the entire Mac Crae Clan," spat Grian. "You two saw with your own eyes how ruthless she was."

"What good is our safety when the folly of it all dooms this world and the next?" accused Aillen.

"We're on our own now, and we have already wasted too much time," finished Fennen.

Grian crossed her arms and huffed. "I know, I know!" she growled, clearly frustrated. "I'm almost ashamed to call myself a

Fianna! Curse this stupid prophecy! Why do we need so many people to fight half a god damn parasite anyways?"

"Because that is the way it was written, and that is the way it must be." The voice that responded belonged to neither Fennen nor Aillen. It came from a man whose hair was as black as Grian's, and whose eyes were windows to a heart that was even blacker.

"Who are you?" demanded Grian, unsheathing her sword. Her brothers did likewise.

"You poor creatures. Do you truly not know who I am?" He smiled seductively, and for a fraction of a second, his human appearance flickered away. He had been...darkness. Pure evil. The Twilight Dragon.

Startled, Grian dropped her sword.

"Do you remember me now, Mother?"

"It can't be..."

The wicked man snapped his fingers, and the cloaking shield that had hidden his seven near-identical SINS shimmered away as his own human disguise had faltered just moments ago. They began to close in on Grian and her brothers. "I am Dr. Adam Ryu III, descendant of the Faeries and Eidoliths, and heir to the Legacy of the Twilight Dragon." He thrust his arm forward and grabbed Grian by the throat, lifting her off her feet and into the air. She grasped at his hand and struggled against his grip as he choked the breath out of her, but it was no use. "And I don't think that you're showing me the proper respect."

Glossary of Terms

pg	Phrase	Translation

French

pg	Phrase	Translation
79	*bonjour*	hello
43	*flocon orage*	snowflake storm
40	*je t'aime*	I love you
46	*neigeux haleine*	snowy breath
40	*oui*	yes
40	*père*	father

Irish Gaelic

pg	Phrase	Translation
5	*is cuma liom*	I do not care
5	*go hifreann leat*	to hell with you
19	*an bhfuil tu damhsa liom*	would you like to dance with me?
20	*cuir sin sios*	put that down
20	*cad is ainm duit*	what is your name?
23	*tada gan iarracht*	nothing is done without effort
23, 107	*ni neart go cur le cheile*	there is no strength without unity
93	*slán*	goodbye
93	*stad*	stop
93	*an bhfuil Gaeilge agat*	do you speak Irish/Gaelic?
93	*tuigim*	I understand
93	*cé as thú*	where are you from?
93	*is as Eidolon dom*	I am from Eidolon
187	*Cad é atá tú a dhéanamh*	what are you doing?

Hawaiian

pg	Phrase	Translation
61, 80, 122, 188	*aloha*	hello or goodbye

About the Author

Kiersten Renée Nichols was born in California in 1992. She now resides with her family in Rhode Island, which consists of her mother, younger brothers, her cat Luna, and her two huskies Shadow and Koda. She graduated from Smithfield High School in 2010, and briefly attended CCRI where she studied English. She first began writing when she was in Middle School under the pen name *Kayari of Midnight*, and some of her old stories are still freely available online to read.

~~~

"Typically the kind of thing I like to read has a hint of drama, a drop of romance, a pinch of folklore, and a superb choice of diction. Magic is also a plus." – Kiersten Renée Nichols

~~~